ACCIDENT OR MURDER?

Grimly, Nick Thorn surveyed the stretch of road where Amanda Hazard found Commissioner Brown dead in the mud. Brown's battered truck was missing a wheel. The high-lift jack lay across the back of Brown's knees, and the jack handle rested on his shoulders.

Nick frowned speculatively. "I think—"

"I know what you think, Thorn. You think Commissioner Brown met with a stroke of bad luck. Right?"

Nick made a neutral sound but, wisely, he kept his trap shut. He was trying exceptionally hard to accommodate his fiancée's tendency to make something from nothing. This accident, Nick concluded, was just that—an accident caused by bad road conditions and inclement weather.

Hazard focused on Nick's expressionless face. "I was mad enough to kill Brown when I came looking for him this morning. If I—an even-tempered, well-adjusted female—was furious at him for his negligent disregard of the road conditions in this district, someone else could have acted upon opportunity!"

Nick grimaced. "Now, Hazard—"

"Brown left a clue in the mud," she cut in quickly. "He etched a scraggly *S* before he expired."

"An *S?*" he asked dubiously. "I don't see a message in the mud."

"It was there before the recent downpour washed it away," Hazard affirmed with a nod of her wet head. "Somebody clobbered Brown and left him dead in the mud. I don't know who or why, but I intend to find out!"

Other Amanda Hazard mysteries
by Connie Feddersen

Dead in the Water

Dead in the Cellar

Dead in the Melon Patch

Dead in the Dirt

DEAD IN THE MUD

An Amanda Hazard Mystery

Connie Feddersen

Kensington Books
Kensington Publishing Corp.
http://www.kensingtonbooks.com

KENSINGTON BOOKS are published by

Kensington Publishing Corp.
850 Third Avenue
New York, NY 10022

First Printing: April, 1997
10 9 8 7 6 5 4 3 2 1

Printed in the United States of America

*This book is dedicated to my husband, Ed,
and our children, Christie, Jill, Kurt, Jeff, and Jon,
with much love.*

One

According to Amanda Hazard, CPA, income tax season was hell.

Every year, when the month of April rolled around, Amanda asked herself why she had chosen this line of work. The hours were grueling, the interruptions continuous, and the days entirely too short.

Thunder rumbled overhead as Amanda scooped up the incomplete tax files she had brought home from her office. Standing at the front door of her rented farm home, she watched rain pour down like Niagara Falls. Not only was it tax time, but it was the spring monsoon season in Vamoose, Oklahoma.

Amanda wheeled toward the closet to retrieve her umbrella and galoshes, but the jingling phone demanded her attention.

Muttering, she snatched up the receiver. "Hazard's Hell, the damned speaking."

"How many times have I told you not to use curse words, doll?"

Amanda sighed inwardly. It was Mother.

"I called about the shower," Mother announced.

Amanda glanced toward the storm door. "We're having a shower in Vamoose as we speak. A real toad-strangler, in fact."

Mother made a snorting sound. "Not *that* kind of shower. I'm talking about your *wedding* shower, doll." Mother cleared her throat and plunged on. "I've decided to give you a shower. It may be the only way I get to meet this country cop you're planning to marry."

"It isn't necessary—"

Mother cut Amanda off with another snort. "Not necessary? Don't you think it's peculiar that this Thorn character refuses to be introduced to your family? Are you sure he isn't after your money, doll?"

"No, he's after my body."

Mother howled like a coyote. "That's a terrible thing to say!"

"It was a joke, Mother."

"Well, it wasn't funny." Mother cleared her throat again. It was her way of beginning a new paragraph. "Now, about your shower, just leave all the details to me."

Amanda put her foot down hurriedly. If Mother organized the wedding shower it would be the most boring, stuffy affair ever. "I'll take care of the details," she said assertively.

"When? In between filing state and federal tax returns for the citizens of that higgledy-piggledy town?"

Amanda gnashed her teeth and listened to the thunder roll and the rain hammer against the roof. "Vamoose is countrified, is all. I happen to like country style."

"You must, since you're planning to marry that cowardly cop who doesn't have the nerve to meet Daddy and me."

Sexy country cop Nick Thorn had plenty of nerve, but Amanda had procrastinated about introducing him to her family. Mother was not the kind of woman a prospective bridegroom needed to meet until it was absolutely necessary.

"I've got to go, Mother," Amanda declared. "I'll be late for work."

"But I've got all these marvelous plans for the shower and the wedding!" Mother wailed. "I have visions of—"

" 'Bye, Mother."

Amanda dropped the phone into the cradle, then scampered to the closet. If Mother took control of the wedding plans, Amanda would insist that she and Thorn elope.

Come to think of it, that was a grand idea, she decided as she grabbed the umbrella and snapped it open.

"Uh-oh," Amanda said when she remembered it was bad luck to open umbrellas indoors. With a shrug, she realized she'd already had the bad luck of starting Monday morning off with a call from her domineering mother.

Shoving her pump-clad feet into her galoshes, Amanda stepped onto the porch. Pete, the three-legged dog, had tucked himself beneath the window—the only dry spot on the porch. Lucky, the duck, was flapping his wings and rooting grass and insects from the water puddles.

It was definitely a day for the ducks of this world, Amanda thought as she sprinted toward her Toyota.

Cursing, she felt the wind whip beneath her umbrella. With an armload of tax files to protect, she was unable to hold onto the umbrella. It escaped her grasp and cartwheeled across the water-soaked lawn.

By the time Amanda plunked beneath the steering wheel, her hair and her silk business suit were drenched. This, she decided, had all the makings of a lousy day.

Cranking the engine, Amanda slipped and slid through her driveway. The windshield wipers slapped and squeaked as she pulled onto the rutted road that led to the highway. The compact car skidded in the mud, then swerved into the deep ruts left by a passing tractor. Amanda could hear water and mud thumping against the underside of her car as she pressed on the accelerator.

"Damn that Commissioner Brown," Amanda growled as she navigated her way down the rutted road. "If that do-nothing clown had spread a new layer of gravel on this road, I wouldn't be blazing my way to work every blessed day!"

The rain was coming down so hard that the windshield wipers couldn't keep pace, and Amanda couldn't see where she was going. When the front wheels of the Toyota dropped into ruts the size of the Grand Canyon, Amanda cursed Commissioner Brown's name out loud.

The car ground to a halt, right smack dab in the middle of the country road. The Toyota was sitting high-center, and Amanda couldn't make it go forward or backward.

You should never have opened that umbrella inside the house, came a taunting voice. *Next time you consider thumbing your nose at superstition, you better think again.*

"Oh, shut up. You sound just like Mother," Amanda grumbled as she shoved the car into reverse, hoping she could get enough traction to free the car. The wheels spun, splashing mud everywhere, but the car stayed where it was.

Amanda sputtered in frustration as she shouldered the door open. She was forced to walk a half-mile to her house—in the wind and rain and mud. Her expensive three-piece silk suit was going to suffer irreparable damage and Commissioner Brown was damned well going to hear about it! This was all his fault. If Brown had kept this country road graded and graveled properly, things like this wouldn't happen!

Amanda came to her feet, her blazing temper steaming in the blowing rain. Her galoshes sank into the rut and water dribbled into her shoes.

"You're really going to get an earful, Brown," she vowed as she slogged down the impassable road.

The county commissioner hadn't done diddly-squat

since he had taken office. It was election year, and Amanda vowed to contribute to Brown's political opposition. Furthermore, she intended to tell Brown exactly that—and more—the instant she got her hands on the telephone.

"Incompetent incumbent," she snarled as she stamped diagonally across the road to reach the grassy slope of the ditch. "I'll—*argh!*"

Amanda hit a slick patch of mud and her feet went flying. She landed with a *kersplat* and hurled a sinfully foul curse at Commissioner Brown's name.

"Oh, yes, Brown is definitely going to hear from me!" Amanda seethed as she crawled on all fours. Her clothes were covered with a layer of mud—and what little gravel was left from Brown's predecessor's days in office.

Amanda's favorite cream-colored suit was mud brown. Her disposition was pitch black.

Swearing and scowling, Amanda crawled toward the ditch before she dared to stand up. Rain dripped from the strings of her blond hair and muddied her eyelashes.

Amanda Hazard was seeing blood-red by the time she staggered to her feet and sloshed through the ditch. Fuming, she sidestepped up the incline of the ditch and stormed across the driveway. Thunder rumbled. It had nothing on Amanda's roiling temper. She couldn't wait to get her muddy hands on the telephone. She was going to give Brown hell!

Circling the house, Amanda entered through the back door that opened into the utility room. She peeled off her ruined ensemble, leaving the garments in a mud puddle on the vintage green linoleum. Wearing only her undies, Amanda stamped through the kitchen, then grabbed the phone book.

She hurriedly dialed the county offices, leaving mud prints on everything she touched. "I want to speak to Commissioner Brown," Amanda demanded.

"I'm sorry," the secretary said in a sweet, soft-spoken

voice. "Dusty is checking the new bridge construction on the western section of the county near his home."

Dusty Brown? Amanda smirked. What a misnomer! His name was MUD!

"Fine, give me directions," Amanda insisted. "I need to speak with him—now. Even if I have to track him down."

In her timid little voice, the secretary told her where to locate Commissioner Brown. Amanda decided Brown had hired this particular secretary hoping her delicate voice would soothe the savage beasts who called to air complaints. Well, it wasn't going to work. Amanda was determined to vent her fury on the source of her frustration— even if she had to slop through ten miles of bad roads to do it!

When she got her hands on Brown, she'd shove his face into a water-filled rut. Then, they'd talk!

After a quick change into Roper jeans, a t-shirt, and cowboy boots, Amanda crammed her "bad hair day" hat down around her ears and made a beeline toward her jalopy truck—which she should have taken in the first place. But she had been afraid she'd snag her silk suit on the cracked vinyl seat.

Dashing through the downpour, Amanda scrambled into the old clunker. With a turn of the key, the gas-guzzler gulped, belched, and finally sputtered to life.

Amanda swerved around the corner, splitting the ruts on the road. While the scraping wipers serenaded her, she mentally rehearsed what she planned to say to Brown: Roads were never graded and truckloads of gravel never arrived to accommodate rural citizens; ruts in the country roads had become trenches; if he had the slightest hope of winning the upcoming election, he'd damned well get his lazy butt in gear and do something!

If not, the incumbent's political opponents would have Amanda's endorsement. In fact, she decided as she slipped and slid down the road, she would attach a cover letter to every tax form delivered to her clients, encouraging voters to oust Brown from office.

With both hands clamped on the wheel, Amanda peered through the smeared windshield. The old truck sputtered as she pressed the accelerator to gather enough horse-power to top the slippery hill. Before she realized it, she had reached the rise and was skidding sideways down the slope. Swearing extensively, Amanda spun the wheel, trying to regain control of the truck.

It was no use. The road was like ice, and she was at the mercy of bald tires and rain-slicked roads. The truck nose-dived into the ditch, slamming Amanda's chest into the steering wheel as it ground to a halt in rushing water.

Shifting from "drive" to "reverse," she tried—unsuccessfully—to plow her way through the ditch, hoping to gather enough speed to veer back onto the road. It was a waste of time and fuel.

Amanda was axle-deep in mud. Water gurgled around the tires and turned to steam as it splattered against the hot engine.

"I'm gonna kill that SOB, first chance I get!" she snarled vindictively.

Swinging the door open, Amanda tried to climb into the truck bed and avoid the rising water. Perching on the tailgate, she sprang toward the road. Damn, who would've thought Vamoosians had to become acrobats to survive? This was absurd! It was an outrage! Commissioner Brown would be sorry as hell that he had pissed off Amanda Hazard. She'd flay him alive with her tongue—cut him to ribbons, reduce him to shreds!

Operating on sheer adrenaline, Amanda stalked along the side of the ditch, avoiding the muddy ruts. God took mercy on her and turned off the overhead faucet—momentarily, at least. The drenching downpour became a sprinkle, preventing her from being soaked to the bone.

As Amanda hiked beside the road, she noticed the

mound of mud heaped along the ditch. Giant tire tracks stood level-full with water. Some crazy fool on a bulldozer must have tried to lumber down this road. It was a wonder the idiot hadn't gotten stuck. What imbecile would be out here on a day like this, trying to work on a new bridge across Whatsit River?

Amanda stopped short when she saw bootprints—two sets—on the east slope of the hill. More tire tracks—from a pickup truck, she speculated—zig-zagged up the steep incline. She frowned when she noticed the widening of one of the tracks.

Watching where she stepped, she approached the flat track. To her amazement, *Goodyear* was imprinted—backward—in the mud. Amanda squatted down to survey the tracks that disappeared over the hill. Then she studied the wider tires of the bulldozer that had veered off in the direction she had come.

Thunder rumbled overhead, announcing another cloudburst. Amanda headed for the ditch, using the traction of the grass to accelerate her speed. She needed to find a farmhouse to call for Nick Thorn's assistance.

Glancing north, she saw a deep ravine lined with trees, and a house in the distance. She considered cutting cross-country, but the way her luck had been running, she would become entangled in the barbed-wire fence and lightning would strike a nearby steel post!

A yipping dog caught her attention as she jogged downhill. Amanda blinked in surprise when she recognized Commissioner Brown's truck. Now, if this wasn't irony Amanda didn't know what was. Brown looked to be stuck on his own impassable road.

So there *was* poetic justice in this world, Amanda thought as she jogged along the side of the road.

Bawling cattle caught her attention. She glanced northwest to see several Herefords, huddled up beside a section of patched fence. As she approached the truck, Amanda noticed an array of prints—boot prints, dog prints, horse and cattle prints.

Did these cattle belong to Commissioner Brown? she asked herself as she veered across the road. It would serve that clown right if his livestock had broken loose and he had become stranded on his own muddy road.

The unbalanced tilt of the battered pick-up drew Amanda's frown. "Brown?" she called out. When she realized the truck was missing a tire, she veered around the vehicle.

The flat tire was lying in the mud.

So was Commissioner Brown.

A clap of thunder broke the eerie silence. Commissioner Brown didn't respond, didn't move. He lay there in his soggy blue jeans and starched shirt. The handle of the high-lift jack lay across his shoulders. The jack, which had fallen off the fender of the truck, lay half-buried in mud.

Amanda circled the sprawled body. Brown's baseball cap sat askew on his head, but she couldn't see his face because it was submerged in the rainwater filling the deep rut.

Amanda squatted down to give Brown a nudge, then laid her hand on his back to check his breathing.

Brown wasn't breathing.

From all indications, he had attempted to jack up his flat tire in the mud. The jack had given way, causing the pick-up to slide sideways, knocking him off balance.

Carefully, Amanda reached out to remove Brown's baseball cap. Blood oozed from the wound on the back of his head. She stared thoughtfully at the jack handle that lay across Brown's shoulder blades. From the look of things, the flying handle had conked Brown on the head. He had fallen facedown in the rut—and drowned in six inches of water.

A fitting end, Amanda caught herself thinking. She had been ready to kill the man, but fate had intervened . . .

Amanda's scrutinizing gaze drifted down Brown's outstretched arm. There, scrawled in the mud beside his fingertips, was an *S*.

Amanda reassessed the scene of this *supposed* accident. Had someone else around Vamoose been mad enough to take a whack at Brown with the jack handle?

It was entirely possible, Amanda mused as she studied the myriad tracks around the truck. After all, *she* had been furious enough with Commissioner Brown to come after him—hell or high water. Who was to say that someone hadn't beaten her to the punch?

The sound of splattering water jolted Amanda from her musings. She saw a black and white Border Collie skid around the corner of the truck. The soggy canine gave Brown a passing glance, then trotted up to Amanda.

While the dog sniffed her jeans, Amanda absently patted its head.

"I'll bet you could answer a few questions if you could talk," she murmured.

The dog appeared to take an instant liking to Amanda. A cold, wet nose nudged her neck. Then a long tongue swept up the side of her face.

"Down, boy," Amanda ordered.

The dog bounded circles around the truck, smudging the prints that Amanda had carefully avoided.

"Come here, you soggy mutt!" Amanda demanded. The dog trotted merrily toward her, the tags on its collar jingling like Christmas bells.

"Bruno?" Amanda said, reading the name on the silver tag.

The dog rose up on its hind legs, planting its muddy paws on her shoulders. With a howl and a squawk, she teetered off balance. Mud splattered as she landed on her back.

The sky opened. Huge raindrops pounded against the metal on the truck and pattered against the trees of the ravine.

Amanda scrambled to her feet. She was about to be drenched—again. She had to contact Thorn before the downpour destroyed the prints and the squiggly S that Commissioner Brown had scrawled in the mud before he fell unconscious. Thorn would never believe this wasn't an accident if the evidence washed away . . .

Wheeling around, Amanda opened the door of the truck, hoping to find a paper to cover the S. When she saw the box of dog biscuits on the seat, she dumped out the treats, then used the box to protect the S. It was the best she could do.

Amanda raced toward the tree-lined intersection to the west. Beyond it was a small house on a hilltop, surrounded by a clump of cedars. To the south, she spotted a spacious brick house. That was where she would make her call, she decided as she broke into a run.

Damn, she was going to have to get into better physical condition, Amanda thought as she huffed and puffed for breath. Bruno didn't seem to have trouble keeping pace, she noticed. The dog was running circles around her as she slogged uphill.

When she reached the intersection, her eyes narrowed in annoyance. In the distance she could see brand spanking new asphalt pavement leading from the brick house to the bridge under construction. Unless she missed her guess, the new road led directly to Commissioner Brown's rural home, then curved northwest to intersect the highway near the small community of Adios.

"Why, that low-down, sneaky creep!" Amanda erupted. "He paved a private access road to his home while the rest of us are wallowing in mud!"

She stamped through the ditch to reach the asphalt pavement. If she had known Commissioner Brown had misused county funds to lay asphalt to his own front door, she would have launched an attack on that corrupt public official months ago! The man had feathered his own nest—

so to speak. Brown had seen to it that he didn't have to drive on hazardous roads. Why, he could make it all the way to the county offices without a problem.

Muttering at the man's audacity, Amanda stalked toward his house to contact Nick Thorn. She wondered if Vamoose's chief of police had the slightest idea what was going on in the outback of this county. Probably not. For all she knew, this unincorporated area might be under the sheriff's jurisdiction.

Bruno plunked down on the mat beside the front door while Amanda covered her hands with the hem of her t-shirt, attempting to gain entrance without leaving fingerprints.

The door wouldn't budge.

Amanda strode around the side of the house to try the back door. To her surprise, it was sagging on its hinges. It looked as if someone had entered by force.

Covering her hand, Amanda twisted the knob. The door whined open.

"Yoo-hoo! It's Amanda Hazard. Is anyone home?"

She pricked her ears, expecting to hear a perp scrambling to make a fast getaway. All she heard was the pitter-patter of rain and the wind rattling the gutters.

Amanda removed her muddy boots before she strode off to locate the telephone. She frowned, bemused, when she noticed the lack of furnishings. A folding table and chairs served as the dining room suite. Two lawn chairs were positioned on either side of the fireplace in the living room.

Odd, Amanda thought as her keen gaze scanned the house. It looked as if someone had cleaned Brown out and he'd been making do.

Spotting the phone on a wooden TV tray, Amanda dialed Thorn's dispatcher and waited several seconds.

"Vamoose PD," came the woman's sing-song voice.

"Hazard here," Amanda said hurriedly. "I need to reach Thorn, PDQ."

"Hi, Amanda. I haven't had the chance to congratulate you on your engagement to the chief. When's the big day?"

"We haven't discussed the date. Listen, Janie-Ethel, I don't want to be rude, but I really need to contact Thorn. I'm stuck in the mud." *Among other things,* she added silently.

"You and everybody else," Janie-Ethel replied. "The chief and Deputy Sykes have had their hands full all morning. These rains have caused problems like you wouldn't believe. We've had reports of fender benders since six this morning."

"Could you relay a message for me?" Amanda questioned as she glanced around the sparsely furnished house. "Have Thorn call me ASAP." She gave the dispatcher the phone number, then hung up.

Was it coincidence that Brown had been found dead in the mud and that his house had been picked clean? Had the thieves returned and Brown happened upon them?

Pensively, Amanda ambled toward the front door. She stared out at the pouring rain. Now that Brown had paved his two-mile-long driveway, someone could have backed a U-Haul up to his porch and carted off his possessions without leaving tracks.

Amanda sank to her knees, then brushed her hand over the mat that lay in front of the door.

Dry as a bone.

When she lifted the mat, she noticed a smudge of mud on the powder-blue carpet beneath. The smudge was still wet. Amanda predicted that someone had covered the stains to conceal their presence in the house.

Interesting, she mused as she stared down the hill to the spot where she had found Brown in the mud. How was she going to squeeze in an investigation of this case when the April 15th tax deadline loomed over her like the ominous gray clouds dumping rain on Vamoose?

Where there was a will, there was a way, Amanda encouraged herself. She would have to sacrifice a little sleep, but that was the price she had to pay to preserve truth, justice, and the American way in the small rural hamlet of Vamoose.

Two

The phone rang while Amanda was replacing the doormat.

"Thorn here. What's the problem, Hazard?"

"My jalopy is stuck in the mud," she informed him. "Can you bring your four-wheel-drive truck out here?"

"At the moment? No," Thorn replied. "It's hooked up to the squad car. Deputy Sykes was racing to the scene of an accident on these sloppy country roads and he became an accident victim himself."

That figured, thought Amanda. The gung-ho deputy was always passing out speeding tickets, but he exceeded reasonable speeds in the name of duty and found his driving skills sorely lacking. The poor man would never measure up to Thorn, no matter how hard he tried.

"Is Benny okay?" Amanda asked.

"Yes, but his pride is bruised and he wrapped the front fender of his black-and-white around a fence post."

"How long before you can pick me up, Thorn?"

"Forty-five minutes. Do you mind waiting?"

"I can wait, but Commissioner Brown is only going to get colder and stiffer."

"What!" Thorn howled. "Good God, you finally did it! Just because he wouldn't gravel and grade these roads! Damn it, Hazard, please tell me you didn't really bump him off."

"I didn't bump him off," she assured him. "Someone beat me to it."

There was a noticeable pause. Amanda could visualize Thorn's thick black brows furrowing over his cocoa-brown eyes while he muttered inwardly about her insistence on crying murder. No doubt, it was going to take some fast talking to convince Thorn that foul play was involved.

"Where the hell are you, Hazard?"

"At Commissioner Brown's house. I found him dead in the mud. Since you're tied up, do you want me to call the sheriff?"

"I'll be there in fifteen minutes."

"I thought you said forty-five."

"I'll drop Deputy Sykes off at Watt's Auto Repair Shop and he can hire a tow truck."

Amanda sagged in relief. "Don't come in from the east. Take the highway to Adios, then turn south," she directed. "You won't have to worry about sloshing through the mud."

"What the hell are you talking about?"

"Commissioner Brown paved the country road from the Adios highway to his home—and part way to the bridge he was constructing for his own convenience. Talk about misuse of county funds!"

"I'm on my way, Hazard."

The line went dead. She put in a quick call to her office, informing Jenny Long, her secretary, that she would be late.

Amanda glanced around the house, determined to make good use of her time. While Thorn was making the drive, she would take a close look around Brown's property. No telling what else she might find besides telltale smudges of mud on the rug.

The master bedroom was strewn with clothes. The king-sized waterbed was unmade. Amanda appraised the untidy room and tangle of sheets, then ventured into the bathroom to check the clothes hamper.

Nothing but garments worn by men, she noticed. Furthermore, there were no stashes of make-up or hairbrushes in the vanity drawers. There was, however, a supply of condoms. Brown, it seemed, practiced safe sex—or planned to. Interesting.

Amanda replaced the hand towel she had used to prevent leaving prints while she searched for clues. Casting one last glance around the bathroom and bedroom, she strode down the hall. When she reached the kitchen, she noticed there were two coffee cups in the sink. Unless Bruno the Border Collie drank coffee with his master in the morning, Brown had entertained a guest in the not-too-distant past.

Thunder rattled the windowpanes and Amanda cursed the downpour. Every tidbit of evidence pointing to foul play was probably being washed away. How was she going to convince Thorn that a murder had taken place? He would take one look at the lopsided truck and the fallen jack, then assume that Dusty Brown's ill-fated accident was an open-and-shut case.

Grumbling irritably, Amanda surged through the front door and stood on the porch. Rain came down in torrents, hammering against the tin roof of Brown's workshop. Since she was already soaked to the bone, she rolled up her pant legs and ran barefoot to the workshop for a quick inspection. Bruno was at her heels.

Although the house was sparsely furnished, the workshop was teeming with tools and supplies. Amanda had never seen so many ratchets, socket sets, portable air com-

pressors, hammers, and wrenches. Heaping sacks of lug
nuts, screws, various electrical tools—tree saws, Skilsaws,
table saws—and air compressor attachments lined the walls
and shelves. A gas-powered generator sat in one corner.
Four step ladders were leaning against the south wall.
Brown had thousands of dollars worth of tools. That, too,
was interesting, she thought to herself.

Dedicated to her clue-finding mission, Amanda dashed
from the workshop to the garage. To her surprise, she
found herself staring at a late model Lincoln with shiny
chrome bumpers and velour interior. Electronic gadgets
and wood paneling lined the dashboard and doors.

"My, my," Amanda said to the ever-present Bruno.
"Brown was certainly making the most of his commissioner's salary, wasn't he?"

Bruno stared up at her and wagged his bobtail.

Nick Thorn, chief of Vamoose police, steered his black
4X4 pick-up through the driving rain. Following Hazard's
direction, he took the long way around Vamoose to the
small rural community of Adios that boasted a service station, a non-denominational church that had been erected
at the turn of the century, and a mom-and-pop grocery
store and bait shop that accommodated weekend travelers
fishing at nearby Buffalo Lake. According to historians,
huge herds of buffalo had gathered in the area to drink
from the natural reservoir.

Taking the narrow blacktop road that skirted the western
boundary of Vamoose County, Nick located the two-mile
paved driveway that led to Brown's home.

He muttered to himself as he cruised through the torren-
tial rain. He had heard that Commissioner Brown had
been focusing considerable time and effort on upgrading
country roads and constructing a river bridge in this sec-

tion of District 1, but Nick never dreamed Brown had been taking such grand care of himself!

The jerk, Nick thought. There had been a time when he had defended Dusty Brown, but the commissioner appeared to have been taking personal advantage of his term in office. If Brown's political adversaries had gotten wind of his pork-barrel projects, the campaign for re-election would have been disastrous. Surely, Brown knew that. Maybe that was why he was concentrating his work force on this area before the election.

When Nick veered into the circular drive, Hazard was standing on the porch, partially covered with mud. Her blond hair was plastered against her face, her t-shirt clung to her ample bustline, and her wet jeans hugged her shapely hips like a coat of paint.

A soggy Border Collie stood at her heels. The dog commenced barking the instant Nick climbed from his truck. The closer Nick came to Hazard, the more the dog objected. Lips curled and teeth bared, the dog assumed his red-alert, prepared-to-attack stance.

"Bruno, sit down and clam up," Hazard demanded, making a stabbing gesture with her index finger.

Amazingly, Bruno circled her legs and came to heel.

"I didn't know you had another dog," Nick commented.

"Bruno belonged to Brown."

Nick arched a dark brow. "Well, he certainly has taken a liking to you. Must be the male in him," he added wryly.

"This is no time to be cute, Thorn," Hazard said as she strode off the porch. "We have a corpse on our hands and two trucks stuck in the mud."

Without ado, Hazard seated herself in the cab of Nick's truck. Bruno hopped into the bed beside the hydraulic hay spear that protruded from the back of the pick-up. From every indication, Bruno had adopted Hazard and refused to let her leave without him.

Nick slid beneath the wheel, then drove in the direction

Hazard indicated. "What the devil were you doing out here in this remote section of the county?" he asked as he plowed his way downhill. "I thought you had too much work during tax season."

"I do. I'm up to my ears, but I took time out so I could come here and kill Brown," she said matter-of-factly. "Someone got here before I did."

Nick winced, then called on his reservoir of patience. He knew the circumstances surrounding Brown's death were going to cause friction between him and his fiancée. This bombshell blond's suspicious nature always came to the fore the moment anyone turned up dead in Vamoose County. True, Hazard had been surprisingly correct several times in the past, much to Nick's astonishment.

But for God's sake, why did Brown have to end up dead now? His timing was lousy. Nick and Hazard were in the process of making wedding arrangements, Hazard was fighting tax deadlines, and Nick had his police duties, cattle to doctor, and windrows of alfalfa hay molding in the meadows. Keeping up with his farming chores and law enforcement obligations had him running in circles.

As it was, Nick and Hazard only managed to see each other once a week—tops. Something was definitely going to have to give when they were married. Nick believed in togetherness. But if he asked Hazard to close her successful accounting business she'd hit the roof. She was, after all, a woman of the nineties—independent, assertive. Not only that, but she was as sexy as hell . . .

The tantalizing thought ended with a splash when Nick halted near Brown's county-issued truck. The instant Nick spotted the corpse his shoulders sagged.

Damn, Brown definitely looked dead. Hazard was right on that count.

"I already checked his vital signs," Amanda said as she opened the passenger door. "He doesn't have any."

Grimly, Nick approached the sprawled form and surveyed the scene. He noted that the battered truck was missing a wheel. He studied the position of the high-lift jack that had fallen across the back of Brown's knees, the metal jack handle that rested on the commissioner's shoulders. Rivulets of rain eroded sections of the muddy road. Heavy downpours had pounded other portions of it flat.

Nick appraised the area a second time, then frowned speculatively. "I think—" he began, only to be interrupted by Hazard's annoyed smirk.

"I know what you think, Thorn. You think what you always think when I'm suspicious of the circumstances surrounding the discovery of a dead body in Vamoose. You think Commissioner Brown met with a stroke of bad luck. Nothing more than cause and effect, followed by a lethal chain of events. Right?"

Nick crossed his arms over his massive chest and forced himself to listen to Hazard's speculations, no matter how ridiculous they were. This time, he promised himself, he was going to avoid argument and conflict, even if this looked like more of an accident than the one Deputy Sykes had had earlier this morning.

Hazard was staring at him defensively, but Nick had the good sense to keep his trap shut and hear her out.

"When I arrived on the scene, there was a variety of muddy prints around the truck," she reported. "Brown's difficulties with a flat tire had 'golden opportunity' engraved all over it. A nudge on the side of the truck could have sent the unstable jack sliding sideways, knocking Brown off his feet. One whack of the jack handle could have scrambled his brains—"

Nick made no comment. He was trying exceptionally hard to accommodate his fiancée's tendency to make something from nothing. This accident, Nick concluded, was just that—an accident caused by bad road conditions and inclement weather.

Hazard focused on Nick's expressionless stare. "I was mad enough to kill Brown when I came looking for him this morning. It is entirely possible that someone else felt the same way."

"Why were you so determined to track him down?" Nick asked calmly.

"Because my Toyota is high center on the muddy, rutted road east of my house and I ruined my favorite three-hundred-dollar cream-colored silk ensemble when I had to wade through the muck to get home!" Hazard erupted like Old Faithful.

Nick nodded pensively. "You were ready to kill the commissioner because of a muddy road and a silk business suit. Don't you think that's a bit extreme, Hazard? You aren't suffering from PMS this week, are you?"

It was the wrong thing to say. Hazard's pretty features puckered in a glower as she shook her forefinger in his face. "Don't try to use that psychological stuff on me, Thorn. If you had been listening carefully, you wouldn't have missed the point."

"There's a point?" Nick tried, really tried, but he couldn't keep the sarcasm from his baritone voice.

Hazard assumed her stubborn stance—feet apart, hands balled on hips, chin tilted to a challenging angle. "The point is," she said through clenched teeth, "if I—a reasonable, well-adjusted female—was furious enough to come after Brown because I could no longer tolerate his negligent disregard for road conditions in this district, someone else felt the same way and saw the chance to act upon it.

"Somebody killed Brown and left him dead in the mud," Hazard added with supreme certainty. "I don't know who or why, but you can bet your bottom dollar I intend to find out."

Nick breathed a long-suffering sigh. "Now, Hazard—"

"Don't start with me, Thorn. I'm having a bad day— and not because of PMS!"

Nick grimaced as her voice rose to an eardrum-shattering pitch.

"You can write up your report and shrug off this murder, but it was no accident. I know better, Thorn."

"How do you know, Hazard?"

"Because Brown left a clue in the mud. He etched a scraggly *S* before he expired."

"An *S?*" he asked dubiously.

"A long, strung-out *S,*" Hazard affirmed with a nod of her wet head.

Nick stared pensively at Brown. "Are you sure he wasn't trying to crawl to safety and his fingers clenched in the mud?" Watching where he stepped, Nick approached the body. "Natural human reaction is to escape danger, you know. Except for timid rabbit types who freeze up and wait until the last possible second to turn tail and run. Brown never struck me as that type of guy."

Nick squatted down to lift the soggy cardboard box beside Brown's outstretched hand. Rain had trickled beneath the box, forming rivulets.

"Well, damn," Hazard muttered. "I tried to preserve the print, but the rain destroyed the evidence. But I swear to you that there was an *S* in the mud when I arrived."

Nick gestured toward his pick-up. "I'll call the medical examiner from my CB, then I'll pull your truck out of the mud. We aren't accomplishing anything by standing out in the rain, exchanging contrasting theories."

"In other words," Hazard grumbled as she slopped back to the pick-up, Bruno at her heels, "I'm wasting my breath, as usual. You don't believe this is murder."

Nick called upon his dwindling reserve of patience while Hazard sat rigidly on the seat, staring at the swishing windshield wipers. How could Hazard cry murder when all evidence pointed to a simple case of rotten luck?

The answer was obvious to Nick. Hazard couldn't resist dabbling in detective work, even if there was nothing to investigate. But to appease his fiancée, Nick promised to take her suspicions into consideration when he and the medical examiner returned to the scene.

"I'll see what the coroner has to say about your . . . um . . . theory."

Hazard's reply to Nick's announcement was a disgusted snort. She knew no one intended to take her suspicions seriously.

Amanda was pure-dee annoyed by the time Thorn pulled her jalopy truck from the ditch and shooed her on her way. When would Thorn realize that her gut instincts and intuitive feminine suspicions were reliable? After all, she had cracked four cases of carefully staged murder—all of which had *looked* like accidents—since she had moved from the big city to Vamoose. By now, it should be obvious that she had dependable bloodhound instincts.

"Well, what did you expect?" Amanda asked herself as she dumped a handful of shampoo on her hair and scrubbed out the mud while she showered. "Thorn may be a hunk deluxe, but he'll never overcome his male mentality. If you're going to marry the guy—for better or worse—you have to tolerate his failing graces. You have known for years than men do not operate on the same high intellectual plane that women do. Their hormones get in their way."

While Amanda rinsed her hair, then dried off, she reminded herself of all the reasons why she was crazy about Thorn. He stirred her physically and emotionally and challenged her intellectually. Those were givens. Since moving to Vamoose, she hadn't met a man who could remotely compare to him.

With that in mind, Amanda decided to dedicate the upcoming years of wedlock to teaching Thorn to respect female intuition and analytical brain power.

Besides, Amanda reminded herself, as she stuffed one leg, then the other, into a clean pair of blue jeans, she was accustomed to handling her unofficial investigations alone. She would call in Thorn when she had the facts, motives and a list of probable suspects.

Amanda smiled wryly, remembering how hard Thorn had tried to remain open-minded while she spouted her suspicions at him. The dear, sweet man, he was making progress. He hadn't scoffed when she'd cried murder. But still, Amanda longed for the day when she announced that foul play was involved and Thorn came immediately to attention.

Someday, she thought whimsically.

Probably when pigs fly.

Until that happened, Amanda would lay the groundwork and do the legwork to solve cases. The first order of business was to make an appointment with Vamoose's most renowned source of background information. Velma Hertzog, the gum-chewing beautician, had cultivated the fine art of gossip into a science. Now that Velma's niece was working in the shop, adding her own two cents' worth of information, Amanda could get the low-down on Dusty Brown.

Amanda headed for the telephone to call for an appointment. Before she could pick it up, a dog fight erupted on the front porch. Hank the tomcat leaped off the chair and hightailed it for cover when canine bodies slammed against the outer wall of the house. It sounded as if Bruno and Pete were battling for territorial rights.

In a flash Amanda was at the door, yelling at the dogs to cease and desist. Not that it did a damn bit of good. Pete and Bruno were in the heat of battle. With ears laid back and fangs bared, the dogs rolled across the porch, getting in their licks—or bites, as this case happened to be.

Seeing the broom beside the door, Amanda stepped

outside to thump both canine fannies. The dogs reluctantly backed off, but Amanda knew there was bad blood between them—and blood dripping from both sets of ears.

This was not going to work, Amanda decided. The newest arrival would have to go. Although Bruno had endeared himself to Amanda—because of his protectiveness—Pete was like family. She couldn't haul off the three-legged dog that one of her deceased clients had bequeathed to her. Elmer Jolly would roll over in his grave!

"Bruno," Amanda said in her most authoritative tone. "Get in the house. Now!"

To her amazement, Bruno slinked inside the door and hunkered down on the welcome mat. He laid his head on his paws and stared up at her with big, sad eyes.

"Call me sentimental, but I can't get rid of you, either," Amanda murmured as she patted Bruno's downcast head. "Maybe you can be my bodyguard while Pete keeps watch outside." She glanced over her shoulder, frowning pensively. "How do you feel about tomcats? Here kitty, kitty!"

Hank took his own sweet time about answering the summons. When he rounded the corner of the hall and spotted Bruno, the cat's hair stood on end. He hissed in warning, but Bruno merely thumped his bobtail on the floor and made no attempt to attack.

Amanda raised a perfectly arched brow as Bruno held position and Hank stalked forward to sniff out the intruder. Bruno was well-mannered in the house, Amanda noted. She wondered if Brown had allowed the Border Collie inside. Obviously.

Keeping an eye on Bruno, just in case he was waiting for her to turn her back before he made a between-meal snack of Hank, Amanda picked up the phone and dialed. So far so good, she mused, cutting Bruno a discreet glance. No blood had spilled on the living room carpet. Hank kept his cautious distance while Bruno sprawled on the doormat to lick his battle wounds.

"Velma's Beauty Boutique." Chomp, pop. "If you need a 'do, we've got the right one for you."

Amanda blinked at the unexpected recording. Velma had gone electronic. Good lord, high-tech had invaded this small-town hamlet.

"At the sound of the beep, leave your name, number and message." Crackle, snap. "We'll be in touch. Have a good one!"

Amanda waited for the beep, then left her name and number. "I need a minimal trim," she clarified. "Nothing drastic."

Checking her watch, Amanda strode off to fix herself a sandwich. At frequent intervals she poked her head around the corner to ensure Bruno was behaving himself. Hank had taken his customary position on the La-Z-Boy recliner. One furry paw rested on the TV remote control. The cat was napping. Bruno was ignoring the cat and pricking his ears each time Amanda checked on him.

"Okay, you big lug," Amanda said, motioning to the dog. "You've proved yourself. Get your soggy butt into the kitchen."

Upon command, Bruno trotted toward her. While Amanda slapped two sandwiches together, Bruno took his position beside the table. When she offered him a ham sandwich, he swallowed it whole.

Amanda made a mental note to stop by Toot 'N Tell 'Em to pick up another sack of dog food.

"Well?" Thorn prompted the medical examiner who had given Brown a thorough going-over.

"Well what?" the coroner asked. He rose from his crouched position. "The man is dead. He caught a high-lift jack handle in the back of the head, fell unconscious, and drowned in the rut. He became a card-carrying jerk after he was elected to his political post, and you're asking me if this could possibly be a homicide?''

Nick nodded. "As a *professional,"* he clarified. "Your *personal* opinion of Brown couldn't be more obvious."

The medical examiner chewed on his bottom lip as he stepped back to assess the scene from four different directions. "There is always a remote possibility, I suppose. But hell, Thorn, anybody with eyes in his head can see the flat tire and fallen jack. Seems to me that Brown was a victim of his own bad road. If you ask me, I'd say Brown got his just desserts. If someone set the stage, you'd think he would've been spotted—bad weather or not. The only prints in and around the truck belong to Brown, livestock and a dog. If anything, I suspect the dog might have bumped into the jack that crashed down on Brown. You gonna arrest the first dog you see?''

Nick frowned. It could very well be that Bruno's rambunctiousness had caused a series of events to take place. Although Hazard had other ideas, Nick and the coroner had arrived at the same conclusion.

All the same, Nick asked the coroner to run the basic tests for time of death and take a closer look at the angle of impact to the back of Brown's skull.

"Okay, Thorn, but this will have to be a hurry-up job," the medical examiner said as he scooped up his bag. "I'm working a homicide down by Pronto at the moment—an obvious one."

Nick helped the coroner load the last remains, then he backed his four-wheel-drive pick-up into position to tow Brown's county-issued truck up the hill.

Within a few minutes Nick had shoved the spare tire into place and tightened the bolts. Putting the vehicle in neutral, Nick pulled Brown's battered truck to the house.

It was becoming increasingly apparent that Hazard's instincts had steered her wrong this time. It had been several months since she had found Will Bloom dead in the dirt, and she was itching to open another unofficial investigation, even if she did have scads of obligations awaiting her at tax time.

Hopefully, the itch would pass, Nick mused. Hazard would find herself so involved with tax returns and wedding plans that she would haven't time to scratch.

This would be a good lesson for Hazard to learn, Nick told himself as he drove to town. She would discover that not every dead body was a murder victim. Occasionally, accidents *did* happen.

"Chief, come in!" Janie-Ethel called over the CB. "There's a report of a traffic accident north of Vamoose."

Nick tensed, hoping Hazard hadn't lost control of her jalopy on her way home.

"Judd Braxton was trying to haul hogs to the stockyards and his pick-up hydroplaned. His stock trailer jackknifed and his pigs are loose on the highway."

"On my way," Nick came back. "Over and out."

He had the unmistakable feeling this was going to be a long, hectic day.

Three

Amanda rattled off instructions to her secretary in specific detail. If she was going to investigate Brown's possible murder, Jenny Long needed a crash course in filling out tax returns. Thus far, Jenny had been delegated the tasks of copying and filing forms and taking calls. Amanda had no choice but to promote Jenny to assistant accountant during tax season.

Jenny had immediately asked for a raise.

Amanda agreed. After all, the single mother had a young son to raise.

"Since I'm paying you the big bucks, I expect perfection," Amanda insisted. "When you transfer these figures to the federal and state forms they have to be accurate. My clients expect that."

Jenny smiled brightly. "I can handle it, boss. I've been taking night classes at the vo-tech so I can be of more help to you."

Amanda blinked in surprise. "You have?"

"I have," Jenny proudly confirmed. "I can handle the

standard forms without a hitch. The itemized tax forms won't be covered until next semester, though."

Amanda beamed in satisfaction. Things were working out better than anticipated. If Jenny could handle the EZ 1040s, Amanda could concentrate on the business accounts and complicated forms requiring detailed deductions and depreciations.

"Sorry to hear you're the one who stumbled onto Commissioner Brown," Jenny said as Amanda sorted the files into two stacks. "I'd probably have passed out if that had happened to me."

Amanda cast the buxom brunette a sideways glance. Jenny was a lifelong resident of Vamoose. She was probably well-versed on the subject of Commissioner Brown.

"Did you know Dusty personally?" Amanda asked.

"Sort of." Jenny quickly alphabetized the files. "Dusty went to school in Adios, but he dated my older sister for a year or so. Back then, everybody liked him well enough. You know, prom king, student of the month and all that. But he changed drastically after he assumed control of his dad's farming operation, then campaigned for commissioner of District 1. Personally, I think his political success went to his head. He was kind of cocky to begin with. After he became commissioner he really got the big head. He hasn't done much for the voters around Vamoose, and I hadn't planned to cast my ballot for him in the primary election."

"Neither had I. Brown has been neglecting the country roads since I moved to town."

"I doubt his wife was going to vote for him, either," Jenny commented as she accepted the armful of files Amanda presented to her.

"His wife?" Amanda did a double-take. Her quick inspection of Brown's home had given no indication of a feminine presence. "I didn't know he had one."

"Sara Mae moved out about six months ago," Jenny

reported. "Dusty has been making the divorce proceedings a genuine nightmare for her. According to my sister, who heard the story from Lydia Shakelford, who's the new waitress at Last Chance Cafe, Dusty was being spitefully difficult and stingy. He wanted the house and the property. All Sara Mae had was the stuff she managed to tote off in a U-Haul before Dusty returned from work."

Amanda stored the information in an open file of her memory bank. Suspect Number One—the estranged wife.

"Was Sara Mae angry about the problems Dusty was causing in the divorce?"

"Angry?" Jenny gave a loud hoot. "Are you kidding? Of course, she was mad. Who wouldn't be? Dusty fancied himself as a roving Romeo while he cruised around the county, deciding which roads and bridges to repair. Word is that the women who accommodated him were the only ones who got a load of gravel dumped on their roads.

"Sara Mae got wind of Dusty's affairs and decided what was good for the goose was good for the gander. When Dusty found out about Sara Mae's new lover, he threw her out of the house. She returned with her boyfriend and they changed the locks to keep Dusty out of the house, but he got furious and broke down the back door. Then the battle was on."

Amanda had noticed the evidence of a forced entry at the Brown home. She had suspected someone had robbed the house. Apparently, Brown was responsible for breaking and entering his own home.

"Who wound up in worse shape after the fiasco?" Amanda inquired. "Dusty or the new boyfriend?"

Jenny gathered the stack of files possessively against her chest. It was evident that she was anxious to put her newly acquired skills to use and prove her competence as assistant accountant. "The new boyfriend," she replied. "Dusty broke a dining room chair over his head and dragged him out the back door. Then he threw Sara Mae over his shoulder. She kicked and screamed until he dumped her right on top of her unconscious boyfriend."

Jenny shook her head ruefully. "All Sara Mae wanted was the king-sized waterbed, dresser and furniture. But Dusty told her she'd gotten everything she was going to get. He contacted his lawyer and froze the joint accounts. She moved in with her new boyfriend—for her own protection, as well as his."

"Who's the new boyfriend?" Amanda had to repeat the question when Jenny focused profound concentration on the Andrews tax file.

"What? Oh, sorry," Jenny apologized. "I guess I'm eager to get started. I really want to prove myself to you, boss. You're my idol, you know."

Amanda didn't have time to be flattered. She had a killer to catch in the heat of tax season. "Who is Sara Mae living with?" she asked for the third time.

"It's Leo Snittiger's son by his first marriage. Sonny runs the bait shop in Adios and rents paddle boats, canoes and rafts at the lake."

Sara Mae and Sonny, Amanda thought as she watched Jenny scan the tax voucher spread across the desk. Both names began with an *S*. She doubted it was coincidence. Both Sara Mae and Sonny had reason to leave Dusty Brown sprawled in the mud.

For several minutes Amanda watched Jenny's nimble fingers hover over the calculator keys. Sure enough, Jenny had been taking her studies seriously.

Amanda was impressed. Jenny had begun to think of her position at Hazard Accounting as a career, not a job. She had come a long way from the ditzy waitress who'd had a crush on Thorn. Amanda was thankful those awkward days were behind them. Having established herself as an amateur sleuth who had a knack for rooting out clever killers, Amanda had no time for feminine rivals who wanted to snatch Thorn away before he tied the matrimonial knot.

Now, if only she could get Thorn to admit that she was as good at detective work as he was. Amanda smiled slyly as she turned on her heels. Maybe she would insist that particular statement be included in the wedding vows.

"I have a hair appointment this morning," Amanda said on her way out the door.

Jenny looked up, her expression dazed. "What?"

Amanda gestured toward her head. "Haircut. I'll be back to check on your progress after lunch—Whoa!"

Amanda braced herself against the open door when Bruno swished past her, refusing to be left behind. The dog had been lying beneath Amanda's desk, quiet as a church mouse.

Jenny grinned in amusement when Bruno came to heel. "That dog has gone ape over you. I've never seen such devotion. Where'd you get him?"

"He adopted me yesterday," Amanda said vaguely.

"Well, he sure got attached fast."

Before Amanda could reply, Jenny had buried herself in her work. Amanda walked away, knowing her clients would be in capable hands. She would have the time needed to investigate the Brown case. Of course, Amanda would have to put in several long nights to complete the complicated tax returns that Jenny couldn't tackle. But lack of sleep was the price gumshoes paid when they couldn't afford to quit their day jobs.

"Hi, hon!" Velma cried when Amanda entered the beauty shop. She waddled away from The Chair to grab Amanda's left hand. "It's about time I got to take a gander at this ring." Crackle, snap.

"Would you look at the size of this rock! Lordy, this diamond must've set Nicky back a few thousand."

Amanda waited for the clientele of the shop to "ooh" and "ahh" over her engagement ring.

Millicent Patch bent her Brillo-pad head over Amanda's hand, then adjusted her bifocals. "I wish my dear Henry, God rest his sweet soul, could have afforded to give me a ring like this. But he was dirt poor when I married him."

Millie tucked her polyester skirt around her plump thighs as she plunked back into The Chair. "Have you and Nick set the date yet?"

"It will probably be sometime after tax season, wheat harvest and field work," Amanda replied. "Thorn might be able to take some time off from patrol duty before fall wheat planting."

Velma gave her dyed red head a dismayed shake. "That doesn't sound the least bit romantic. Both of you are letting your careers stand in the way of happily ever after. You should be working your business obligations around your wedding."

"My clients might object if I requested extensions on their tax returns and flew off for a honeymoon," Amanda pointed out.

Velma waved a beefy hand. "Well, pooey on your stuffy ol' clients. As for me, I don't care if I have to file for an extension. Uncle Sam can wait to get his greedy mitts on my money."

Beverly Hill seconded her aunt's declaration. "You go, Aunt Velma! Like, I think we need to start a tax rebellion. It worked for George W. and the minutemen. Why not for us? Giving so much of my paycheck to the government is a real bummer. Like, why do I have to pay Social Security anyway? The fund will be defunct by the time I'm old enough to retire."

"And can you believe the way Uncle Sam wastes hard-earned tax dollars?" Millie tut-tutted in disapproval. "Why, it's outrageous. If my dear Henry was still alive, he'd be up there in Washington leading the protest. If the government functioned as efficiently as private business we wouldn't be drowning in a sea of national debt!''

Amanda had her own firm opinions on the state of national affairs—tax revenue in particular—but she had come to the salon to glean information about Dusty Brown, not discuss politics.

Artfully Amanda steered the conversation toward Brown, before the rabble-rousers joined ranks to march to Washington. Amanda could imagine the reaction when a convoy of pick-up trucks arrived at the Pentagon, demanding tax cuts that were always promised and never delivered. Small-town America would probably be laughed off Capitol Hill.

"I suppose everybody heard about Commissioner Brown," Amanda said for starters.

"Of course, we did, hon." Velma positioned herself behind The Chair to snip the wiry frizz from Millie's gray hair. "Since Beverly set up her police scanner radio in the storeroom, we know everything that goes down in Vamoose." Snap, pop. "Can't say our pig-headed commissioner is going to be missed."

Now we're getting somewhere, Amanda thought as she took the vacant seat at Bev's new manicure table.

"Dusty wasn't too popular around here?" Amanda baited.

Bev bit. "Popular? Like, no stinkin' way! You should've heard the complaints that were buzzing around the shop after the news reached us."

Bev plopped her pudgy body into her chair. Her black Shirley Temple curls bounced against her shoulders like metal springs. "I'll give you a manicure while you're waiting for Aunt Velma," she said as she plucked up the nail file.

Amanda nodded. What could the rookie beautician do to screw up fingernails? It couldn't be worse than the disastrous haircut Amanda had received at Bev's hands a few months earlier.

Bev laid Amanda's left hand in her palm. "My mama went, 'Somebody oughta shoot that Commissioner Brown for his incompetence'. And I went, 'You can say that again!' The roads in our district are atrocious. Like, you have to have a four-wheel-drive truck to get anywhere when it rains."

By now, Amanda had grown accustomed to Bev's adolescent lingo, even if it had taken some getting used to.

"I'll tell you what, though," Bev yammered as she filed Amanda's nails. "I swore Isaac Marcum was going to strangle Commissioner Brown outside Last Chance Cafe a few months back. Like, wow! Isaac went for Brown's throat with a vengeance. My daddy had to pry them apart before they beat each other black and blue."

"Isaac Marcum?" Amanda repeated curiously.

"Isaac is the Vietnam vet who lives down the road from Brown," Velma put in as she placed the finishing touches on Millie's 'do. "He had been badgering Brown to remove the cluster of trees and Johnsongrass from that blind intersection." Chomp, chomp. "Isaac predicted that somebody was going to have a terrible wreck if Brown didn't bulldoze that ditch. Sure 'nuff, it happened. It was Isaac's teenage daughter who got killed. The poor man went berserk."

Although Isaac's name didn't begin with an *S*, Amanda mentally jotted down another possible suspect to interrogate.

"Salty lit into Brown like gangbusters," Velma went on as she grabbed the aerosol hairspray.

"Salty?" Amanda repeated, bemused.

"That's Isaac's nickname." Crackle, chomp. "He's known for his four-letter-word vocabulary. When he blows his stack, curse words fly like bats from a cave. Since his daughter died, Salty sits out there at his house like a hermit, drawing his disabled vet pension and brooding. He rarely comes to town, except to gather his rations. Lives off the land mostly, practicing all the survival skills he perfected in the war.''

"I—" Amanda clamped her mouth shut and held her breath when the choking fog of hairspray filled the salon. Several minutes of silence followed. Nobody dared to breathe until Velma opened the door to let the sticky particles drift outside.

The ozone layer was about to take another direct hit.

"What the heck—?" Velma yowled when Bruno dashed inside to take his place at Amanda's feet.

"My bodyguard," Amanda introduced, patting the dog with her free hand. "Bruno doesn't like to be out of my sight."

Bev looked down at the dog, then sniffed. "If I had a bodyguard, like, I'd have held out for Kevin Costner."

"I wasn't offered that choice," Amanda replied.

"That's Bruno?" Velma chomped her chewing gum and blinked her fake eyelashes. "Are we talking about Brown's dog?"

Amanda nodded while Bev Hill meticulously applied a coat of nail polish.

"Well, go figure," Velma said as she shook out the Pepto-Bismol-colored cape that had been fastened around Millie's neck. Split ends of gray hair fluttered to the floor. "I heard tell that Brown had to bribe Bruno with dog biscuits to persuade him to ride in the truck. It doesn't say much for a man when his own dog hates him. The minute Brown wound up dead, Bruno latched onto you."

"*Nobody* liked Brown?" Amanda questioned.

"Like, who could?" Bev put in, then bent her curly head over Amanda's hand. "Brown thought he was hot stuff after he was elected. Like, if I was his political opponent in the upcoming election, I'd be relieved to have him out of the way. Anybody opposing Brown would be a shoo-in this time. Brown has turned friends into enemies."

Amanda rose to her feet when Velma motioned her to

The Chair. Her discreet investigation momentarily forgotten, Amanda gestured her wet fingernails toward her head. "Just shape up my 'do, Velma," she requested. "I've decided to let my hair grow out for the wedding. Thorn likes long hair best."

"Don't worry about a thing, hon." Pop, smack. "When the time comes for the ceremony, I'll style your hair for nothing. It'll be part of my wedding gift to you. I've got some great ideas for your ceremonial hairstyle. You'll love 'em!"

Amanda doubted it. She'd had more than her fair share of bad haircuts and outlandish styles since she'd moved to Vamoose. But there was no place like Beauty Boutique to acquire investigative leads. Already, Amanda had the names of several suspects to question.

Velma took brush in hand and tugged on Amanda's hair. Amanda clamped hold of the armrest to prevent being uprooted.

"And don't you worry about the wedding shower, hon," Velma went on. "Bev and I have decided to give you the best darned shower you could hope to have. Aren't we, sugar?"

"Like, yeah!" Bev enthused as she scampered over to finish painting Amanda's nails. "Nothing but the best for Vamoose's favorite couple. It'll be just swell. Aunt Velma went, 'Why don't you be in charge of decorations, plates and napkins while I do the invitations and order the cake?' I went, 'Cool!'"

Amanda inwardly winced. She wasn't sure which would be worse—having Mother or Velma commandeer a wedding shower.

It was too close to call.

"Now, don't start fretting when I start clipping your hair," Velma forewarned as she scooped up the scissors. "This is a preliminary trim for your wedding 'do. Your hair will grow into this statement-making cut." Pop, pop!

Amanda braced herself for the worst and prayed for the best.

"What are your accent colors for the wedding, hon?"

Accent colors? Hell's bells, Amanda hadn't given those insignificant details a thought. "I haven't decided."

"I've always been particularly partial to Prussian purple and passion pink."

Oh, God . . .

"Both colors look flashy with white." Snap, crackle. "You *are* wearing white, aren't you?"

"It's my second marriage," Amanda chirped, feeling the arrangements for her wedding spinning beyond her control.

"But it's Nicky's first, ya know." Velma grabbed a handful of blond hair, holding it at a sixty-degree angle from the crown of Amanda's head. "You can't deprive Nicky of tradition. It should be a humongous wedding."

"I was thinking of a small, private affair."

"Nonsense!" Velma protested. She set to work with industrious zeal. "You have to invite everyone in Vamoose. This is small-town America we're talking about. Everybody has been planning to attend since news of your engagement swept through town. Folks will feel hurt and left out if they aren't invited."

"Like, Aunt Velma is right on," Bev chimed in as she worked feverishly on Amanda's nails. "It'll be the social event of the year. I know I'd be hurt if I wasn't invited." Bev's eyes widened in alarm. Her incandescent-green, half-moon-shaped eye shadow disappeared into the creases below her brows. "Like, I *am* invited, aren't I?"

Amanda said the only thing she could possibly say. "Like, sure you are, Bev."

When Bev beamed in satisfaction, her painted-on Marilyn Monroe mole disappeared into the crevice in her jowls. "Cool!"

Amanda bit back a wail when Velma took a wild whack

with her scissors. A clump of hair drifted to Amanda's shoulders. All those months of letting her cropped hairdo grow out had been in vain!

"Now, don't panic, hon," Velma said as she focused her attention on the left side of Amanda's head. "I'm experimenting with a bi-level 'do that will take some time to perfect." Whack, snip, snip. "You'll need to come back next week for phase two."

Velma glanced down at her niece. "Bev, hon, pencil Amanda in for next Friday, will you?"

Bev rose from her squat, then set the nail polish aside. Hurriedly, she added Amanda's name to the appointment book.

Amanda was too stunned to object. Her wide-eyed gaze was glued to the mirror. Velma had chopped her blond hair in layers, making the side of her head look like a shingled roof!

Yikes! Thorn was going to throw a ring-tailed fit when he saw the disastrous by-product of Amanda's fact-finding mission.

"Oh, before I forget." Chomp, crackle. "The Vamoose Fire Department is hosting a Donkey Basketball game as a fundraiser. I know you and Nicky won't mind riding for the town team."

"I—"

Velma didn't take a breath as she circled The Chair, whacking and snipping the right side of Amanda's hair. "I'm in charge of rounding up riders and candidates for Donkey King and Queen."

Velma cracked her gum so near Amanda's ear that she flinched.

"The queen and king titles are determined by how much money the candidates raise for the fire department," Velma added.

"I don't think I want to—"

"Of course, you do," Bev broke in as she resumed work

on Amanda's nails. "Like, Vinita Frizzell has been begging to be a candidate. You can't let her win. She doesn't have your class and style."

A woman needed class and style to be Donkey Queen?

"I don't believe I know Vinita," Amanda wheezed as she watched Velma bear down with scissors.

"You haven't missed much," Bev sniffed. "Her husband, Homer, works for the country road department. While poor Homer is running the road grader, Vinita slinks around in her Spandex body suits, trying to drive the male population of Adios crazy. The woman refuses to work, and she doesn't even have a driver's license, for Pete's sake. Homer has to haul her around all the time. Personally, I think the woman has too much time on her hands."

Velma gave her dyed red head a remorseful shake. "Talk about being oversexed. Vinita can't see past her own body. She had a nose job, boob job and liposuction to shape herself up and call more attention to her feminine assets. She comes in here once a month for bleachings. If one black root on her head is exposed, she goes bonkers."

"And talk about a haystack of brittle straw," Bev added. "Vinita's platinum hair looks like ripe wheat. Like, she freaked out when I trimmed her hair too short. You should've heard her ranting and raving at me. She made me give her two free cuts, because she said I screwed the first one up so bad. When Homer brought her in this morning, she even made me dye her roots for free!"

Amanda had been paying little attention to the discussion of Vinita's idiosyncracies, but the instant Bev mentioned that Homer Frizzell worked for Brown's road crew, she took notice. Now here was a man who probably had the inside track on Brown's professional life. Amanda made a mental note to question Homer. He might provide productive links to other possible suspects. Heck, he might even be one himself! At this point, Amanda was not prepared to rule out anyone. Not even the temperamental Vinita.

"I wouldn't wait too long to begin collecting donations as Donkey Queen candidate," Velma advised as she scooped up a comb. "You'll need to begin immediately if you're going to beat out Vinita. She's been hitting everyone up for three days, demanding donations. It wouldn't be good for your image to become first runner-up to that sexpot."

Amanda gulped when Velma teased her hair. The strands stood at attention and Amanda thought she looked as if she had plugged herself into an electrical socket.

"I'm going to experiment with this spray-on color," Velma announced as she latched onto the aerosol can. "We'll find just the right shade to match your accent colors before the wedding."

Psssst . . . Fizzzz . . .

A florescent-pink fog hovered around Amanda's head as Velma circled The Chair.

"Like, wow, Aunt Velma, that washable tint does make a statement, doesn't it?" Bev stood aside, waiting for the gooey particles to cling to the ends of Amanda's teased hair. "Awesome! Just think how that color would look when combined with spray-on glitter!"

The thought made Amanda want to throw up.

"Now, we'll top it off with hair spray to seal in the color," Velma announced. "Next week, we'll try Prussian purple."

"With glitter!" Bev added. "Definitely go with the glitter, Aunt Velma."

Velma studied Amanda's reflection thoughtfully. "Or maybe incandescent pearl. We'll try both to see which effect we like best."

Patting Amanda's shoulder, Velma smiled into the mirror. "I'd cover my head before I went outside," she advised. "It's raining again. Wouldn't want that tint to bleed."

Slack-jawed, Amanda scooted off The Chair. She barely remembered paying for the cosmetic catastrophe, barely recalled walking from the salon with Bruno at her heels.

If this outrageous 'do was any indication of the creation Velma and Bev had in mind for her wedding, she'd have to be married with a paper sack on her head!

Following the beautician's suggestion, Amanda covered her head and dashed through the rain to clamber into her truck. Removing the newspaper Velma had placed over her head to avoid raindrops, Amanda stared at herself in the rearview mirror. Lord, she looked as bad as Dennis Rodman of the Chicago Bulls!

Shakily, Amanda glanced at the dog. ''Well, Bruno, what do you think?''

Bruno whined, lay down on the seat, and covered his head with his paws.

Amanda inhaled a bracing breath and cranked the engine of her truck. If man's best friend couldn't bear to look at her, Amanda hated to imagine what Thorn would have to say.

Four

"Oh, my God . . ." Jenny Long's face lost all color. Stunned, she stared at her boss. "What happened to your hair?"

Amanda strode across the office to retrieve the tax files. "I forgot to put the newspaper over my head before I dashed in here. Is it that bad?"

"Bad?" Owl-eyed, Jenny stared at the cosmetic disaster. "What *is* that stuff?"

"Washable tint, or so Velma says." Amanda glanced down at her fingernails—and screamed.

Bruno howled sympathetically from his guard post beside the door.

Amanda had been too preoccupied with the haircut Velma had given her to notice what Bev had done to her hands. Her fingernails had been filed to sharp points and painted florescent yellow. On each finger, a happy face stared back at her. Black pointed hats formed the peak of each nail and shiny, industrial-strength lacquer prevented the creative designs from chipping.

Pink hair and happy-face fingernails? Good grief!

When Amanda recovered from her shock, she wheeled toward the door. "I think I better work on these tax returns at home since I look like a sideshow circus freak. Can you hold down the fort?"

"Sure thing, boss." Jenny scurried from behind her desk to add one more file to Amanda's stack. "Sara Mae Brown dropped in while you were at the beauty shop. She wants you to handle the estate taxes and final returns for Dusty."

Amanda smiled to herself. This was the only bright spot in a catastrophic day. Getting her happy-face hands on Brown's tax receipts might offer a few clues to solve the murder that Thorn had shrugged off as an accident.

"Better wear this," Jenny advised, snatching up a copy of the *Vamoose Gazette*. "If that hair color keeps bleeding, it'll blind you while you're driving. I'd hate for you to have a wreck on your way home."

Amanda nodded her thanks before walking out into the rain. She was sure the dripping dye was destroying her vision as she drove home, because she swore she saw pigs darting across the highway.

Things were looking up, she thought optimistically. Next thing she knew pigs *would be* flying!

When Nick Thorn finally chased down the last of the hogs that had run wild after Judd Braxton's traffic accident, sundown was settling on Vamoose. Nick had yet to find time to tow Hazard's Toyota from the middle of the muddy road.

Switching on his headlights, Nick sloshed down the road leading to Hazard's farm home. He had received a call from the medical examiner, and he felt obligated to pass along the information to Hazard.

Not that she would be satisfied with the coroner's conclusions, Nick thought as he hooked the heavy-duty chain to the car bumper. Returning to his truck, Nick eased the compact car backward. The plastic bumper crackled like popcorn. Nick grimaced when he glanced back to see one side of the flimsy fender dangling.

"Well, hell," he muttered as he towed the car into Hazard's driveway. This tin-can car would need an appointment at Watt's Auto Body Shop.

Swiftly, Nick unhitched the chain from the mud-splattered car, then tugged on the dangling bumper. The damned thing gave way and fell in the mud.

"Nice work, Thorn. Maybe you can get a job with a demolition company in your spare time."

Nick glanced toward the darkened doorway. He couldn't see Hazard, but he didn't miss the dismay in her voice. She was none too pleased with the condition of her Toyota.

"You need to consider trading cars," he said as he strode up the sidewalk. "When we're married, you'll need a 4x4 truck. This foreign car of yours has been nothing but trouble since you moved to Vamoose. It can't hold up on rough roads and muddy ruts."

"Fine. I'll go truck shopping after tax season . . . You aren't planning on coming in, are you?"

Nick stopped short, staring at the darkness that concealed Hazard from view. "I'm your fiancé. Of course, I'm coming in. We have wedding arrangements to make, and I'm starving to death. It's been a long, hectic day on the police beat."

"I'm snowed under with tax returns. Maybe we should postpone making wedding plans for a few days."

Nick squinted through the storm door, seeing nothing but Hazard's indistinguishable silhouette among the shadows. "I also wanted to let you know what the coroner had to say about Commissioner Brown."

"You can tell me from here. I'm not presentable."

Nick frowned warily. Something was up. Hazard was trying to get rid of him. Well, it wouldn't work. Being engaged allowed a man certain undeniable rights. One of them was seeing his fiancée after a hard day's work.

Hooking one muddy boot heel on the edge of the porch, Nick removed his footwear.

"I really don't think you want to come in here, Thorn."

"Why not?"

"Because Bruno has been extremely protective of me. He might bite you."

Nick's dark brows jackknifed. "You let that dog in your house?"

"Bruno insisted."

"Well, so do I."

Nick whipped open the glass storm door and surged inside. He didn't look down when Bruno growled beside his stocking feet. Nick couldn't. His bug-eyed gaze was glued to Hazard's wild hairdo. Solidified globs of passion pink clung to her hairline.

"What the sweet loving hell happened?" he yelled.

Hazard's chin went airborne. "Thanks for the moral support, Thorn. Where's the sympathy and concern expected from a devoted, caring fiancé?"

"Well *sorry*, Hazard," Nick snorted. "But anybody who tries to glean information on a nonexistent murder case at Velma's Beauty Boutique usually gets what she deserves."

Hazard's eyes narrowed in annoyance. Nick had promised himself that he would handle Hazard's compulsion for detective work better than he had in the past. Unfortunately, he'd had a frustrating day on patrol. His patience had been worn paper-thin. He'd wanted to kick back and relax. Instead, he'd been greeted by a fiancée who couldn't keep from poking her nose into investigations and had ended up with a hairdo from hell.

"You're wasting time, money and hair tint on Brown's case," he blurted out tactlessly. "The medical examiner called this afternoon with the results of his testing. Brown died about eight-thirty this morning. The angle of the blow to his skull indicated nothing suspicious. No fingerprints, other than Brown's, were found on the tire tools, jack, or pick-up. This was nothing but a case of bad luck, Hazard. You ruined your hair for nothing.''

"I told you that Brown tried to leave a message in the mud," Hazard said sharply.

"The man was trying to crawl to safety, not writing his last will and testament. You've got nothing substantial to go on."

Hazard pointed a happy-face finger toward the La-Z-Boy recliner. "Take a load off your feet and I'll pop some frozen dinners in the microwave while I tell you what I've turned up."

When Hazard spun toward the kitchen, Bruno trotted after her. Nick plunked down in the chair, then heaved an exhausted sigh. He asked himself—and not for the first time—why he hadn't fallen for a normal, laid-back kind of woman who could cook a decent meal and didn't have an obsessive fetish for self-appointed criminal investigations.

Once married, could he ever look forward to coming home to a delicious casserole, a goblet of wine and casual discussions about the weather, home improvements—anything except unauthorized investigations?

"Thorn, I turned up several possible leads while I was at the beauty shop," Hazard called from the kitchen.

The answer to his silent question was "no," Nick concluded. Ah well, he thought as he shoved away the pushy tomcat that tried to nest on his lap. Life with Hazard had never been dull. He'd just spend the rest of his days taming her investigative tendencies. There were arousing and tantalizing ways to distract Hazard, he reminded himself with a grin.

"Did you know Dusty Brown was in the process of getting a divorce?"

Nick laid his head against the back of the chair and stared at the ceiling. "No, I didn't."

"Rumor has it that Sara Mae and her boyfriend sneaked in to haul the furniture from the house and Brown returned home unexpectedly to clobber the boyfriend. And guess what else?"

Nick was too tried for guessing games. "What else, Hazard?"

"Sonny Snittiger and Sara Mae's names start with *S*. The estranged wife and lover both have motive and opportunity. They could have been waiting at the house, saw the chance to hike through the ditch and hammer Brown on the head with the handle of the high-lift jack."

Okay, Thorn, Nick thought to himself. *Be a good sport and play along with Hazard while she's nuking your supper.* "What else did you turn up during your scalping and dye job at the beauty salon?"

Hazard poked her head around the corner and smiled. Clearly, she approved that he was showing token interest in this nonexistent case.

"Remember the young girl from Adios who was killed in the traffic accident last fall?" she prompted.

Nick nodded his dark head.

"She was Isaac Marcum's one and only child. Isaac had been badgering Brown to clear the dangerous intersection of trees and underbrush for a year. Isaac tried to choke Brown after his daughter died in the crash. Isaac blamed Brown.

"Revenge is a strong motive. And as it happens, Isaac lives on the hill overlooking that stretch of road where Brown had his flat tire."

"Salty," Nick murmured, remembering the vet's well-earned nickname.

"Precisely. The *S* thing again."

Hazard emerged from the kitchen. Oven mitts covered her hands. Nick eyed the steaming plastic plates of greasy fried chicken and gooey mashed potatoes and lost his appetite. He preferred to cuddle up with Hazard and make a feast of her.

Nick took the microwave meals from her hands and set them on the floor.

"Thorn! What are you doing!" Hazard yelped when Bruno trotted over to gobble up the food in four gulps.

Rising from his chair, Nick scooped Hazard into his arms and turned toward the bedroom.

"I thought you were starving," Hazard murmured as she curled her mitted hands around his shoulders.

"Starving for you, Hazard. Always for you," he purred seductively.

Later, to Nick's amused delight, he felt those happy-face fingernails raking playfully over him. He reassured himself that he could tolerate Hazard's compulsive investigative urges and unappetizing meals for the next hundred years or so . . .

Amanda giggled to herself as she peeled the label off a plastic Miracle Whip jar. The evening she had spent with Thorn had been exceptionally gratifying. Thorn hadn't blown a gasket when he saw her wild hairdo. True, he had made a couple of snide remarks, but he hadn't completely lost his temper. Progress, she thought. And Thorn had actually listened to the information she had collected without inserting negative comments.

Yessiree, Thorn was coming along nicely. He hadn't volunteered to open an official investigation, because he had yet to be convinced Brown's supposed accident was murder, but he hadn't yelled at her, either.

Instead, he had carried her off to bed. Amanda grinned remembering how they had spent the evening before strolling hand-in-hand to the kitchen to munch on cheese and crackers.

Willfully, Amanda stifled her wandering thoughts and focused on the business at hand. She printed in bold letters on the new label she had stuck on the Miracle Whip jar: Hazard for Donkey Queen. Asking for donations for the community fundraiser was a perfect excuse to tote her jar around the county and pose questions to possible suspects.

With jar in hand, Amanda strode outside to see the sun peeking through the scudding clouds. She was going to interrogate suspects by day and figure tax returns by night. Being a conscientious businesswoman, she couldn't neglect her clients. But the trail of murder would get cold if she delayed.

"Come on, Bruno, let's go catch a killer," she called to the dog.

Bruno and Pete greeted each other with a good morning snarl, then ignored each other.

As had become his habit, Bruno hopped onto the seat and stuck his snout out the window on the passenger side of the jalopy truck. Amanda shoved the gas-guzzler into gear and drove off. After fishtailing through a mile of mud, she reached the highway, then pointed the truck north. The curved road took her through the sleepy little community of Adios that was situated near Buffalo Lake.

Amanda glanced sideways when she passed Snittiger Bait Shop. The place was locked up tighter than a sealed oil drum. The couple was either lying low or off celebrating Brown's demise.

Amanda made a mental note to track down the twosome after she interviewed Isaac Marcum.

Veering onto the newly-completed asphalt road that led to Brown's home, Amanda soon discovered why the bait shop was closed. To her suspicious surprise, Sara Mae and Sonny were hauling furniture *into* the house. It looked as if the widow intended to take up residence ASAP.

Amanda applied the brake, deciding to delay questioning Isaac Marcum. Bruno growled at the twosome on the porch. Interesting, Amanda thought as she snatched up her Donkey Queen donation jar. Bruno knew who had clubbed Dusty on the head. Maybe his growl was his way of pointing out the killer.

"Amanda Hazard, isn't it?" Sara Mae looked noticeably uncomfortable as her mascara-lined eyes leaped from Amanda to Sonny, then back again. "What are you doing out here?"

Quickly Amanda appraised the green-eyed, strawberry blond who was dressed in trim-fitting Wranglers and a western blouse. Then Amanda cast the lean, six-foot-tall man a discreet glance. The wholesome-looking couple appeared to be normal enough, attractive even. But Amanda reminded herself that outward appearances could often disguise some nasty behavioral patterns. She didn't know the widow and her lover well enough to pass judgment—yet.

Amanda pasted on a cheery smile as she gestured a happy-face nail toward her jar. "I'm collecting donations for my candidacy of Donkey Queen. The Vamoose firefighters are planning a fundraiser."

Although Sara Mae's gaze zeroed in on the telltale pink tint and choppy hairdo Amanda was sporting, she didn't comment. "Well, um . . . I suppose we could contribute to a worthy cause." She turned to the man who stood beside her. "Do you have any cash on you, Sonny?"

"Sonny Snittiger?" Amanda asked, as if she didn't know. She extended her hand, waiting for Sonny to raise his gaze, which was focused on her sharp-pointed, flourescent nails.

"Nice to meet ya," Sonny drawled.

"So . . . you're moving back into the house, I see."

Amanda decided to let the merry widow know, right there and then, that she was aware of the situation.

Sara Mae shifted the box of dishes to one shapely hip. "It is my house, now, all of it," she said defensively. "Dusty was giving me fits about splitting the property, but I'm aware of the law. Joint acquisition, you know. What was his was half mine. Now, it's all mine, because that son-of-a—"

Sara Mae slammed her mouth shut—fast—then composed herself. "Dusty is gone and I have legal rights to this property. His daddy may continue to call me with his threats of lawsuits, but I intend to live here, and so will Sonny. We're getting married after the funeral, whether Papa Brown approves or not!"

A murder, a funeral and a wedding? Amanda's thoughts reeled. Apparently, Sonny and Sara Mae didn't give a damn what anybody thought. They were staking their claim on Dusty's inheritance. It made Amanda wonder how long the couple had plotted to dispose of Brown. Once Dusty was dead and gone they had moved very swiftly.

"I know what you're thinking," Sonny said as he pulled a dollar bill from the roll of cash in his jeans pocket. He crammed the money into the slot Amanda had cut in the lid of her jar. "You think we had something to do with Brown's death."

"I do?" she said innocently.

"Of course, you do." Sara Mae's civil expression turned sour. "Everybody in Vamoose County knows that when somebody bites the dust—or mud, in Dusty's case—you start interrogating suspects. I guess Sonny and I are at the top of your list. But for your information, we didn't have anything to do with Dusty's accident. Did we, Sonny?"

"Nope, not one thing," he seconded when Sara Mae nudged him with her elbow.

Since Sara Mae and Sonny were wise to her ploy, Amanda took the direct approach. "I happen to know that Sonny and Dusty came to blows when you tried to remove furniture from the property without informing him. I also heard that Sonny got pounded senseless. Injured pride can be a strong motivation." She stared directly at the attractive young blond man. "Both of you could have hiked down the road to give the unstable truck a shove, then finished Dusty off with a blow to the head."

"We weren't anywhere near Dusty's truck!" Sara Mae snapped.

"No? Then where were you?"

"At the bait shop," Sonny spoke up quickly.

"At eight-thirty?" Amanda countered. "I just drove past your shop and noticed it was closed. If you closed down today, you could have closed down yesterday. It won't take me long to find out from folks in Adios if you stepped out for a while."

"Now, listen here, Amanda," Sara Mae shouted. "I showed good faith by turning Dusty's tax receipts and estate information over to you. I haven't even asked for my dog back. He seems satisfied where he is, and you're welcome to him."

Sara Mae was trying to butter her up, Amanda thought to herself. Too bad the *un*grieving widow didn't know Amanda Hazard couldn't be buttered.

"Rest assured that the accounts and receipts will be handled with conscientious efficiency," she replied. "But one has nothing to do with the other. I'm the one who found Dusty dead, and I saw the footprints around the truck. I also saw the *S* that Dusty etched in the mud. He was trying to expose the killer's name before he collapsed."

The comment got the expected results. Sara Mae and Sonny's faces turned as white as iodized salt.

"Now then," Amanda continued, feeling herself on solid interrogative footing. "Why don't you tell me exactly where you were when Dusty died. Hiding the truth will only arouse more suspicion—as if this upcoming wedding of yours isn't enough to raise eyebrows."

"You can't pin this on me!" Sara Mae railed, losing her cool. "All right, yes, we were at the house—"

"Sara, hush," Sonny snapped. "We have the right to

consult an attorney. We don't have to answer Hazard's questions!"

"If you're smart, you will," Amanda countered. "Concealing information looks highly suspicious. Answering my questions will be a snap, but if Thorn comes calling, I can guarantee that he'll have you squirming in your skin. You might not have seen him grilling suspects, but I have."

"Okay," Sara Mae muttered as she pivoted on her heels. "We'll tell you what you want to know while we're unloading dishes."

"No, we won't!" Sonny objected adamantly. "If you're going to blab to Hazard, then I'm outta here. Besides, I've got a bait shop to run."

To Amanda's disbelief, Sonny stalked off the porch to unhitch the flat-bed trailer from his car. Bruno, who was still inside the jalopy, barked his head off. Now why, Amanda asked herself, would Sonny refuse to answer questions if he didn't have something to hide?

When Sonny zoomed off, Sara Mae broke down and bawled. "Now see what you've done?"

Sara Mae blubbered her way into the house to set the box of dishes on the kitchen counter. Through streams of tears that caused mascara to streak down her cheeks like zebra stripes, Sara Mae tossed silverware and utensils into the drawers.

"You can't honestly admit that Sonny wasn't with you at eight-thirty yesterday morning, can you?" Amanda questioned as she propped herself against the doorjamb.

"We were both at the house at seven-thirty," Sara Mae said between sniffles.

"Was Dusty here?"

Sara Mae shook her strawberry blond head as she carefully lifted stoneware plates from the cardboard box. "Dusty was here for a few minutes."

"Long enough to pick another fight with Sonny?" Amanda ventured.

Sara Mae nodded reluctantly. "My estranged husband turned into a full-fledged jerk after he was elected county commissioner. He got even worse during the divorce proceedings. I nearly starved to death because he froze our joint bank account and wouldn't let me withdraw living expense money. If Sonny hadn't taken me in, fed and housed me, I don't know what I would've done.

"I couldn't get a job anywhere except at the bait shop," Sara Mae confided. "Dusty followed me around and withdrew every application I filled out, saying he didn't want his wife working. He was the one screwing around on the side and he blamed *me* for the bad publicity caused by the divorce. He said I was ruining his political career. Ha! He did that with no help from me!"

Amanda kept silent and watched Sara Mae stack dishes in the cabinets. She had the intuitive feeling that Sara Mae wanted to air her frustrations, here and now.

"Just ask Ervin Shakelford if Dusty wasn't a master at twisting truths to his benefit," Sara Mae muttered bitterly.

Turning on her boot heels, the widow propelled herself through the hall to retrieve another box from the trailer. Amanda fell into step behind her. Since she was here, Amanda decided, she may as well make herself useful.

"Shakelford is the Republican candidate, right?" Amanda inquired as she scooped up a box labeled: Very, very breakable.

Shakelford with an *S*, Amanda silently reminded herself.

"That's right," Sara Mae confirmed as she retraced her steps to the kitchen. "Dusty was conducting a mud-slinging campaign from the word go. He had yet to win the primary and he'd already lambasted Ervin every chance he got. After the divorce became public knowledge, Dusty spread the rumor around the county that Ervin was having an affair with *me*, but that he quickly broke it off when Dusty discovered the truth. Talk about political homicide! Ervin was ready to kill Dusty when he got wind of that particular story. And believe you me, that was only the beginning of Dusty's vicious rumors.''

Amanda knew Ervin Shakelford had much to gain from Brown's demise. The man also had a double motive. Ervin wanted to win the election, and he had undoubtedly spent a great deal of money trying to compensate for Brown's damaging accusations.

But there was still the matter of Sonny Snittiger's whereabouts yesterday morning, Amanda reminded herself. She wasn't going to let herself become sidetracked by the information about Shakelford.

''What happened when Dusty showed up at the house yesterday?'' Amanda inquired.

''You mean after he called me a slut and Sonny a deadbeat golddigger?''

''Yeah, right after that.''

''I told Dusty that I was taking the waterbed and dresser and that I was going to start pawning off all those damned tools of his if he didn't give me the right to withdraw half the money in our joint account.''

''And Dusty said . . . ?'' Amanda waited for Sara Mae to fill in the blank.

Sara Mae lifted the crystal goblets with trembling hands, then set them carefully on the shelf. There was a long moment of silence before she answered.

''He said the only way I'd get the money was over his dead body.''

Appropriate choice of words, Amanda decided. No wonder Sara Mae was reluctant to respond to that question.

''Then Dusty told Sonny that he'd find a way to ruin his bait shop business. And when Sonny and I were down to broke, Dusty vowed he'd pull a few strings at the county welfare office so we couldn't draw one red cent.''

Geez, Dusty Brown was really a piece of work, wasn't he? It seemed his idea of climbing the ladder of success was stepping on as many people as he could grind with his boot heels.

Amanda had the unshakable feeling she could use the phone book as an alphabetical listing of possible suspects in this case. As of yet, no one had a kind word to say about Dusty Brown. Since his election to public office, he'd transformed into a conniving, lying, egotistical monster. Surely the man had realized his days in public office were numbered. He could have raised only two votes in the upcoming election—his own and his father's.

Or could it be that Dusty was so full of self-importance that he thought no one could defeat him?

"Did Dusty provoke Sonny into another fight yesterday?" Amanda pressed ever onward.

An uneasy expression claimed Sara Mae's blotchy face. She refused to reply.

Amanda gave the shaken widow a verbal nudge. "Who took the first punch yesterday, Sara Mae?"

Sara Mae swallowed audibly as she placed another goblet on the shelf.

"Do you want me to take this line of questioning up with Sonny? If you refuse to answer, I will, you know."

"Dusty threw the punch," Sara Mae spewed out. "He caught Sonny in the solar plexus with an unexpected blow that drove him to his knees. Then Dusty stood there and laughed while Sonny tried to draw breath. Dusty told Sonny that he was worthless scum who deserved no better than to take up with a slut like me."

Amanda could visualize the scene with vivid clarity. After being thoroughly insulted and taken to his knees, Sonny had been furious enough to want revenge. He definitely had reason to dispose of Brown. But then, so did Sara Mae. She had been refused funds, prevented from finding employment and humiliated several times. How much harassment could a woman tolerate before she lost her cool and exploded in rage?

"What did you do when Dusty clobbered Sonny?" Amanda asked softly.

Sara Mae's shoulders shook. She broke down and cried her eyes out.

Amanda sympathetically patted the woman's clenched fist. "You'll feel ten times better after you get this off your chest," she said. "The truth will set you free."

Really corny, Hazard, Amanda criticized herself. But Sara Mae fell for it, bait and hook.

"I took a swing at Dusty, but he ducked away, then he laughed that infuriating laugh I had come to hate. When he strutted to his truck to drive away, I was so upset that I ran into the house and bawled." Sara Mae wiped away her streaming tears. "That's the truth. I didn't hike downhill to club Dusty. I might have if I had known he was stuck in the mud, but I didn't know. Sonny came inside later and said we should leave, because he had to open the bait shop."

Amanda put two and two together and realized Sara Mae couldn't account for Sonny's whereabouts. Sara Mae had been having a good cry—in private, or so she said. She couldn't testify that Sonny had not left the premises. Nor could Sonny testify that he had been with Sara Mae the entire time.

"Would you like a ride into Adios?" Amanda asked belatedly.

Sara Mae blotted her bleeding mascara on the sleeve of her blouse. "No, I'd rather stay here and put the house back in order. Sonny and I could both use some time alone. It's been a hectic twenty-four hours."

Amanda picked up her Donkey Queen donation jar and quietly exited the house. "Well," she said to herself. "You might be able to cross this *S* off your list."

Amanda sank onto the seat of the truck to give Bruno a pat on the head. Then she gave the matter of Sara Mae second consideration. Better not be too hasty about discarding Sara Mae as a suspect, she advised herself. A woman could have brained Dusty as easily as a man. And furthermore, Amanda had yet to hear Sonny's version of the incident.

After several cranks of the ignition, the truck finally started. Amanda putt-putted around the circular driveway and glanced uphill. Her next destination was Isaac Marcum's home.

Good thing Bruno was along, Amanda thought. Crazy as Isaac was reported to be these days, Amanda might need a bodyguard whose bark was as bad as his bite.

Five

Nick veered into the parking lot at Last Chance Cafe. According to the dispatcher, Velma had sent him a summons to meet her for a coffee break. Nick couldn't imagine what the emergency conference was about. He supposed he'd find out soon enough.

Ambling inside the restaurant, Nick was greeted by a chorus of "Hi, chief." Farmers filled the red vinyl booths to capacity, complaining about the wet weather and discussing the effects the soggy conditions might have on their wheat crop and cattle.

Velma had tucked her hefty body in Nick's favorite booth in the corner of the cafe. After years on the Oklahoma City police force, Nick had adopted Wild Bill Hickok's habit of keeping his eyes open and his back against the wall—just in case.

When Velma spotted Nick, she motioned for him to join her. "Hi, sugar. How's everything with my favorite hunk of a cop?"

"Dandy." Nick smiled at the plump beautician as he slid onto the seat.

"I've already ordered your coffee. It should be here eventually." Velma cast the young waitress an irritated glance. "Lydia is slower than Christmas. Don't know how she landed the job Faye Bernard vacated when she decided to go to college full time." Chomp, crackle, snap.

"Maybe Lydia's father had something to do with it," Nick chuckled. "Ervin Shakelford probably paid the owner of Last Chance to let his daughter work here. Lydia has so many campaign buttons pinned to her chest it's a wonder she doesn't trip and fall on her face. She's been campaigning for her dad while she takes orders."

"Don't I know it," Velma smirked. "Wait 'til you see the buttons she's wearing today. One has Ervin's smiling mug and his name printed in blood-red letters. The other one says, 'I'll grade the road to victory'."

Velma frowned thoughtfully. "Wonder who is going to be chosen as interim commissioner now that Brown is gone. That somebody will be a shoo-in as the Democratic candidate for District 1."

Nick had to agree with that reasoning. With Brown out of the way there would be no need for a Democratic primary. Lord, when Hazard came to that conclusion, she would be up at the courthouse sniffing for information and adding another name to her list of suspects.

Could it possibly be—? Naw, Nick quickly reassured himself. He and the medical examiner had found no evidence that Brown's deadly mishap was anything but an accident.

"Amanda put me in charge of the wedding shower," Velma announced as she gestured a pudgy finger toward her guest list.

Nick's eyebrows rose. "She did?"

Velma nodded. "I thought we'd have the shower the weekend of the Donkey Basketball game."

The beautician broke into a cagey smile as she glanced at Nick. "Oh, by the way, Amanda is a Donkey Queen candidate."

Nick blinked, astounded. "She is?"

"Doing her civil duty, of course." Snap, snap. "I've signed both of you up to participate in the ballgame. Knew you wouldn't mind supporting a worthy cause by riding for the town team. We've got to provide our brave firemen with those fancy fireproof suits, you know."

Nick resigned himself to the fact that he was going to climb on a donkey and make an ass of himself for a good cause. He wondered if Hazard would be able to keep her seat on the back of a contrary donkey while racing up and down court with a basketball tucked under her arm. If nothing else, the fundraiser should be worth a few laughs.

Velma smiled slyly as she chomped her chewing gum. "Sure hope some other handsome stud doesn't raise enough money to be crowned Donkey King. There are several young bucks around here who've had the hots for your fiancée since she came to live in Vamoose. Can you imagine the kind of kiss some of those guys would try to plant on Amanda's lips after the crown is placed on her head? Whooee, that could be really embarrassing for you, Nicky."

"How do you know Hazard will be crowned queen?" Nick asked, feeling the rise of possessive jealousy. Hazard was *his* woman. He didn't want anyone getting their itchy fingers on her.

"Amanda is the best-known female in town," Velma insisted. "Who wouldn't donate to her cause? Can't have Vinita Frizzell crowned queen. That would make the Vamoose Fire Department look bad. Amanda definitely has more class and style."

Velma lifted the jar that she had tucked on the seat beside her. She had taken the liberty of printing Nick's name in bold letters, announcing his candidacy for Donkey King. "I know you'll want to enter the race," she said as she placed the jar in front of him. "It'd be nice if Vamoose's most noted couple was reigning royalty."

Reluctantly, Nick accepted the jar that had a five-dollar bill inside it. Obviously, Velma had contributed to his cause.

"Now then, back to the guest list," Velma hurried on. "I—"

"Vote for Ervin Shakelford. He's the man who can put the county roads back in shape and keep a sharp eye on the county offices under his jurisdiction," Lydia Shakelford interrupted as she set the coffee cups on the table.

"About time," Velma muttered after Lydia sauntered away. She focused her fake-lashed gaze on Nick. "I know you'll want your mother to attend the wedding shower. I don't have her phone number since she and your dad retired and moved to Texas to bask in the sun. This will be the first time your mom has met Amanda, won't it?"

Nick squirmed in the booth. He wasn't sure he wanted Hazard to meet Mom until the wedding. That would be soon enough. "I doubt Mom would want to drive all the way back here for a shower."

"Not come?" Velma hooted. "Of course she will. Everybody's mother comes to her son's wedding shower. It's tradition."

"Maybe it is, but—"

"Give me her number and I'll extend the invitation," Velma cut in.

Nick felt decidedly uncomfortable. "I . . . uh . . . haven't told Mom that I'm getting married yet."

"What?" Velma's eyes popped and she nearly swallowed her chewing gum. "Why not, Nicky? She'll want to know something as important as that. Why, she thinks you and your brother Rich are the perfect sons."

And no woman on God's green earth would be good enough for two perfect sons, Nick silently added. Hazard thought *her* mother was meddling, domineering and manipulative. Well, Mom had a few noticeable flaws that would drive a daughter-in-law nuts!

"I'll . . . um . . . tell Mom, then I'll invite her to the shower," Nick said belatedly, and without much enthusiasm.

"When are you going to tell her?" Velma eyed him suspiciously. "The night before the shower? Oh no you don't, Nicky. I'll take care of this shameless oversight and smooth it over for you with your mom." She patted his hand and winked. "Trust me, sugar. This shower is going to be the biggest bash you've ever seen, exceeded only by your wedding ceremony."

Nick grimaced at the thought. "I had planned to make the wedding an intimate ceremony."

"You can't do that!" Velma croaked. "You'll disappoint Amanda. She's planning to invite the whole town. I've asked Billie Jane Baxter and the Horseshoe Band to come home from Nashville to perform for the fundraiser. While I had Billie Jane on the phone, I asked her to sing for the reception dance at your wedding. She said she'd be happy to help out her home town and her accountant."

Nick sank a little deeper in his seat.

"This is a big deal, Nicky. You can't exclude your fellow Vamoosians! Everyone wants to be on hand to see you and Amanda tie the knot!"

"Hazard agreed to this?" Nick bleated.

"Good grief, Nicky, you're behaving as if you're ashamed to show off your bride!"

"That's not the case—"

"Good. Then you just leave everything to me and Bev. The shower and wedding will be humdingers!"

Dazed, Nick staggered from the booth, oblivious to the murmur of conversation around him. He had considered asking Hazard to elope—had intended to bring up the subject last night. Unfortunately, he'd gotten sidetracked to the bedroom.

He'd never dreamed Hazard had visions of a gigantic wedding with all the pomp and pageantry of British royalty!

If things between Hazard, Mom and Mother didn't go well at the shower, the wedding could evolve into a feud between the Hazards and the Thorns. Good thing Nick was a cop. A law officer might be needed to keep the peace!

Nick and Hazard definitely needed to put their heads together and discuss their wedding plans before the arrangements mushroomed into full-scale disaster.

His mind whirring with the unpleasant prospect of the meeting between Mom and Hazard, Nick drove out to patrol the area around Vamoose. Things would work out, he tried to convince himself. Mom wouldn't lay down the law at Hazard's feet, ordering her to become the humble, devoted kind of wife Nick supposedly deserved. Mom wouldn't disapprove of Hazard because she couldn't cook, didn't sew and insisted on juggling a career with marriage . . . would she?

Deep down inside, Nick had the queasy feeling that Mom could become every bit as difficult to handle as Hazard's mother.

Come to think of it, Hazard had been careful never to let Nick meet her mother in person. Maybe it was for the same reason. Nick hadn't said much about Mom . . .

Amanda killed the engine of the jalopy and stared at the run-down home nestled in a grove of trees. Glancing south, she studied the blind intersection she had driven through to reach Isaac Marcum's farm. She understood why Isaac had wanted the county corner cleared of trees and underbrush. If she had been driving her compact car she couldn't have seen who was coming until she was in the middle of that intersection. Traveling in a truck wasn't much better, she reminded herself. The lay of the land, and the line of trees and underbrush, made it impossible to see a vehicle approaching from the west until it was too late.

As it had been too late for Isaac's daughter . . .

Composing herself, Amanda clambered down from the truck. Bruno bounded across the seat, refusing to be left behind this time.

"What the hell do you want, woman?" came an unfriendly snarl from the side of the house.

Amanda pulled up short, her heart pounding like a jackhammer. Bruno growled as he stalked forward. Amanda saw the rifle barrel protruding from the corner of the house.

"Bruno! Come here—now!" she ordered hurriedly.

"What are you doin' with that son-of-a-bitch's dog?"

"He took a liking to me." Amanda gave her best imitation of a sunny smile. "Mr. Marcum . . . Isaac . . . I was hoping you would donate to a worthy cause." She lifted her plastic jar. "I'm a candidate for Donkey Queen. The proceeds from the donkey basketball game will provide Vamoose's fire department with new protective gear."

Amanda held her ground when a long shadow fell across the unmoved grass. With the spitting end of the rifle pointing at her, then at Bruno, the recluse stepped into view. The image of Howard Hughes in his later years instantly sprang to mind as Amanda appraised Isaac Marcum. Shoulder-length white hair and a long beard surrounded his leathery face. Though Isaac couldn't have been more than 47, he looked as if he was pushing hard at sixty. Wrinkles and creases testified to each hard, trying experience life had dealt him.

A dangerous glint flickered in his cavernous eyes. He pinned her with a glare that suggested he'd like to turn her into roadkill.

Hmm . . . Essentially, wasn't that what happened to Brown?

"You came a helluva long way out here for a damned

donation, little lady. You think I don't know who you are and what you're about?''

Bruno growled protectively when Isaac, dressed in camouflage fatigues, crept forward with the silence of a trained guerrilla fighter. Although Isaac had a noticeable limp, he was still extremely intimidating.

According to Velma, the disabled vet had gone over the edge after he lost his daughter. If Isaac had disposed of Brown, he could easily dispose of Amanda. With his background, he could field strip Amanda and no one would know what had become of her for weeks—years, maybe.

You and your bright ideas, Hazard, the cowardly side of her nature muttered at her. *Get the hell out of here while you still can!*

What? You're turning chicken? the assertive part of her character spoke up. *Plow your way through this difficult situation the way you usually do.*

"Isaac?" Amanda squared her shoulders, then advanced a few steps. "May I call you Isaac?"

"I prefer Salty," he said in a hostile voice.

"Salty it is then." Amanda smiled brightly—or tried to. "Is a dollar donation asking too much? I'd settle for fifty cents if—"

Amanda slammed her mouth shut when Salty pounced at her. Bruno crouched and went on immediate attack. His jaws clamped around Salty's combat boots. With swift efficiency, Salty flipped over the rifle and popped Bruno with the butt end of the weapon. The dog whined and sprawled on the ground—dazed.

Isaac's dark-eyed gaze swung from the stunned dog to Amanda. "The mutt never was that protective of Brown. How'd he get so damned attached to you?"

Amanda ignored the question and cut straight to the heart of the matter. No sense pussyfooting around with this hard-boiled vet, she decided.

"You're no fool, Salty," she said boldly. "If you know

who I am, then you know the real reason I'm here. I'm investigating Brown's death. I was the one who found him dead in the mud."

"I know. Saw you down there."

The comment caught Amanda off guard. "You did?"

"Yep."

"Well, why didn't you come get me instead of letting me tromp around in the mud to call for help? That wasn't very neighborly of you."

"Look here, little lady," he scowled. "I already did my good deed by serving hell's sentence in 'Nam. Since then I've lost a wife and buried a daughter. And as far as that bastard Brown is concerned, I wouldn't have cared if he laid there in the mud and rotted for a couple of months. Cocky son-of-a-bitch deserved what he got, and anybody who wanted to help him is no friend of mine."

From the sound of things Amanda was at the top of Salty's shit list. Animosity sizzled through the steamy morning air like an electrical current. Amanda decided to use the tactic that had worked so effectively with Sara Mae. If she could get Salty talking, maybe he'd put his hackles down and reveal a tidbit of information.

Calmly as you please, Amanda strode forward to seat herself on the rickety wooden steps. "You lost your wife? I didn't know that. I'm sorry, Salty."

Isaac snorted derisively. "The bitch ran off with another man and left me with my baby girl. Best thing that ever happened. I made sure Molly was nothin' like her mama."

The hitch in Salty's voice indicated the depth of emotion he felt for his departed daughter. Amanda's tenderhearted tendencies, cultivated from living in the close-knit community of Vamoose, put a sentimental lump in her throat.

"I'm sure you raised Molly right," she murmured.

"Damned right I did. Raised her to be honest, polite and courteous. She was smart as a whip, too. Had her whole life ahead of her, but that cocky son-of-a-bitch killed her and didn't even apologize!''

Amanda inwardly flinched when Salty's voice hit a loud pitch. She waited, giving Salty the chance to bare his troubled soul.

''I told the worthless bastard that intersection would get someone killed. I tried to clear out part of the ditch with a machete, but a bulldozer was needed to clean it up.

''Brown's predecessor always took care of that intersection while he was in office, but not Brown. He was too busy taking care of *himself*. You saw that goddam asphalt expressway he built to his house, the expensive bridge he was building so he'd have his private shortcut across Whatsit River to check on his property and livestock to the south.''

Salty gestured the barrel of his rifle toward the mound of mud and concrete piers that were to be used to span the river. ''My little girl died in a wreck at the blind corner while Brown was misusing county funds to pay for his own pork-barrel projects. I've been sitting up here on this hill every goddamn day, watching those goddamn bulldozers and graders repairing the goddamn road and construct the bridge. Brown could have had those dozers clean out the dangerous intersection while they were coming and going from here. But, hell no. The son-of-a-bitch just smirked when I asked him to do ditch work. Said he had better things to do than clean trees for some loony vet and his squirrelly daughter.''

Amanda sensed the grief, fury, bitterness and outrage seething in Salty. Clearly, the man's world had come crashing down when he lost his daughter. And just as clearly, Amanda realized Salty had been keeping surveillance on Brown's comings and goings. Salty had been trained to reconnoiter. He knew how to stalk, how to conduct a surprise attack. It wouldn't have taken much effort for Salty to

sneak up on Brown while the commissioner was changing a
tire in the mud.

Problem was, Amanda wasn't sure she could blame Salty
for taking advantage of opportunity. No telling how long
Salty had waited for just the right moment to pounce.

Amanda's gaze drifted to Salty's hands, which were
clenched tightly around the rifle. Salty was wearing cream-
colored work gloves. Mud stains discolored the tanned
hide . . .

Amanda tensed when she noticed flecks of red splattered
on the gloves. She had the queasy feeling the stains had
come from blood—Brown's, to be specific.

"Did Brown offer the slightest consolation after Molly's
traffic accident?" Amanda questioned softly.

Salty, who had been staring southeast, jerked his shaggy
head around. His eyes narrowed into hard slits. "Hell no.
After the funeral, I saw Brown outside Last Chance Cafe.
I told him I held him responsible for what happened to
Molly and that her death was on his conscience. Brown
just tossed me one of his arrogant smirks and told me to
go crawl back in my hole on the hill."

"And you lost your temper with him," Amanda speculated.

Cold black eyes bore down on Amanda like drill bits.
"I'd have killed that bastard right where he stood if Clem
Hill hadn't pulled me off."

Beverly Hill had mentioned that incident, Amanda
recalled.

"You want me to be sorry about Brown? Well, I'm goddamn not! I've imagined a dozen different ways to torture
him and take him out. I've watched him come and go
from his house, watched him lure in his women after he
kicked out his wife. The man wasn't worthy of respect or
consideration. Eye for an eye, I always say."

Amanda wondered if Salty realized how incriminating
that comment was—or if he even cared.

"I saw a lot of men die in 'Nam. None of them deserved it. They were fighting for a cause they believed in—though nobody back here in the States seemed to give much of a damn about us. But Brown deserved what he got!"

Amanda let silence settle in the grove of trees surrounding the dilapidated home. "Did you see that Brown got his due?"

A strange, indecipherable expression settled into Salty's leathery features. It could have been a sinister smile—or not. With Salty it was hard to tell. His grasp on sanity was slippery.

"Yeah, I saw it," he said cryptically.

Amanda cocked her head to study Salty from a different angle, trying to read the underlying truth in the remark. Did his admission carry a subtle meaning? If she had heard him correctly, Salty had said he *saw* it, not that he *saw to* it. She wondered if he was trying to lead her off the track.

Amanda's thoughts evaporated when Salty reached out to haul her to her feet. The firm grip on her arm loosened, then fell away when Salty dug into the pocket of his camouflage suit.

"Here's a buck for your jar, little lady. But damned if I know why anybody would want to be crowned Queen Ass of Vamoose."

"Come to think of it, neither do I," Amanda replied, staring straight into those dark, tormented eyes. Oddly enough, she no longer felt threatened by him. Salty's killing fury had been focused exclusively on Commissioner Brown. Although she considered him a highly probable suspect—or at the very least a key witness—she was no longer intimidated.

Spinning on her heels, Amanda strode toward her truck. Bruno trotted behind her.

"Hazard?"

Amanda halted, then glanced over her shoulder at the recluse.

"You've got guts. I like that. But you've got the weirdest hairdo and fingernails I ever saw," Salty said before he wheeled around and limped away.

After several unsuccessful attempts to start the truck, the engine groaned to life and Amanda was able to drive off. "Well damn, Bruno. Here I am actually liking the man who most likely killed Brown."

Bruno stared out the open window. Amanda reminded herself that the dog showed no more regret over the loss of his master than Salty did about the passing of his country neighbor. From all indication, both Salty and Bruno were glad to have Brown gone.

Nick pulled into Thatcher's Oil and Gas to fuel the patrol car. Hiking his sagging breeches over his rounded belly, Thaddeus Thatcher lumbered from the service station.

"Want me to fill 'er up, chief?"

Nick nodded.

"So when's the big day?" Thaddeus asked as he poked the nozzle into the neck of the gas tank.

"We haven't decided."

"Talk around town is that the wedding is going to be the social event of the season. My wife has already started shopping for a new dress. I might even buy a new sports coat for the occasion."

Thaddeus braced his stocky arm on the side of the squad car and stared at the shiny foil that was wrapped around the gift lying on the front seat. "You're already buying stuff for your fiancée? Big mistake," Thaddeus said with a shake of his silver-blond head. "Women start expecting that once you start. What'd you get for Hazard?"

Nick glanced at the gift beside him. "A cellular phone. She's been stranded often enough to deserve one."

"Reckon so. Would've helped her out considerably if she'd had a mobile phone when she found Brown in the mud."

"My thoughts exactly."

"Guess you heard the county appointed Sam Harjo as interim commissioner until the November election," Thaddeus said as he leaned over to grab the nozzle. With a squeeze of his hand he squirted a few more gurgles of gas into the tank. "Wonder if Harjo will become the Democratic candidate now that Brown's gone. Somebody told Ab Hendershot, who told Willy Rhymes, who told me, that Harjo was planning to run on the Democratic ticket after he and Brown had it out at work several times. Always was a lot of bad blood between Brown and his road foreman."

Nick knew Sam Harjo never had any kind words for Brown. According to Harjo, working for Brown was a stint in hell. Nick had picked up Harjo by the side of the road a few months ago. Harjo had been spitting mad when Brown had sent him out on the bulldozer, as if the foreman was an underling. Harjo had gotten stuck and he'd cursed Brown all the way back to the county commissioner's workshop.

Here was another piece of information Nick wasn't anxious for Hazard to get wind of. Sure as hell, she'd make something of it.

Thaddeus wiped his hands on the red rag he kept in his hip pocket. "Anything else I can do for you, chief?"

"No, a full tank should do it."

"Be sure to let Gertrude and me know when you set the big date. I plan to close down the station early so I can get spiffed up."

Nick drove toward his house to grab a sandwich for lunch. Much as he didn't want to do it, he had to call his parents to announce the wedding and the preliminary shower. He wasn't anxious to be drilled with questions concerning Hazard.

Mom was a master at that.

Amanda veered into the parking lot at the bait shop. To her surprise, the shop was doing a driving business. Several cars and trucks, hitched to boat trailers, filled the parking lot to capacity. Two little tykes scampered at their father's heels, jabbering excitedly as they approached the shop. Two old coots, obviously long-time fishing buddies, were jawing about lake conditions as they ambled from the shop, toting a bucket of minnows and stink bait.

Amanda presented her jar to customers who were coming and going, collecting several dollars for the fundraiser. After the crowd thinned out, she entered Snittiger's Bait Shop.

Sonny glared at her. "You're like a rash that won't go away," he grumbled. "I already donated to your cause."

"But you refused to answer my direct question," she countered.

Sonny sighed, then braced his hands on the counter. "I already told you I have nothing to say on the subject of Dusty Brown, except that he was a bastard from the word go. He treated Sara Mae like dirt since the day she married him. I've been in love with her since ninth grade, but she never knew that. Now that I have my chance with her, I'm not letting anything stand in our way."

Especially not a jerk of a husband, Amanda thought to herself. Sonny was as protective as Isaac was vengeful. Both men had it in for Brown. Since no one cared if Brown was gone, it could take months to question everyone who held a grudge against the man!

Keeping that in mind, Amanda didn't waste more time. "Where were you at eight-thirty yesterday morning, Sonny?"

"What did Sara Mae say?"

Amanda shook her head warningly, causing the layers of her hair to flap like loose shingles in a stiff breeze. "I've heard Sara Mae's version of the story. Now I want to hear yours."

"She didn't do it," Sonny blurted out.

"So who did? You had all the opportunity and motive anyone might need to put Brown out of your misery."

Sonny slammed his fist against the counter. Jigs, corks and lures rattled in their plastic containers. "Until I'm served with an official warrant I've got nothing to say. If you want to bark up every tree in search of clues, then fine and dandy. Just leave me out of it!"

"Then point me toward another tree that stood as much to gain from Brown's demise," Amanda challenged.

"No, I'm not planning to make this easy for you."

"Then I'm never going away, Sonny. I'll be here long after your last customer leaves."

The unpleasant possibility of spending the entire day with Amanda was apparently more than he could stand. Sonny finally relented.

"Okay, you win." Sonny stared at her for a long moment. "Try tracking down the guy who was driving the bulldozer in the mud yesterday. He crossed paths with Brown, too. I could hear them yelling at each other between downpours."

If Amanda wasn't mistaken, Sonny Snittiger knew exactly what had happened the previous day. It made her wonder if Sonny was covering for Isaac, who was covering for Sonny. It could have been a conspiracy for all Amanda knew.

Ponderously, Amanda appraised Sonny, wondering if she had twisted his arm into sending her on a goose chase.

"Off the record, I think you're involved up to your eyebrows," she told Sonny candidly.

A goading grin spread across Sonny's striking features. "Yeah? Then why don't you try to prove it, Hazard?"

Amanda spun around and walked away. She really hated it when probable suspects called her bluff.

Fact was, Amanda had very little to go on. What if she was wrong about the incident? What if Brown's death really was an accident? What if the stringy *S* she had seen in the mud beside Brown's hand meant nothing at all? What if Thorn was correct in thinking that Bruno might have bumped into the truck, causing a chain of events that left Brown dead?

Amanda didn't want to accept the possibility that her keen feminine instinct had a glitch. Gut feeling still told her that Commissioner Brown had *not* ended up dead in the mud by accident!

Six

The phone was ringing off the hook when Nick came through the door of his farm house. Hurriedly, he snatched up the receiver.

"Thorn here."

"You're getting *married*?" Mom questioned. "You proposed to some woman named *Hazard*? Good gad, Nicky, the name alone should alert you to trouble. What is she? Some two-bit airhead? She can't be from sound rural stock, not if you've been keeping your engagement secret from your own mom and dad. Your brother didn't even know you were engaged! I know that for a fact, because I had the OSBI office track Rich down so I could ask him!"

"Hi, Mom. Nice to hear from you. How are things in Texas? Is Dad still playing his customary rounds of golf three times a week?"

"Don't try to sidetrack me, Nicky," Mom scolded. "Velma Hertzog called information to get our number so she could invite me to a wedding shower that I had no idea you were having. Who is this *Hazard*ous person anyway? A relative of Velma's?"

"No, just a friend." More like an informant, Nick silently amended.

"Where did this person come from?" Mom grilled him.

"She's Oklahoma City-born and bred."

Nick could hear Mom's groan of dismay—all the way from Texas. "A big city girl? Oh, Nicky, you didn't! What use is she going to be to you on the farm? Who's going to cover your farming emergencies while you're keeping the police beat? Can the dingy woman even drive a tractor?"

"Hazard can hold her own in most situations," Nick felt compelled to say in his fiancée's defense.

"I'll just bet she can." Mom sniffed caustically. "What does Hazard do for a living?"

"She's an accountant, a very good one."

There was a noticeable pause. "An accountant for whom? The Oklahoma Tax Commission? The IRS? One of *those* kinds of accountants who nit-picks over tax returns and conducts audits?"

"No, Hazard opened her own office in Vamoose after leaving the firm of Nelson, Blake and Cosmos in Oklahoma City."

"Has she been married before?"

Nick hesitated before answering, "Once."

"How long? How long ago? She's not on the rebound, is she?"

"She was married for a couple of years, but that was over seven years ago."

"What happened? Did she cheat on her husband?"

"Mom . . ." Nick said warningly.

"She did cheat, didn't she?" Mom continued relentlessly. "You'd tell me if she didn't."

"She was the cheat*ee*, not the cheat*er*."

"What's wrong with her that caused her hubby to do that?"

Was it any wonder Nick had procrastinated in announcing his wedding plans to his mother?

"I do not intend to discuss this with you, Mom. I'm over thirty," he reminded her. "I don't have to answer to anyone nowadays."

"Don't get smart with me, Nicky. I'm the only Mom you've got. And your dad and I have a right to know if you're marrying some floozy who'll besmirch the family name."

Nick rolled his eyes heavenward, begging for divine patience. He hadn't tolerated the likes of this round of questioning since he'd gone out on dates as a teenager.

"Hazard *is* planning to quit her job to be a good farm wife and stay at home to raise your children—I hope."

"I doubt it. This is the nineties, Mom. Things have changed since you and Dad lived on the farm."

Mom sighed audibly. "I don't see how this mismatched marriage can possibly work out. I don't want you to go through the big *D* like your older brother did. It broke poor Rich's heart, you know. I told him it was a mistake from the beginning, but did he listen?"

"Mom—"

"Don't you dare confirm a wedding date until Dad and I get there to check out the situation. You hear me, Nicky? And you can bet your sweet bippy that I'll be there for this wedding shower. I've got a long list of questions to ask this Hazard woman."

"Mom—"

"We'll stay with you," Mom rushed on. "And I better not find any of Hazard's clothes stashed in your closet, either. You know what I think of premarital live-in arrangements."

The sound of the phone being slammed into its cradle rattled Nick's eardrums. Hearing the hum of the dial tone, Nick hung up. "That went well," he muttered sarcastically.

Nick could see it all now. His mom and Hazard's mother would square off at the shower, sizing each other up. Clash of the Titans—in technicolor and surround sound—he thought, as he threw three sandwiches together and chased them down with a beer. Maybe he never should have proposed. If he had an inkling what a big to-do it would turn out to be, he might have left things the way they were.

Amanda collapsed in her recliner. It had been another hectic day. She had stayed up until all hours of the night working on complicated tax vouchers for several clients. She had labored over her calculator until her eyes blurred and her brain short-circuited. Then she trudged off to bed to catch a few Zs.

When the alarm clock blared at her, Amanda pried herself from bed and staggered into the shower. She stopped by the office to check on Jenny Long's progress with the standard tax forms, and found them stacked in alphabetical order. Each entry had been neatly typed and double-checked for accuracy.

During lunch at Last Chance Cafe, Amanda collected donations for her candidacy. Then she placed a call to the county courthouse to glean information about the Brown case. She had discovered that the road foreman, Sam Harjo, had been driving the bulldozer the day Brown died. In fact, Harjo's dozer was the only piece of heavy equipment that had been taken out that rainy morning.

Amanda found that to be an interesting piece of information. Furthermore, her suspicions multiplied when she asked who had been appointed interim commissioner.

Wouldn't you know, it was Sam Harjo.

Nursing her Diet Coke, Amanda set her tax files on the end table and reflected on the incidents leading up to her discovery of Commissioner Brown's body. After her pickup had slid across the slick road and nose-dived into the ditch, Amanda had hiked uphill to see the broad tracks left by a bulldozer. That was also where she had seen the pick-up tire flatten out and noticed the Goodyear imprint spelled backward in the mud . . .

Amanda froze in mid-sip, her mind shifting into high gear. She began to speculate on possible explanations. Now that she thought about it, she realized Brown's tire must have gone flat at the crown of the hill, near the dozer's tracks. When the tire lost air, the weight of the pick-up had mashed the Goodyear imprint into the mud.

So why hadn't Brown changed tires at the *top* of the hill rather than driving to the *bottom?* And why, she wondered, hadn't the bulldozer operator offered to lend a hand?

Amanda checked her watch. It was 4:35. If she hurried, she might be able to intercept Sam Harjo at the county's machine shop before he clocked out at five.

Amanda guzzled her soda for an extra-added dose of caffeine, then bounded from her chair. "Come on, Bruno. I want to gauge your reaction to the temporary commissioner."

Thus far, Bruno had growled at every possible suspect, then bit the most likely one on the ankle. Not that it had fazed Salty Marcum, Amanda reminded herself on her way out the door. Salty had just whacked the dog on the head. It was entirely possible that Salty had taken the jack handle in hand and whacked Brown.

Amanda whizzed off, vowing to keep an open mind. She had to piece together the incidents leading up to Brown's death before she perfected her theories. Once she had listed the chain of events in chronological order, she could determine who had committed the murder—and why.

To Amanda's disappointment, she arrived at the machinery barn minutes after Harjo had clocked out. Several members of the road crew were sitting on the tailgate of a pick-up, sipping longnecks. All male eyes focused on Amanda as she strode toward the blue-collar crowd. Some of the more brazen men erupted in wolfish whistles.

Amanda bristled in irritation when the men stared at

her body before they looked her in the eye. She had a fetish about being reduced to a sex object by the male of the species.

"I'm Thorn's fiancée," she said, gesturing to the over-sized diamond on her hand. "He gets riled when I'm harassed."

"You're Thorn's broad—I mean, babe?" Chuck Gilhaney asked out the left side of his mouth. He squinted at her through the smoke that curled from the cigarette dangling from the right corner of his lips. "My, my, Thorn can really pick 'em, can't he, fellas?"

The group of men sniggered. Amanda bared her teeth. "I'm here to ask questions about Brown's death," she said in a no-nonsense tone.

The announcement had a startling effect on the men. They glanced everywhere except at Amanda. Now why was that? she wondered.

"You there." Amanda pointed a happy-face fingernail at Chuck Gilhaney. "How long did you work for Brown?"

"Four hellish years," Chuck replied, then took a drag of his cigarette. "Today was the first day I didn't get my butt chewed out for nothing." He lifted his longneck in a toast, then chugged a drink. "That's why I'm celebrating. Of course, our foreman enforces the one beer limit, so that's all the celebrating we'll do. Whatever Harjo says goes around here."

Amanda stared at the muscle-bound man beside Chuck. "What about you? Have you worked here long?"

"Five years," Homer Frizzell replied.

"Did you get along with Brown?"

Homer smirked. "I hated him, same as everybody else around here. Nobody *got along* with Brown. We just tolerated him."

A concurring murmur rippled through the cluster of men who were perched on the tailgate.

"You wanna know what it was like to work for Brown?"

Ron Newton questioned as he peeled the label off his beer bottle. "It was the shits—'scuse my French. He barked orders like a drill sergeant. When one of us said it was time to grade the roads and gravel certain sections of the district, Brown told us to keep our mouths shut and our thoughts to ourselves."

"His favorite comment was, 'You aren't getting paid to think, asshole,'" Homer Frizzell quoted. "'Just do what the blankety-blank I tell you or I'll hire some other stupid, blankety-blank moron who will.'"

Amanda was reasonably certain that none of the men in the road crew would be attending Brown's funeral the following morning. Work, she predicted, would continue as usual at the commissioner's barn. These men were delighted they no longer had to deal with Brown's intimidation and ridicule.

Amanda suspected Brown had lorded over his employees, relishing the power of his position. If it were true that a man's worth was judged by the attendance at his funeral, Brown had accomplished very little in life.

When Chuck Gilhaney scooted off the tailgate, the other men followed like a flock of sheep. "If you're implying there was something fishy about Brown's death," Chuck said as he ground his heel into the cigarette butt, "don't expect any of us to care who did it—if anybody did."

"Yeah," Ron Newton chimed in. "Some things are better left alone, I always say. Could be that all of our collective curses caused Brown to met with a twist of fate. If prayers are answered, maybe curses are, too."

Amanda trailed after the muscle-bound man who had the misfortune of being the last one to pile into his truck. "Were you here the morning Brown sent Sam Harjo out to run the bulldozer in the downpour?"

Homer Frizzell stopped short, then glanced over his bulky shoulder. "How'd you know about that?"

"I've been checking around," Amanda said evasively. "So . . . were you?"

"Yeah, I was here. We all were. Brown came swaggering into the shop, demanding that Harjo do some work around the new bridge piers on Whatsit River. Harjo told Brown to stick it where the sun don't shine."

Amanda raised her eyebrows. "Harjo didn't take guff off Brown, I assume."

Frizzell grinned, displaying the silver cap on his front tooth. "Harjo stood up for all of us, and for himself. He didn't take any crap from Brown, because he was challenging Brown to fire him."

Amanda frowned, bemused. "Harjo doesn't need a job?"

"Sure he does, but he . . ." Homer looked away. "He had something on Brown. If Brown fired him, Brown was afraid Harjo would go public."

"Harjo was blackmailing Brown?" Amanda asked.

"I didn't say that." Frizzell made a grab for the door latch. Clearly, he was anxious to be on his way. "Harjo was planning to run against the incumbent in the Democratic primary. Our foreman was planning to use his inside information to control Brown's big mouth."

"If Harjo was defeated in the primary, did he plan to pass along this information to Ervin Shakelford? The uncontested Republican candidate?"

Frizzell slid beneath the steering wheel. "I don't know how and when Harjo planned to use what he knew. All I know is that he's a damned good road foreman and he'll make a damned good county commissioner, because he knows the ropes and he knows how to get things done. Even when Brown ordered him to do the worst jobs around here, hoping Harjo would up and quit, Harjo stood his ground."

"Essentially, you're saying Brown wanted Harjo to quit so he didn't have to fire his foreman," Amanda paraphrased.

"You got it, sister."

Amanda rolled the information around in her mind, then nodded in understanding. "If Brown *fired* Harjo, the foreman could use the fact to his advantage at election time. But if Harjo *quit*, Brown could use the incident for more mud-slinging."

Frizzell nodded as he dug into his pocket for his keys. "I can almost hear Brown calling Harjo a quitter. He lived to harass anyone who stood in his way. But Brown met his match in Sam Harjo. That is one tough son-of-a-bitch. If I was in a fight, I'd want him on my side. All of the guys on the road crew feel that way. We would walk through walls if Harjo asked us to. As for Brown, none of us would've given him the time of day if we didn't have to."

Pensively, Amanda watched Frizzell unroll the pack of cigarettes stuck in the sleeve of his grimy t-shirt. She glanced at the tattoo on his bulging arm muscle. From the look of him, Homer was the mechanic who kept county machinery operating efficiently.

"Can you tell me where to find Harjo?" Amanda asked before Homer drove away.

Frizzell chuckled as he lit his cigarette. "You don't quit, do you, lady?"

"No," she proudly affirmed. "Not when I'm on the trail of truth and justice."

Frizzell blew a few smoke rings in the air, then cranked the engine. The old truck sputtered, then purred like a kitten. Yep, Amanda assured herself. Homer was a master mechanic who kept this bucket of rust in proper working order.

"Brown got his due," Homer said matter-of-factly. "*That* is the truth and the justice."

Amanda's shoulders slumped as Frizzell drove away. Was she the only one in the county who cared to know if Brown had died accidentally or on purpose?

Sure as hell looked that way.

* * *

Amanda rubbed her bleary eyes, then took a sip of coffee that was doctored with enough cream and sugar to neutralize the bitter taste. It was ten o'clock at night and she still had hours of calculations ahead of her. She took another gulp of coffee, wishing she could inject much-needed caffeine straight into her veins. Doing double duty as an accountant and a self-appointed detective was zapping her energy and straining her brain.

Blankly, she stared at Harry Oglebee's tax receipts. She wished the old farmer had tallied his expenses instead of delivering them to her in a shoebox. The old codger was going to pay extra for her time and effort, Amanda promised herself.

The shrill sound of the phone broke the silence. Amanda poked her forefinger on the numerical column so she wouldn't lose her place, then snatched up the phone.

"Hazard Accounting. Hazard here."

"I know who you are, doll. I'm your mother. For heaven's sake, you sound as if you're at your office."

"I am, sort of." Amanda stifled a tired yawn.

"Your daddy and I were wondering if you had our tax returns completed. I always like to look them over before I mail them in."

In other words, Amanda thought to herself, Mother didn't trust her not to screw up. "Your returns should be ready by the first of next week."

"Why aren't they ready now?" Mother whined. "We're family, after all. Doesn't that entitle us to certain privileges?"

"I do your returns for *free,*" Amanda reminded her. "That is your *certain privilege.*"

"My, aren't we grumpy this evening," Mother said with a disdainful sniff.

"Speak for yourself, Mother."

"Don't be snide, doll."

"Wonder where I learned it?" Amanda said under her breath.

"Pardon, doll?"

"Nothing, Mother. I'm really busy here. I've got more tax returns to tally than I have time."

"Then I'll be brief."

That'll be the day, thought Amanda.

Mother cleared her throat and switched topics. "I've got my ideas for your wedding shower lined out. I chose Victorian accent colors—all pastels. I plan to have the event catered at the country club."

Amanda specifically remembered telling Mother to butt out. It was just like Mother to take over, despite objection. Well, Amanda wasn't going to let her get away with it. "You'll have to cancel your plans, Mother. Velma Hertzog is handling the shower."

"Who?"

"The beautician."

"Are we talking about the woman who gives you those disastrous haircuts? You've got to be kidding!"

"I couldn't be more serious, Mother."

"No daughter of mine is going to have a second-rate shower engineered by some rinky-dink beautician from Nowheresville!"

Amanda held her tongue—and it was no small feat.

"I planned to invite all my friends."

"You mean the ones who showed up for the shower for my first marriage?"

"Well, yes, doll. My friends are all high society, you know."

Lord, the affair had been so dull that Amanda had nearly died of boredom. No way was she going through that again!

"Sorry, Mother, but I'm letting Velma handle it. She doesn't have children and she's looking forward to giving this shower."

"Well, let her adopt somebody else's kid!" Mother ordered, as only Mother could. "I want to be in control of this shower!"

The doorbell clanged and Bruno barked his head off.

"I've got to go, Mother. Someone is here."

"Who? Thorn? A little late for a social call, isn't it?"

"We're engaged, Mother."

"Is that a dog I hear in the background?" Mother questioned. "Don't tell me you keep pets in the house! Pops never said anything about it after he spent a couple of months with you."

Amanda's grandfather never told Mother anything he didn't have to. Neither did Amanda.

"You'll be overrun by fleas and ticks and the place will smell like a kennel," Mother yipped. "Really, doll, I thought I trained you better than that."

"Gotta run, Mother. 'Bye."

The forceful knock rattled the door hinges, provoking Bruno to send up another loud bark. Amanda dropped the phone in its cradle and dashed to the door. Bruno sniffed the threshold, his ears laid back, his teeth bared.

"Down, Bruno," Amanda commanded, but the dog continued to growl and snarl.

Forcefully, Amanda wedged herself between the dog and the door. To her surprise, it wasn't Thorn who stood on the porch. A tall, brawny figure of a man in faded blue jeans, wearing a Resistol cowboy hat and scuffed boots, appeared before her. His face was shadowed by the brim of his hat, leaving only a hint of a square chin that boasted a five o'clock shadow.

"Hazard, I hear you want to talk to me," the man said in a low, gravely voice.

Although Bruno was raising a ruckus, the man didn't seem the least bit intimidated. His fearlessness reminded Amanda of Isaac's reaction to Bruno's attack.

"The name is Sam Harjo."

One tough son-of-a-bitch, according to Homer Frizzell. Amanda didn't know whether to let the big brute inside or call Thorn.

Sam tilted his head back ever so slightly. The interior lights from the house reflected off golden brown eyes that reminded Amanda of a stalking cat. A very large, formidable cat. The jungle variety that gobbled domesticated accountants in one gulp.

Marshaling her courage, Amanda stepped back a pace to pat Bruno on the head. Still, she didn't unlock the storm door.

"Well? You wanted me, Hazard. Now you've got me. Are you going to let me come in or not?"

Amanda met Harjo's penetrating stare. She found herself comparing the sinewy mass of strength and muscle to Thorn. An equal match, Amanda mused, except that Harjo's voice, posture and physique reminded her of the younger Clint Eastwood, when he'd starred in those spaghetti westerns.

When Amanda unlocked the storm door, Harjo took his cue. Bruno bolted forward to intercept the intruder.

"Bruno, heel!" Harjo demanded in a lethal but quiet voice.

To Amanda's amazement, Bruno halted in mid-bark and dropped to his haunches. Harjo sauntered over to plant himself on the sofa. Mutely, Bruno followed him.

Amanda frowned at Bruno's odd behavior.

"Do you have anything to drink, Hazard? I'd like to wet my whistle before you grill me with questions."

Amanda surveyed the ruggedly handsome man who had sprawled negligently on her couch. Though she considered herself a courageous soul, there was something about this man that made her wary. She could easily picture him slamming a scuffed boot against the side of Commissioner Brown's truck, sending the jack sliding into the mud. It would have taken only one fell swoop powered by those muscled arms to render Brown senseless.

Quickly, Amanda shook off the vision and strode into the kitchen. "I've got coffee brewing," she said over her shoulder. "Will that do?"

"I like mine black," he replied.

Amanda poured two fresh cups of coffee. When she re-entered the living room, Sam was thumbing through her latest issue of *Tax Reform Quarterly*. He glanced up, studying her with amber-colored eyes.

"You actually read this stuff, Hazard, or is it all for show?"

"I have to keep updated on changes in state and federal tax regulations. Of course I read that stuff."

Sam sank back against the sofa and regarded her for a long, pensive moment. "You're a rare combination, Hazard. A head for figures and a figure to stop traffic. Brains and beauty. From what I've seen, there aren't too many of your kind on the planet."

Amanda didn't know whether to be insulted or flattered by the man's straightforwardness. For certain, this younger version of Clint Eastwood had set her back on her heels—and kept her there.

"Mind if I ask you a question before you pump me for information, Hazard?"

"Fire away, Harjo."

"Why are you so damned insistent on making a big deal of Brown's death?"

"Because I have the sneaking suspicion that Brown had help reaching the Great Beyond."

Harjo smirked. "The man's headed for hell in a hand-basket. He was a creep with a capital *C*. The power of political position worked on him like fast-acting poison." He glanced down at Bruno, who lay complacently beside the couch. "Even his own dog couldn't stand him."

Again, Amanda eyed Bruno curiously. After sending up

his initial protest, Bruno had allowed Harjo to make himself at home. Now why was that?

"The dog certainly took up quickly enough with you," Harjo added. "He never put up a fuss when he was with Brown. I guess Bruno doesn't want anybody messing with the good deal he's got going now."

Amanda continued to stand there holding the steaming coffee, silently appraising the dominating male presence that had entered her home. For a long moment she made comparisons and speculated on how Harjo fit into the incidents leading to Brown's death.

"Take a load off, Hazard. And quit staring at me as if you're trying to decide how dangerous I am," Harjo insisted. "You can sit down and relax. I've got more sense than to strangle you in your own house."

Amanda didn't know how to take that remark, either. Although she had remained on alert, ready to cut and run to the phone at the first sign of trouble, she found herself sinking onto the La-Z-Boy recliner. Since Harjo insisted he was harmless, Amanda went from defense to offense.

"I know you were driving the bulldozer on the stretch of road where I found Brown," she said. "Did you speak to Brown the morning he died?"

"Yep."

"About what?"

"The idiocy of taking out a dozer in the rain. That was Brown's style. He got his kicks from devising situations that were difficult for me to plow my way out of."

"He liked to make you look bad," Amanda paraphrased. "Why?"

"He hated my guts for several reasons. What really got his goat was that I never let him walk all over me. I came to the defense of the road crew under my supervision and he strongly resented that. Brown despised having his authority defied."

Harjo's lips quirked in a wry smile. "You didn't know Brown personally, did you?"

"No, I didn't, but I was ready to kill him the morning I got stuck—twice—on bad roads."

"You and half the citizens of Vamoose County," Harjo added. "The man isn't worth your time and effort, Hazard. He was one of those agitating people who could walk into a room and piss off everyone in it in less than five minutes."

No one painted a complimentary picture of Brown, Amanda reminded herself—and not for the first time. Maybe she should drop this investigation. It was time-consuming, distracting, and not well received.

Yet, Amanda couldn't back off. Unanswered questions were driving her nuts. A habit of her chosen profession, she supposed. Accountants were trained to account for everything. Right down to the last penny, the last detail.

"Homer Frizzell told me that you had something on Brown."

Sam outstretched his arm to grab the coffee cup. Sinewy muscles peeked at Amanda from beneath the hem of his short-sleeved t-shirt.

Sam choked on the strong coffee. "Damn, Hazard," he wheezed. "This tastes like tar."

"It keeps me awake while I'm figuring tax returns."

"Make sure you've had several cups of it when you figure Brown's taxes. Wouldn't want you to miss anything."

Amanda beetled her brows. "What's that supposed to mean?"

"The commissioner whose death you're hell-bent on avenging was embezzling money from the county." Sam took a small sip of his coffee, made an awful face, then set the cup aside. "Brown also refused to sign a contract with a machinery company unless he received a kickback. All those cattle you saw standing by the fence near Brown's truck were bought and paid for with kickbacks. All the purchases Brown made for the county came with the same kind of fringe benefits.''

''Were you planning to disclose his dirty dealings during the primary election?'' Amanda questioned.

For the first time since Harjo arrived, he looked uncomfortable. That was saying a lot for a man who was reported to be difficult to intimidate.

''Let's just say Brown knew I had the weapons at my disposal.''

There was something Harjo didn't want to confide. Amanda wondered what and why, but she didn't probe deeper. The hard expression on Harjo's bronzed face indicated that he had said all he intended to say on the subject.

''So Brown came out to check on you while you were supposed to be working the area around the new bridge,'' Amanda prompted. ''I don't suppose he had come to cut a deal with you before the upcoming primary.''

Harjo's brow rose in surprise. ''Damn, Hazard, you're good.''

''Am I also accurate?''

Reluctantly, he nodded. ''Brown offered to split his kickbacks down the middle if I would drop out of the primary and be satisfied to keep the position of foreman.''

''And you refused,'' Amanda predicted.

''In so many words, yes.''

Despite this watered-down version of the incident, Amanda suspected there were a great many four-letter words exchanged that morning. She wondered if Brown had picked another fight. Brown had obviously been on a rampage after confronting his estranged wife and Sonny Snittiger.

Amanda appraised Harjo critically, then decided Brown would have to be crazy to physically attack his foreman. Harjo looked as if he could make mincemeat of a man in two seconds flat.

''Did Brown try to tamper with your dozer to retaliate

for your refusal to cooperate? Was he planning to leave you out in the rain and on foot?''

Sam did a double-take. "What the hell are you, Hazard? Some kind of psychic?''

"No, just a practical analyst," she said. "Brown couldn't browbeat you. I've learned that much about you from your road crew. Brown couldn't battle a man like you physically and expect to win. All that's left is attacking your equipment and leaving you stranded. And that," she added pensively, "seems to have been Brown's style. From what I've learned, Brown had turned goading and ridicule into an art form.''

Sam nodded in agreement. "You've certainly got that right.''

Amanda was glad she had a few things right in an investigation that was moving at a snail's pace!

"When I refused Brown's bribe, he stormed over to jerk on the dozer's fuel line. When he snapped it in two, I decided to give him a taste of his own medicine. I used my pocket knife and a hammer to stab his tire. I had intended to have it out with him—then and there, once and for all.''

A flash of memory leaped to mind. Amanda recalled the flattened tire track and the backward imprint of Goodyear in the mud. Harjo had caused Brown's flat tire.

"Brown ordered me to change his flat," Sam continued. "I told him to fix it himself. He got mad and took a swing at me with the tire tool.''

Although Harjo was giving an impassive account of the incident, Amanda suspected emotions had been roiling and tempers flying at the time.

"You disarmed him," Amanda guessed, then stared intently at Harjo. "What did you do for a living before you hired on as foreman?''

Sam's full lips pursed as he eased back on the sofa. "I was a hit man for the mob.''

Amanda hoped he was pulling her leg. She gave Harjo credit for possessing a dry sense of humor, then waited for him to tell her the truth.

"I had no trouble handling Brown because I was a wrestler in high school," he told her without blinking.

That explained the bulk and brawn, and accounted for the ability to fend off a physical threat. But Harjo had not directly answered Amanda's question. Again, she had the feeling that Harjo wasn't being completely honest with her. She would have to devise a way to check his file at the courthouse. There had to be a résumé and list of previous employment filed somewhere.

"What happened after you countered Brown's attack?" she inquired.

"Brown vowed to make my life so miserable that I would finally quit my job. He also swore that he would fix it so that I would be accused of taking kickbacks from the tool companies and machinery suppliers we dealt with. Then he—"

A muscle ticked in his jaw and his expression closed up. "Brown gave the dog a kick in the ribs, because he couldn't vent his temper on me. Then I helped Brown back into his truck."

Amanda imagined Harjo had bodily planted Brown in his pick-up.

"When Bruno whined and took off, Brown yelled at him to come back. Brown tossed several dog biscuits in the truck bed to lure the dog with him. Then Brown drove off on his flat tire. He went as far as he could go before the loss of traction caused him to get stuck in the mud."

Amanda frowned, wondering just how much of the incident Harjo had purposely omitted. She knew he was supplying carefully guarded answers.

Sam could have sprinted downhill to pounce on Brown while he was trying to change the tire. Sam had been threatened and bribed and had plenty of reason to dispose of his obnoxious boss. Accepting the position of interim commissioner and seeking the Democratic candidacy could have been accomplished in one blow—literally.

Or . . . Amanda mused as she watched Sam rise from the sofa, Sam Harjo could have seen Sonny Snittiger or Isaac Marcum sneaking up on Brown. Harjo could have looked the other way and let Brown get his due.

All three men had perfect motive and opportunity to bump off Brown. They could have been protecting each other, because each man had strong feelings about seeing Brown dead. And for damned certain, Brown had developed a knack of making his associates so furious that they lost their cool.

"How did you repair the dozer and leave the scene before I arrived to find Brown?" Amanda asked.

"I bent the fuel line back into position with my bare hands and duct-taped it together so I could drive back to the commissioner's barn," Sam replied as he strode toward the door in lithe, pantherlike strides.

"One more question," Amanda demanded.

"Don't push it, Hazard. I've been as cooperative in your unofficial investigation as I plan to be."

Amanda swallowed the question she wanted to ask, then scooped up the plastic jar that sat on the coffee table. "Will you donate to my Donkey Queen fund, commissioner?"

The unexpected question caught Harjo off guard. He stared at the jar, then at Amanda. Plucking his wallet from the hip pocket of his jeans, he pulled out a twenty-dollar bill, folded it in fourths, then poked it through the slot in the lid.

"Twenty bucks? Is this a bribe, commissioner?"

"No," he said, repocketing his wallet. ""I gave Vinita Frizzell a ten-spot. But don't tell her husband I'm showing favoritism."

"Why are you?" Amanda asked, tilting her head to assess the tall, dynamic figure of a man.

His hand brushed very lightly over the curve of her jaw. Amanda froze to the spot. Was Sam Harjo coming on to her? It certainly felt like it!

"Because I like you, Hazard," he replied in a velvety-soft voice. "You've got class and smarts. If you ever decide to slip that engagement ring off your finger, let me know."

Amanda simply stood there staring at Harjo as he opened the door and stepped out into the darkness.

"See you around, gorgeous."

Amanda was still standing there, her tongue welded to the roof of her mouth, clutching her plastic jar to her chest, when she heard Harjo drive away. Was that big stud of a male trying to butter her up so she'd drop her inquisition about the possibility of murder?

Legs wobbling, Amanda sank down on her chair and stared out the door. Was Harjo the kind of man who would try to use premeditated charm on a woman, so she would cut him some slack?

Despite Homer Frizzell's previous remarks, and her uncertain impressions about this personal interview with Harjo, Amanda wasn't sure she knew the new commissioner well enough to decide if he would use his noticeable physical attributes for persuasive tactics.

Put quite simply, Amanda didn't know what to think.

Seven

Amanda groaned groggily, unaware of what had awakened her. Her eyes drifted shut, her fatigued body begging for a few more hours of sleep.

With the tax filing deadline looming in the near distance, Amanda had devoted the past two days—and nights—to calculating tax returns. She had poured over the stacks of receipts, calling a halt at four in the morning because she hadn't been able to see anything except a fuzzy blur. Her highly efficient brain had gone on the blink.

The roar of heavy machinery in the still morning air brought Amanda to a higher level of awareness. Rolling onto her side, she squinted at the digital clock—7:59 a.m.

Bemused, Amanda leaned over to separate the louvers on the mini-blinds. To her astonishment she saw a convoy of county vehicles approaching her home like a herd of mechanical dinosaurs. Homer Frizzell and Ron Newton were manning the faded yellow road graders that lumbered past the house, smoothing over the deep ruts. Chuck Gilhaney was driving a dump truck heaped with gravel. A bulldozer plowed through the south ditch, scooping up gravel that had been washed off the road, then piled it beside Amanda's driveway.

It was the first time in living memory that Amanda had seen an entire work crew pass by her house. Brown, she now knew, had concentrated the work force at his command on the roads in the northwestern sections of the district near his home.

And suddenly Amanda was receiving preferential treatment. Why?

Her wary gaze drifted to the rear of the convoy. The county-issued truck that had once belonged to Brown was parked in the middle of the road. The tall, shadowed figure of a man was propped leisurely against the side of the truck. Amanda nearly swallowed her tongue when she realized Sam Harjo was staring directly at her bedroom window, smiling that lopsided smile she had become acquainted with two nights earlier.

Deep suspicion loomed over Amanda when Sam Harjo tipped his Resistol hat in silent greeting. Amanda snatched her hand away, letting the blinds settle back into place.

This was the most awkward situation she had ever encountered. She wasn't sure if she was being courted or bribed into dropping her investigation.

Two nights earlier, Sam Harjo had made Amanda decidedly uncomfortable. The fact was that she had been more than a little rattled by his dynamic presence in her home. She kept comparing Harjo to Thorn, finding both men equal in appeal . . .

"Good grief, Hazard. What can you be thinking? Harjo is a prime suspect in Brown's murder. The man had opportunity, motive and a helluva lot to gain. You're an engaged woman, for heaven's sake!"

Exasperated by emotions she wasn't wide awake enough to cope with, Amanda crawled from bed, then shrugged on her clothes. With the everfaithful Border Collie at her heels, she marched outside and made a beeline toward Sam Harjo.

"Okay, Harjo, what are you trying to pull?" Amanda demanded as she halted before the new commissioner.

Sam pushed away from the side of the truck, staring down at her with those hypnotic golden eyes that were surrounded by long, thick lashes. "Have you got a problem with me, Hazard?" he asked in a low, husky voice.

"I most certainly do!" Amanda erupted in bad temper. "Are you bribing me or something? Brown never graded my road, so why are *you*?"

He cocked his head slightly, regarding her from beneath the shadowed brim of his hat. "Are you always this cranky in the morning, Hazard?"

She bared her teeth. Although Amanda was an early-morning person—except when she'd stayed up half the night figuring tax returns—the effect Harjo was having on her was rapidly souring her disposition. "I'm habitually cranky, if you want to know. Lately, I've had little sleep, and your noisy convoy of heavy machinery woke me up!"

A roguish grin quirked his lips. "I could arrange to wake you up gently," he offered in an ultrasexy voice.

Amanda, who rarely let a man get the better of her, found herself retreating a cautious step. "What do you want, Harjo? For me to drop this investigation because you're going out of your way to be charming and accommodating?"

"Is that what you think is happening here?" he countered.

"That's exactly what I think is happening here."

Amanda stopped breathing when Harjo reached out to tuck a recalcitrant strand of blond hair behind her ear. Lack of sleep must have caused some chemical imbalance in her brain, she decided. Her heartbeat accelerated, her skin tingled.

Too much work, not enough proper nourishment and not

enough rack time, Amanda quickly diagnosed. Those were the reasons why she was suffering this odd reaction to Sam Harjo. He was a murder suspect, she reminded herself—again.

"Maybe I'm just doing my job," he said in a caressing voice. "And maybe all I want is your vote, come election day."

Amanda wheeled around and stomped off. Clearly, she was in no condition to deal with a man of Harjo's capabilities. She needed coffee to kick-start her sluggish brain.

"From now on, you can expect this stretch of road to be cared for properly," Harjo called after her. "And Hazard?"

"What?" she asked, glaring over her shoulder at him.

Harjo smiled wryly as his penetrating gaze glided over her body. "You've got your t-shirt on inside-out."

Face blazing with color, Amanda stomped back to her house. She was not prepared for what seemed to be happening. She was an engaged person. Sam Harjo could not possibly be getting to her, no matter what his ulterior purpose!

When Amanda re-entered her house, the phone was blaring at her. She snatched it up, anxious for a distraction. "Hazard here."

"Hi, hon." Chomp, crackle. "I know we were going to give you phase two of your new 'do tomorrow afternoon, but I have a cancellation this morning. Sara Mae Brown isn't keeping her appointment."

Amanda's mind shifted gears, though not as quickly as usual. She suspected Sara Mae and Sonny had eloped. The *un*grieving widow would have the county gossips flapping their jaws when word of their hasty wedding got out.

"You wanna come in for your trim?" Velma asked.

"What time?" Amanda leaped at the chance of leaving the vicinity where Harjo loomed.

"Soon as you can get here."

"I'm on my way."

Tugging at the hem of her t-shirt, Amanda turned the garment right side out. By the time she grabbed her purse and keys, Bruno was at the door waiting for her. In a short span of time, the dog had associated the jingling of keys with Amanda's departure. Bruno had no intention of being left behind.

Refusing to glance in Harjo's direction. Amanda piled into her truck. Hurriedly, she switched the ignition.

Nothing.

After three unsuccessful attempts, Amanda pounded her doubled fist on the steering wheel.

"Can I be of help?"

Amanda shrank back when she realized Harjo was standing beside her truck. The man moved with the silence of a cat!

A handy talent if you wanted to sneak up on somebody and club him over the head with a jack handle.

Willfully, Amanda brought her accelerated pulse rate under control. "Damn thing won't start," she muttered, staring straight ahead.

"Probably a dead battery."

"You probably know a lot about *dead*," she grumbled under her breath.

"Pardon?"

"Never mind. I have a hair appointment and I'm running late."

Harjo shot a glance toward the Toyota—with its front bumper dangling on the ground. "I'll take you into town," he volunteered. "We'll stop by Thatcher's Oil and Gas so you can buy a new battery."

"I don't want to ride with you," Amanda blurted out.

Harjo opened the door, latched onto her elbow and towed her off the seat. "Why not, Hazard? Afraid of me?"

"Yeah," she flung back as he propelled her toward his county-issued truck. "Afraid I might end up like your predecessor."

Harjo never broke stride. He simply ushered Amanda to the battered truck. Bruno followed closely at Amanda's heels, then hopped into the bed so he wouldn't be abandoned.

Amanda inwardly groaned when Benny Sykes cruised past in the squad car. The deputy recognized her and waved. Amanda sank a little deeper on the seat and hugged the passenger door. Harjo smiled as he drove past the city limits sign that read: If you like it country style, then Vamoose.

When they reached the service station, Thaddeus Thatcher glanced up from the flat tire he was repairing. Amanda watched his curious gaze bounce from her to Harjo. He was making all sorts of speculations, Amanda predicted.

"Hazard's truck has a dead battery," Sam called to Thaddeus. "Can you fix her up with a new one? I'll stop by to pick it up after I take Hazard to her hair appointment."

Thaddeus arched a graying brow as he cast the couple a contemplative glance. Amanda considered strangling Harjo right on the spot. She had the unmistakable feeling that he intended to get considerable mileage out of this incident. In fact, she wondered if he had sneaked up to tamper with her truck so she would have to rely on him.

When Thaddeus lumbered off to retrieve a new battery, Harjo cruised away. Amanda noticed that Harjo made a spectacular display of waving at the clientele in the parking lot at Last Chance Cafe as he passed.

Amanda gnashed her teeth and glared at the commissioner.

"I don't like being used or manipulated, Harjo," she growled. "You didn't have to detour into Thatcher's first, so Thaddeus could see us together." Amanda glowered at him good and hard. "For a man who claims that he detested the way Brown operated, you've certainly picked up his unscrupulous habits in one whale of a hurry."

Harjo didn't reply until he had stopped in front of Velma's Beauty Boutique. He shifted beneath the wheel and laid a sinewy arm on the back of the seat. "In the first place, I'm nothing like Brown," he said, holding her steady gaze. "And 'B,' politics is tricky business. Even when you're aware of the dirty secrets revolving around you, innocent people can get caught up in the boiling cauldron. Timing, I'm afraid, is extremely important."

"Like being seen with me this morning?" she said, eyeing him speculatively. "The citizens of Vamoose see me tooling around town bright and early in the morning with the political hopeful who has been selected as interim commissioner. And since I'm reasonably well known, you are given an automatic vote of confidence because of our association. Is that one of those dirty little tricks and clever timing skills you're referring to?"

His hand glided off the seat to brush playfully against the tip of her upturned nose. Amanda immediately shrank back into her own space.

"I won't deny that I want to win the election," he told her flat-out.

"At any cost?"

Harjo ignored the baiting and continued. "I have discovered that there are two sides in politics. The side the public sees and the ugly side where means sometimes justify the end result. I'd like to make a few changes in the way deals are made behind closed doors, but I have to get voter approval before I have the authority to make changes.

"I could also use a respectable, credible campaign manger. I'd like you to take the job."

Amanda's jaw sagged. Was she being baited, charmed and/or manipulated again? Harjo could be using the clever strategy on her. Maybe he intended to win her over, flatter her, then bribe her into dropping her investigation of Brown's death.

Without replying, Amanda opened the door. To her

dismay, she saw Velma's, Bev's and Millie Patch's faces plastered against the windows of the salon. The threesome was all eyes and imaginative speculation.

Well, damn! No doubt the women had seen Harjo's light, teasing caress.

Accusingly, Amanda darted Harjo a glare. He was smiling that Clint Eastwood smile again. Amanda climbed from the truck with more speed than grace. Bruno bounded from the bed to follow Amanda inside.

When Amanda opened the salon door, the three women scurried for position, trying to pretend they hadn't been spying on her.

"Hi, hon," Velma said brightly as she motioned Amanda toward The Chair. "Fine morning, isn't it?"

"Swell, just swell," Amanda muttered as she plunked onto the seat.

"I didn't know you were so well acquainted with our new commissioner." Crackle, snap.

"He was grading the roads near my house," Amanda explained in a rush. "My truck wouldn't start, so he gave me a ride to town."

The three women glanced discreetly at each other, but Amanda intercepted the speculative looks in the mirror.

"If you say so, hon." Pop!

Amanda flinched as if she had been shot. "I do say so."

"Fine, hon," Velma patronized.

While Velma gathered her scissors, brush and comb, Bev scurried around in front of Amanda to rub off the happy-face polish with industrial-strength nail polish remover. "Do you think Sam Harjo will defeat Shakelford in the election?" she asked the salon at large.

"Don't know," Millie Patch said as she pulled the hair dryer over her head, then crossed her polyester-clad legs at the ankles. "For sure, Sam has come up through the ranks in the county work force. He knows the how-to's and what-for's to get things done."

"And he'll earn himself extra votes when he plays in the Donkey Basketball game." Velma cracked her chewing gum as she massaged Amanda's scalp with instant conditioner. "He volunteered to be one of the king candidates, too."

Amanda went utterly still. "Oh? When did you coax him into doing that?"

"Like, she didn't have to," Bev put in as she dabbed on more nail polish remover. "When Sam found out who the queen candidates were, he asked to sign up."

"Nothing like competition to rack in the cash for the fire department." Velma eyed Amanda as she plucked up a hair brush. "How long have you and Sammy been chumming around together?"

"We are *not* chumming around together," Amanda said through her teeth. "He gave me a lift into town."

"Like, are you trying to make Thorn jealous?" Bev asked as she clamped her meaty fist around a bottle of fire-engine red polish.

"Certainly not!" Amanda erupted.

All three women glanced at one another again. Amanda silently groaned. Her defensive reply suggested there might be another reason why she was seen with Harjo.

You have to watch what you say—and how you say it—when you're roosting in a gossip's nest, she reminded herself.

"You're the first woman Sammy has been seen with in public for a long time," Velma reported as she brushed Amanda's hair.

"My mama said Sammy has kept to himself the past few years. That heartthrob has lots of eligible women wishing he'd pay attention to them."

"Why hasn't he been on the dating circuit?" Amanda asked, watching in the mirror while Velma snipped an uneven clump of hair.

"He's very particular—like Nicky." Crackle, chomp.

"That and the fact that Sammy lost part of the family

ranch a few years back,'' Millie added as she poked her head from the dryer. ''It was a real blow to his pride, you know. He had to take the job with the road crew to make ends meet.''

Amanda had the suspicious feeling Sam Harjo had gone bankrupt. So that's why he had been reluctant to answer her question about previous employment. He was a poor financial manager, like her ex-husband, no doubt.

''Mama said Sammy tried to save the family farm,'' Bev said while she painted Amanda's nails. ''But Ben Harjo—that was Sammy's daddy—had gone so far into debt before he died that there was no way out. Sammy managed to salvage only 80 acres of the 640 acre farm. Even though Sammy was doing a good business training dogs, it wasn't enough to pay the loans.''

''Training dogs?'' Amanda blinked like a faulty florescent bulb.

''Like, sure.'' Bev gestured her curly head toward Bruno, who waited patiently beside the door. Her Shirley Temple curls bobbed around her plump cheeks. ''Dogs are his first love, or so Mama says. Sammy trained Bruno and gave him to his sister, but Dusty claimed the dog as his own.''

Amanda felt the color drain from her face. ''Sara Mae is Sam's sister?'' she chirped.

''Yes.'' Snip, whack. ''That's why Sara Mae threw such a fit about the house and property that Dusty tried to keep for himself. That land and house where Dusty and Sara Mae lived once belonged to the Harjos. Old man Brown bought it, then Dusty and Sara Mae bought it from him when they were married.''

Red warning flags waved in Amanda's mind. No wonder Harjo had been playing up to her. There was a lot he hadn't told her during their interview. There was more than political conflict between Dusty Brown and Sam Harjo. No question about it, Amanda decided—Sonny, Sam or Sara Mae could have snubbed out Dusty and not one of them would dream of ratting on the other. Sara Mae wouldn't dare implicate her own brother or her soon-to-be—if he wasn't already—husband.

Or, she thought pensively, Isaac Marcum could have done the deed and the other suspects kept silent because the crazy old hermit had done them a stupendous favor.

"Sure is going to make the king and queen contest interesting with Nicky and Sammy in the running, isn't it?" Velma said, jostling Amanda from her ponderous thoughts.

Amanda forced herself not to react to the baiting comment. She sat in The Chair like a slug.

"Sammy can do a little campaigning for the election while he's collecting donations. Smart man, that Sammy. He'll make a good commissioner. He knows how to cover all the bases."

Smart, Amanda mused, did not adequately describe that tall, sexy man. But she didn't add her two cents' worth to the conversation, for fear of providing fruit for the gossips' grapevine. Enough damage had been done already.

"Just lay back for a minute, hon," Velma instructed. "I need to give you a quick wash so I can remove the last of that temporary tint. Your hair seems to be extremely porous and retains dye."

No kidding, thought Amanda. Hard as she tried, she couldn't completely rinse the passion pink from her blond hair.

Before Amanda could brace her freshly painted fingernails on the arm of The Chair, Velma whirled her around and tipped her backward. A spray of water dribbled into Amanda's ears as the nozzle hovered over her head. Shampoo bubbles floated across the room as Velma scrubbed vigorously, then sprayed away the excess suds.

"You're gonna love this new conditioner," Bev enthused as she dumped the fragrant goo on Amanda's head.

Strawberry? Amanda mused as Bev worked her chubby

fingers through the clump of wet hair. Cold tingles raced across Amanda's scalp. It felt as if Bev had rubbed strawberry-scented Ben Gay on her head!

"This revolutionary new gel conditions and adds amazing body," Bev said as she pulled the reddish globs through each strand of Amanda's hair.

The last thing Amanda needed was additional body. Her hair was as thick as a Pyrenees sheep dog's to begin with!

"Just a quick rinse," Velma advised the rookie beautician. "Make sure you don't wash out all that conditioner."

More water streamed down Amanda's temples as Bev rinsed out the conditioner. A towel floated over Amanda's head before Bev brought The Chair upright. Amanda swore her head had been clamped into a vice when Bev applied pressure to squeeze out the water.

While Velma combed out Millie's hair, Bev grabbed the blow dryer and brush. In a flurry, she circled The Chair, styling and drying Amanda's partial cut.

"There you go, Millie," Velma said, assisting the older woman to her feet. "All set for your afternoon bridge party. Play a trump for me."

Smacking her gum, Velma focused her fake-lashed eyes on Amanda's wet head. "Too much thickness here," she said as she grabbed the thinning scissors. After several random whacks, she turned to her niece. "Mix up some tint in the spray bottle for me, Bev. I want to try out the combination of colors we've worked up for Amanda."

Amanda was struck speechless when she glanced in the mirror. Her hair stuck out in all directions. There was entirely too much height on top of her head to compliment the shape of her face. She looked as if her head had exploded!

Snip, clip. "You're gonna love this style once it's perfected, hon. You'll be a real sensation at the wedding shower."

Velma leaned close, staring at Amanda through the mirror. "The shower is still on, isn't it? I mean, this new development with Sammy is just one of those passing fancies associated with the bridal jitters, isn't it?"

"Velma—"

"Now, you know me, hon." Chomp, chomp. "I wouldn't breathe a word about this to anybody, but some folks might think it looks highly suspicious to see Sammy bringing you into town at this time of the morning. Some folks—not me, of course—might wonder if Sammy had been there with you all night."

"All night!" Amanda yelped, aghast.

"He was?" Bev blinked owlishly. "Like, wow! The plot thickens! Sure hope Nicky doesn't get wind of this!"

"He and I were not—" Amanda slammed her mouth shut when the door creaked open. To her dismay, Sam Harjo's hunk of a masculine physique filled the doorway to overflowing.

"He who?" he asked casually.

"He *you,*" Velma answered as she took one last whack with her scissors. She eyeballed Sam for a pensive moment. "What do you have to say for yourself, Sammy?"

"Not a thing. I prefer to be known as a man of action, not words."

A slow, wicked grin slid across Sam's lips. His unwavering gaze fixed on Amanda as he reached down to scratch Bruno behind the ear. Amanda wanted to leap from The Chair and put a stranglehold on the man's neck. Sam let the comment hang in the air, giving the professional gossips ample time to leap to their own imaginative conclusions.

"If you're about finished with Hazard, I'll take her back home," Sam said as he rose to full stature.

Amanda gnashed her teeth. The situation was becoming worse by the second.

"Bring that spray over here, Bev," Velma ordered. "Don't want to keep the new commish waiting."

Bev dashed forward with the spray bottle clamped in her fist. With each squirt of the bottle, a spray of glittered lavender settled on Amanda's bushy head. Damn it, now she looked *worse* than Dennis Rodman—if that was possible. Her fluffy hair was coated with sparkling purple. Even Sam Harjo looked the other way, his broad shoulders shaking in silent amusement.

"All done," Velma proclaimed proudly. "So what do you think?"

Sam's tawny gaze glided back to Amanda. "Gorgeous," he murmured. "Absolutely gorgeous . . ."

Amanda managed to contain her fury until she had paid for the latest cosmetic calamity and stepped outside. "Don't you ever do that again," she seethed as she flounced onto the seat of the truck. "Take me home this very second, and use the back road to get there."

"Don't you think that will invite more gossip?" he asked reasonably. "Everyone watching will think we have something to hide if we sneak out the back way." He paused momentarily and stared at Amanda, ignoring her outlandish hairdo. *"Do* we have something to hide, Hazard?"

"No, we do not! I am an engaged person!" she all but yelled at him.

Sam glanced pointedly at her left hand, which now boasted red polish with white stripes that were reminiscent of candy canes. "So . . . why aren't you wearing your ring?"

Appalled, Amanda glanced at her hand. She had forgotten to slip the ring on her finger after doing last night's supper dishes. If Sam had noticed the absence of the ring, then so had Velma, Bev and Millie.

Oh my God . . .

"Just take me home, Harjo. Then stay away from me. Stop messing with my life."

"The way you're messing with mine by trying to pin a murder on me that didn't happen?" he countered as he drove straight down Main Street.

"Why didn't you tell me Sara Mae was your sister and that you are the one who trained Bruno?" she flung accusingly.

"You didn't ask me."

"Why did you suddenly decide to run for Donkey King?"

"Because it's free publicity. I can't afford expensive advertising for my campaign," he explained logically.

"And that's another thing," Amanda fumed, wagging her candy cane-coated finger at him. "You neglected to mention that the Browns bought your family farm when you went belly-up."

"My, you've had a busy morning, haven't you?" He glanced directly at Amanda's wild, colorful hairdo. "Is that where you gathered information for this unofficial investigation? At the beauty shop?"

Her chin went airborne. "I collect facts whenever and wherever they can be gathered."

"And I'm making myself visible in town to remind voters that I'm running for office."

"At my expense," Amanda quickly pointed out.

"It doesn't have to be at your expense."

Amanda's gaze narrowed on him. "Are you blackmailing me, Harjo?"

Sam applied the brake as he turned into Amanda's driveway.

"Well?" she demanded impatiently.

He half turned to stare at her, his expression solemn. "I thought I made my intentions clear the other night, Hazard."

Amanda's brows flattened on her forehead. The way Sam was staring at her lips gave her the distinct impression that he would have kissed her, there and then, if she had given him the slightest invitation. That smoldering look of his was doing strange, unexplainable things to her blood pressure.

Amanda climbed down from the truck with undo haste.

This case was becoming more frustrating and complicated by the day!

"I'll replace the battery for you," Sam offered.

"No, I'll do it myself," she insisted as she unfastened the tailgate. Bracing her legs beneath her, Amanda hoisted up the heavy battery. Waddling, she toted the battery to her truck.

She swore she heard Sam chuckling as he drove away.

If the battery hadn't been so damned heavy Amanda would have hurled it at him. On second thought, that would have assured him that he was getting under her skin.

While Amanda hooked up the new battery, she asked herself if forgetting to replace the engagement ring on her hand was a subconscious indication of bridal jitters and doubts.

What the devil was the matter with her? She was engaged to Tom Selleck's look-alike—minus the mustache.

And who showed up? A younger version of Clint Eastwood, a man who might very well have several hidden agendas.

While Amanda replaced the battery cables, she asked herself if she was trying a little too hard to pin Brown's murder on Sam Harjo. Maybe she *wanted* him to be the guilty party so she would have the perfect excuse not to like him . . .

"Good gad, Hazard! What is happening?" she asked herself as she slammed down the hood of the jalopy, then promptly locked herself in the house.

Eight

Nick stared out the back window of his Allis Chalmers tractor, checking on the hay rake he was pulling behind it. The metal teeth of the rake picked up the windrows of alfalfa hay that had been doused with rain and flipped them upside down to air out. Left unattended, the hay— for Nick's flock of sheep and cattle herd—would rot in the fields.

Nick whimsically wished for a spell of hot, dry weather, then glanced at the clouds piling high on the horizon. One more downpour and this hay would be moldy and worthless.

Ah, such were the trials and tribulations of farmers. Having to depend on the fickle moods of Mother Nature was tricky business.

"One dry day is all I ask," Nick said to the powers that be. "Twenty-four hours and I can bale this hay and haul it away. Give me a break here . . . please?"

Nick had taken two days off from patrolling Vamoose so he could tend to his farming chores. He had been raking hay meadows around the clock. If the threatening sky was any indication, his efforts would be for nothing.

In the distance, Nick saw the convoy of county workers in their dump truck, graders and bulldozers. The new commissioner wasn't wasting any time, Nick noted. Road repair was in full swing. Hazard should be pleased. From the look of things, the farm that Hazard had inherited from one of her departed clients would soon be surrounded by passable roads.

When Nick twisted in his cushioned seat, he noticed the black-and-white racing toward him. Something must be cooking, Nick predicted. Vamoose's gung-ho deputy was headed in Nick's direction.

Nick pushed the hydraulic lever to raise the rake, then he cut diagonally across the meadow to reach the patrol car that halted at the gate.

As Nick stepped from the tractor, Benny Sykes bounded from the squad car. His mirrored sunglasses reflected sunlight. Benny struck his serious business pose—feet planted askance, hands clasped behind him.

"Got a problem, Sykes?" Nick asked as he worked the kinks from his spine. Riding across rough fields was hell on a man's back.

"Problem?" he repeated. "No, *I* don't, chief, but I think *you* do."

Two black brows rose. "I do?" That was news to Nick. "Did my house burn down while I was out here working?"

"No, worse," Benny said gravely. "Somebody is trying to steal your fiancée."

"Hazard has been kidnapped?" Nick choked out. "What happened?"

"Kidnapped isn't entirely correct, chief." Benny whipped off his sunglasses and stared grimly at Nick. "Hazard has been seen all over town with Sam Harjo. Early this morning, too."

An uneasy sensation twisted in Nick's gut. He'd been

afraid Hazard would stumble onto Harjo if she delved into this accident that she had insisted was murder. Damn, if there was one man in Vamoose County that Nick would have preferred Hazard steer clear of, it was Sam Harjo.

"Well?" Benny prompted impatiently.

"Well what?"

"Well, aren't you going to do something? Velma said Sam dropped Hazard at the salon, then came by to pick her up. They were cruising down Main Street together. I saw them myself, *very early* this morning!"

"Were they breaking the law?" Nick asked as calmly as he knew how.

"No, but I drove by Hazard's place after I saw them coming into town. Get this, chief. Harjo had his crew out there grading and repairing Hazard's road. She's got a new layer of gravel from her driveway to the highway!"

Nick glanced over his shoulder, watching the county crew working the road a half mile away.

Benny followed Nick's gaze. "Well, damn, Harjo is fixing the road around the property that Elmer Jolly bequeathed to Hazard! That should tell you something, chief. Hazard's access roads are getting first priority. Nobody else has gotten preferential treatment from the new commish."

"What am I supposed to do? Arrest Harjo for doing his job?"

"No, but you better have a man-to-man talk with him," Benny advised. "He's trespassing into your territory. A man would have to be blind not to see that."

"Hazard can take care of herself," Nick said.

"Maybe she needs to be reminded who she is engaged to." Benny shoved the sunglasses onto the narrow bridge of his nose. "According to Velma and Bev, your fiancée wasn't wearing her ring at the salon this morning. While you're out here in the boondocks, turning windrows of hay so they can dry out, that interim commish is *making hay* while the sun shines!"

"And if I don't get this hay raked and baled before another round of rain, my livestock will go hungry this winter," Nick countered.

"So you're placing your livestock before your crumbling engagement, is that it?" Benny raked his hand through his thinning hair. "Fine, chief, don't heed the warning. And don't come whining to me when Harjo beats your time. He's running for Donkey King, too, if you hadn't heard."

Great, Nick mused. Just what he needed—competition from a worthy male rival.

"While you're out here, Harjo has been all over town, campaigning and collecting donations for the ballgame that will be held in two days. This is no time to be runner-up, chief. There's more at stake here than a donkey crown."

Wheeling around, Benny flounced on the seat, slammed the door, and sped off.

Nick stared after his deputy for a long moment. Sighing tiredly, Nick paced toward his tractor. There were times when a man had to leash his possessive tendencies and back off. This was one of those times, Nick told himself. He and Hazard were being put to the test. Nick supposed he was getting what he deserved after what he had done to Hazard during the case that left Will Bloom dead in the dirt.

And let's not forget the way you behaved while Hazard was trying to figure out who had left Elmer Jolly dead in the cellar, he thought with a grimace. Nick had dealt Hazard a few emotional blows during their conflicts over investigations. He had the unshakable feeling that the things he had done—to annoy Hazard when she infuriated him—were coming back to haunt him.

The most sensible thing Nick could do was rake his hay and cross his fingers. He could hope the obvious attention Hazard was getting from the new commissioner didn't become serious. If it did, this engagement—which Mom strongly opposed—might get called off!

Amanda did everything she could think of to remove the glittery purple tint from her hair. Nothing worked. Finally, she gave up and pulled the "bad hair day" hat down around her ears. With firm resolve, she drove out to the area where she had found Brown dead in the mud. Something about the scene of the crime niggled at her, something she was certain she must have overlooked during the distraction of filing tax returns and dealing with the unexpected attention from Sam Harjo.

Amanda stopped her jalopy just beyond the ruts and distorted prints that had dried in the road. Although rural traffic had smeared the shallow indentations, evidence of cattle tracks still trailed off into one bar ditch.

Amanda ambled along the edge of the road. Had the cattle broken through the fence before or after Brown stopped to repair the flat Harjo had caused? Or had someone purposely spooked the cattle? To cover incriminating tracks, perhaps? To distract Brown before the oncoming attack?

Amanda stared at the two houses that sat atop the hills to the west. Had Sonny Snittiger jogged downhill to have his revenge? Had Isaac Marcum sneaked up to vent his bitterness on Brown? Or had Harjo crept up to hammer Brown's head?

There was also the possibility that Sara Mae had not remained inside the house, as she claimed. She could have gone through the back door while Sonny was in the workshop, as *he* had claimed. If Sara Mae was as bold as her brother, she could have dealt effectively with her two-timing, double-dealing husband.

A woman could have leveled a lethal blow and then told her sob story when approached for questioning, Amanda reminded herself. That would certainly explain why Sara Mae and Sonny had lit out to tie the matrimonial knot. They had become conveniently unavailable for further questioning and had time to corroborate their stories.

And let's not forget that, married, they could refuse to testify against each other in court.

How convenient.

When Amanda considered how much Sara Mae and Sonny had to gain from Brown's death, suspicion mushroomed. But then, when she glanced northwest to see the run-down house tucked in the canopy of cedar trees, she couldn't rule out Isaac Marcum's vicious hatred for Brown. Isaac had only one bright spot in his tormented life. That bright spot had been blotted out, because Brown had been too busy accommodating himself to rid the county roads of a blind intersection. Molly Marcum was the price paid for Brown's neglect.

Amanda spun around, then recoiled when she saw Isaac Marcum, dressed in combat fatigues, poised beside her truck. Bruno crouched at her heels and growled.

"If you know what's good for you, little lady, you'll go home where you belong—and stay there," he warned in a scratchy voice.

Isaac's slurred tone indicated that he had been drinking heavily. Amanda wondered if it was a daily occurrence.

"Brown deserved to die, and I hope he's roasting in hell," Isaac muttered.

"Did the cattle break loose before or after Brown died?" she asked.

The cold rage dwindled from Isaac's eyes. He smiled faintly as he shot a glance toward the grazing livestock. "Before and during. Though that doesn't make a shit's worth of difference. It didn't have nothing to do with anything."

"No?" Amanda pressed.

"No," he confirmed.

"Who rounded up the livestock?"

"Not Brown," Isaac replied, propping himself on the barrel of his rifle.' 'He didn't dirty his hands with menial jobs. Always paid someone else to do it."

"Like who?" Amanda quizzed.

Isaac compressed his lips and smiled that enigmatic smile.

Amanda stared across the pasture, mentally rehashing the sights and sounds of the morning she had discovered Brown's body. "What about the horse? Did it make a difference?"

Isaac grinned mischievously. "What horse?"

"The one that left its tracks around Brown's truck," she answered, as if he didn't know. He did know. Amanda was pretty certain Isaac knew exactly what had happened. Problem was, his hatred for Brown prevented him from admitting to the crime or speaking out as an eye witness. In Isaac's opinion, Brown had received his comeuppance, and whoever saw that he got it was going to get off scot-free.

"Don't see no horse in the pasture, do you, little lady?" Isaac taunted.

"No, but it had to come from somewhere, because I noticed the tracks."

Isaac gestured his silver-colored head toward the road. "Don't see any tracks now, do you? Must've been your imagination. All that excitement over finding Brown in the mud, I suspect."

Thunder grumbled overhead. Amanda glanced skyward. Another round of rain would effectively destroy what was left of the crime scene.

She suspected Isaac was praying for rain.

Intimidating though Isaac could look, with his scraggly hair and the wild gleam in his eyes, Amanda strode boldly toward him. "I intend to find out who killed Brown," she told him point-blank. "I have all the reason in the world to suspect that you're the one who did it."

"But you can't prove it," Isaac reminded her with a devilish grin. "Can't prove a damned thing, little lady."

It occurred to Amanda just then that Isaac wanted her to think he had done it—whether he had or not. And if he hadn't, he was wishing he had. He thought it was his right, his duty.

Amanda also imagined that Isaac Marcum would not utter a single word in his defense if he were brought to trial. He had nothing to live for. He was withering away in that house on the hill, lost to memories of a war gone sour and a daughter who had been taken before her time, nursing a hatred for the man he held responsible.

"Get in the truck, Isaac," Amanda said abruptly.

"What for?"

"Because I said so." Amanda glanced at Bruno. "Get in the back, boy—Isaac will be riding shotgun."

Isaac regarded her for a long, quiet moment. "You always this bossy, little lady?"

"Most generally." Amanda planted herself in the truck and switched on the ignition. The truck hummed on its new battery.

Isaac plopped on the seat. Cradling his rifle on his thighs, he propped his arm in the open window. "Where are we going?"

"To my house. You need a shave and a haircut and a decent meal."

"They give those things in jail, so I've heard tell. Lawyers always see that their clients are spiffed up before they appear in court."

Amanda drove off, serenaded by rumbling thunder.

"You're taking a dangerous chance with me, you know," Isaac murmured a half mile later. "You could end up like Brown while you're out here in the middle of nowhere."

Amanda glanced at the gloved hand clenched around

the rifle barrel. No identifiable prints, she thought to her-self. Maybe this was a mistake. Maybe taking pity on this tormented vet wasn't such a good idea.

"Cops claim that the most difficult crimes to solve are the ones where the vehicle turns up one place, the body somewhere else and the weapon is lost forever," Isaac commented.

An eerie tingle skittered down Amanda's spine, but she shrugged it off. She told herself that Isaac was bluffing. The only man he wanted to see dead was gone.

She was reasonably safe in Isaac Marcum's company.

She hoped . . .

Amanda handed Isaac the mirror after she'd clipped his shaggy hair and trimmed his beard so that it hugged his jaw rather than scraped his chest. "Well, what do you think?" she asked.

Isaac studied his reflection, then flicked Amanda a glance. "I think this is the worst haircut I ever had. I look as bad as you do."

Amanda motioned Isaac on his way. "Make yourself at home in the living room while I sweep the hair out of the utility room. Then I'll fix us some lunch."

After sweeping hair into the dustpan, Amanda stepped outside. She swore she saw a shadow move beside the corner of the house. Cautiously, she tiptoed in the direc-tion the "shadow" had taken. She couldn't see anyone, but she had the uneasy sensation she was being watched.

Was someone keeping tabs on her? Was someone afraid she would coax Isaac into telling what he knew?

A series of clucks went up inside the chicken house. Amanda glanced suspiciously around the area, wondering why Pete wasn't barking in alarm.

"Pete!" Amanda called out. "Come here!"

The dog was nowhere to be found.

Amanda strode back inside to snatch up the rifle Isaac had propped against the arm of the recliner. "Mind if I borrow this? Somebody is sneaking around my henhouse."

When Amanda clutched the rifle, Isaac grabbed her wrist and quickly disarmed her. "I'll check it out. You stay here."

"No, I'm coming w—"

Isaac wheeled around, his eyes glittering dangerously. "Stay put," he hissed at her. "If you follow me against my orders, I might mistake you for the prowler."

Amanda gulped hard. She had seen that wild look in Isaac's eyes on a few occasions. She couldn't help but wonder if he didn't go just a little mad in situations that reminded him of his days in 'Nam. He looked like a soldier mentally preparing himself to patrol enemy territory.

Reluctantly, Amanda stayed where she was—smack dab in the middle of the living room with Bruno sprawled at her feet. She looked down at the dog and asked herself why she hadn't let Bruno step outside with her when she spotted the "shadow." It would have been the smart thing to do.

Amanda didn't hear a single sound as Isaac moved across the tiled floor to reach the back door. The man hadn't lost his knack, she realized. He could still stalk in silence.

If she couldn't hear him leave the house, was it any surprise that Brown hadn't heard him sneak up that morning on the road?

Suspicious, Amanda hurried to the window. She watched Isaac cradle the rifle across his arms, his right hand hovering on the trigger. He limped toward the henhouse, then flattened his back against the outer wall.

No, Amanda mused as Salty Marcum disappeared around the corner. He had definitely not lost his battle instincts. But then, she suspected he had been visited by the horrors of war on a regular basis. The man had remained alert and ready for years.

Several minutes later, Isaac hobbled around the henhouse with Pete hopping alongside him. Amanda could have kicked herself for letting Isaac convince her to remain in the house. He could have used the opportunity to rendezvous with whomever was lurking outside.

Had that someone wondered if Isaac planned to reveal what he knew? There was no need to fret on that count, Amanda thought to herself. She was pretty sure Isaac wouldn't confide the truth, even if he were tortured within an inch of his life.

"Found your dog," Isaac said as he came through the back door. "Caught himself a baby rabbit. Was trying to bury it beside the henhouse."

Amanda eyed Isaac suspiciously as he retraced his steps to sprawl in the recliner. She glanced out the window, noting that Pete didn't scuttle off to check on his evening meal.

She would bet money that Isaac had been in conference with someone and that Pete had been tossed a tasty snack to keep him quiet.

"Who did you talk to outside?" she demanded to know.

"Just the dog," Isaac replied with a wry grin. He picked up the TV remote and surfed the channels.

Amanda sighed in frustration. Isaac was one tough nut to crack. Spinning on her heels, Amanda headed for her alphabetically arranged cabinets to retrieve ingredients for their meal. Tuna on a shingle was her specialty. She was smart enough to know when she had hit a dead end. Isaac Marcum would take the knowledge of Brown's death to his grave. Guilty or innocent, Isaac had nothing more to say on the subject of Dusty Brown.

Damn, Amanda thought while she ate her tuna. This case was exasperating. She had suspects galore and motives aplenty. Yet, evidence was so sketchy that she was beginning to wonder if she could solve this mystery. All she had to show for her efforts was a key witness—or prime suspect—

who came to lunch and offered not one tidbit of pertinent information.

She had, however, convinced Isaac to attend the fund-raiser basketball game the following evening. Isaac claimed that seeing Amanda riding a donkey while playing basketball would be worth a few laughs. If nothing else, Amanda had convinced the hermit to appear in public, after locking himself in seclusion for years.

When Amanda dropped Isaac off late that afternoon, she glanced toward the corral beyond his house. There was no horse penned up. No horse grazing with Brown's cattle in the pasture down the hill.

Interesting that Isaac wanted her to think she was mistaken about the horse, she mused as she circled the section, checking nearby pastures for horses.

As the sun sank behind the bank of gray clouds that formed vaporous mountains on the horizon, Amanda veered east, then south. She came upon a small, wood-framed farmhouse similar to the one she rented. In the pasture beyond the house was a deep, tree-lined ravine that cut diagonally southwest.

Amanda studied the rugged terrain intently. Her gaze circled the area, noticing the dirt path that led to a trailer house nestled against the knoll of ground that protected the home from cold winter winds.

Amanda had intended to cruise past the small farm . . . until she saw the silhouette of a man against the backdrop of clouds.

It was Sam Harjo.

Amanda turned into the driveway, wondering why her path kept crossing Sam's. Was it only his role in the events leading up to Brown's death that drew her to him?

Or was it the man himself?

"Don't be ridiculous," Amanda scowled at her betraying

thoughts. "You are engaged to Thorn. Or at least you are supposed to be. Just because you haven't heard a peep from him in almost a week doesn't mean a thing."

So why haven't you called to check on him, Hazard? It works both ways, you know.

"Maybe Velma was right. Maybe this reluctant interest in Harjo is a by-product of bridal jitters. You have one failed marriage to your credit. Maybe you're afraid you'll blow it with Thorn."

Muttering at herself, Amanda climbed down from her truck. She was here on a fact-finding mission, nothing more. The engagement ring was back on her finger and she was digging for clues.

Having had that sensible talk with herself, Amanda strode toward the small pen where Sam was training a Border Collie to work with a flock of sheep. Harjo carried a shepherd's crook in his hand. The young dog was dragging a nylon cord that had been attached to his collar. Ten ewes were bunched against the fence, staring at the prowling dog.

Sam had positioned himself between the dog and the sheep. As the dog trotted in a half-moon pattern, Sam called, "Get out." Then he dragged his cane across the ground. The dog immediately backed away from the sheep.

"Come by," Sam ordered quietly.

The dog began to move in a clockwise half-circle. Fascinated, Amanda propped herself against the fence post to watch the dog being trained by repetitive commands.

When Sam glanced over his shoulder, Amanda smiled faintly. "You do good work, Harjo."

"Thanks, Hazard." He inclined his head toward Bruno, who watched interestedly from outside the pen. "If you want to see a real pro at work, you should see your dog in action. Brown never gave Bruno a chance to prove his worth, because Brown didn't bother to learn the commands. All he did was punish the dog when he tried to work cattle."

Amanda glanced down at Bruno, then frowned thoughtfully. Isaac had told her the cattle were out on the road before and during Brown's attempt to change the tire. He had also said it was of no consequence.

Was Isaac trying to throw her off track again? Quite possibly, thought Amanda. Isaac, after all, wanted her to drop the matter of Brown's death like a hot potato.

"Bruno, come up," Sam ordered.

Bruno ducked under the fence and came immediately to heel.

"Come by," Sam instructed softly.

Bruno made a semi-circular sweep, keeping his distance from the huddled flock.

"Bruno, walk on."

The dog approached the sheep, causing the flock to move along the pasture fence in single file.

Sam strode forward to position himself between the sheep and Bruno. "Bruno, come up."

Bruno trotted along the fence line, forcing the sheep into the middle of the pen.

"Outrun," Sam called to the dog.

In smooth precision, Bruno began to move the flock toward Sam, swinging in a half-moon pattern behind the sheep.

While Bruno was moving the sheep forward, Sam backed toward the gate that led into another small pen. With the gate standing open, Sam ambled toward Amanda. Giving Bruno the command, the dog gathered the sheep and funneled them through the gate.

As Amanda watched Bruno perform his task, she reflected on the first time she had seen the Border Collie— or rather, heard him. She frowned pensively in thought.

"Does Bruno ever bark when he's working with livestock?"

Sam propped a muscled arm over the fence. "With cattle he'll bark," Sam clarified. "Larger livestock require greater intimidation to force them where they are reluctant to go. Sheep are relatively timid and can be stared down. With the exception of blockheaded rams," he added with a grin.

Amanda was well aware of the contrary nature of rams. She and Thorn's ram had butted heads on a few occasions.

"The problem Bruno had with Brown's cattle wasn't with the livestock. It was with Brown," Sam explained. "The stupid idiot was forever giving the wrong commands to Bruno. When the dog did what he had been trained to do, Brown took a switch to Bruno. Left alone, Bruno is smart enough to know what needs to be done with a herd."

He indicated the open gate in which Bruno stood, refusing to let the sheep return to the smaller pen to graze. "The dog was specifically trained to hold a herd while you repair downed fences. He was also taught to drive a herd toward you, or herd them down a fence line. In my opinion, Bruno was a helluva lot smarter with livestock than Brown was. Bruno was punished and never rewarded when Brown had him."

"No wonder Brown had to bribe Bruno with dog biscuits," Amanda mused aloud.

Sam half turned, pinning Amanda with an unblinking stare. "What does it take to get you to *come by?*" he asked quietly.

A second earlier, Amanda had been assimilating the facts Sam had offered. She had found herself on the verge of investigative discovery . . . until Sam posed his provocative question. He was staring at her the same way Bruno was staring down the sheep—quiet, watchful, poised for action. Her analytical thought processes scattered like a covey of quail.

"Are you trying to complicate my life, Harjo?" she asked him flat-out.

"Why are you here, Hazard?" he questioned her question.

"I'm investigating an accident that could very well be a murder. It seems to me that you are in the thick of it."

"That's the only reason?"

Amanda spun on her boot heels. "It's getting late and I have a stack of tax forms waiting. It's going to be another long night." She glanced back at the Border Collie. "Come on, Bruno! We're going home."

The dog abandoned its post, forcing Sam to close the gate before the sheep made a run for it. Amanda refused to look back, refused the invitation she had seen in Sam's amber-colored eyes. If she didn't take a wide berth, she was never going to figure out the chain of events leading up to Brown's death.

The whinny of a horse caught Amanda's attention as she made a grab for the door latch of her truck. Her head swiveled around to see the blood-red gelding pinned on the back side of the barn.

The horse . . .

Warning bells clamored in Amanda's mind. Her gaze swung back to the man silhouetted by gathering darkness. Had someone on horseback helped Bruno round up the cattle that had escaped from the pasture that fateful day? Did that someone leave the bulldozer atop the hill, mount a horse, and ride down to confront Brown one final time?

Amanda's attention shifted southwest. From the driveway she could see across the rolling pasture to the section of road where she'd found Brown. It wouldn't have taken long to jog to this house, mount up, and follow the ravine to the valley beside the road.

Shakily, Amanda slid onto the seat of her pick-up, then drove off. She kept remembering that Isaac insisted there was no horse in the pasture with the cattle. She kept recalling the sound of the barking dog as she slogged through the mud to see Brown's stalled truck on the road.

Had Bruno been gathering the cattle and herding them through the broken fence that morning? Had Brown's killer patched the fence before riding off on horseback, clinging to the tree-choked ravine so as not to be noticed? Who was to say that Sam Harjo hadn't driven the grader the short distance to his home and traded his mode of transportation for a horse?

Isaac certainly wasn't pointing an accusing finger and Brown wasn't around to identify his killer. But he had left a clue in the mud. An *S*.

Sam Harjo . . .

Again, Amanda asked herself if Sam's apparent interest in her was a ploy to persuade her to drop her investigation. The man had made use of his earthy sensuality more than once during their short acquaintance—and he used it extremely well, much as she hated to admit it.

Was it premeditated charm or the real thing?

"You better solve this case pronto," Amanda muttered to herself as she drove home. "Either that or give it up entirely."

She glanced down at the dog lying on the seat, his head resting on his paws. "I wish the hell you could speak, Bruno," she said wistfully. "You're the only one I trust."

Nine

Nick came through the back door of his house, serenaded by the first splatters of raindrops. He had been working 24 hours straight, and he was dead on his feet. He had gone from one hay meadow to the next, raking and airing out windrows of alfalfa. As soon as one hay field was dry enough to bale, he hitched up the baler to his tractor and made endless circles.

A steady downpour pattered against the back door as Nick flicked the lock into place. Perfect timing, he thought as he trudged toward the bathroom to take a shower. He stunk to high heaven and itched from the leafy stems of hay that had drifted inside the collar of his shirt. His eyelids were at half-mast and he was hungry enough to gobble down Hazard's "shit on a shingle"—and like it.

Nick glanced at the clock on his way through the kitchen. Five in the morning. The rooster might be up and crowing, but Nick was ready to hit the sack. A few hours of sleep and maybe he'd feel like his old self again.

After a quick shower, Nick returned to the kitchen to retrieve the makings of a sandwich from the refrigerator.

The answering machine winked at him while he slapped ten wafer-thin slices of ham on bread. Reaching out, he punched "play" and waited for the messages.

"Nicky? Are you still alive out there?" Chomp, snap. "It's Velma. Just called to remind you about the Donkey Basketball game on Friday night. Be at the high school gymnasium about seven-thirty so the owner of the donkeys can give everybody their instructions."

There was a distinct pause. Nick spread mayonnaise on both slices of bread while he waited.

"I don't want to meddle in your business, hon—"

"Yeah, right," Nick smirked. "Meddle" was Velma's middle name.

"—but since you've been out of circulation, Sam Harjo has been hanging around your fiancée. I don't need to tell you that he's no average Joe, do I, Nicky?" Crackle, snap. "If you start taking Amanda for granted you could be in serious trouble! After that stunt you pulled during Will Bloom's murder case, you're probably getting what you deserve. But, dang it, boy, you better do something before this wedding gets called off!"

The answering machine beeped, signaling the end of Velma's message. Nick sighed, exhausted, then slapped his sandwich together.

"Hi, it's Mom. Is everything okay up there? Dad and I have decided to drive up from Texas for the wedding shower. We need to meet this Hazard person—and soon. We have some reservations about this marriage."

Nick wondered if Hazard was having them, too.

"It's frustrating not to know if this woman is exactly right for you. But I plan to find out real soon."

The answering machine clicked off. Nick frowned as he chased a bit of sandwich with a cola. No message from Hazard. Why hadn't she called? She knew he was raking and baling hay in a fiendish rush to beat the rain. The least she could have done was call to say hello.

You could have taken a minute to call, Thorn. So why didn't you? he asked himself.

Nick pondered that question as he finished off his supper . . . or breakfast. He knew why he hadn't gotten in touch with Hazard—even though no one else would understand. The fact was that he had to let things work out for themselves—or not.

And besides, Nick reminded himself as he trudged off to bed, he was just too damned tired to talk to Hazard. He might say the wrong thing when he didn't have all the facts. He figured he would find out which way the wind blew at the Donkey Basketball game.

From all reports, Sam Harjo would be there. During the game, Nick would get the feel of the situation between Hazard and Harjo. Until then, he wasn't going to pay the slightest attention to local gossip.

Sighing heavily, Nick sprawled on his bed. He was asleep the instant his head hit the pillow.

Amanda grabbed her purse and keys. Bruno met her at the door. "Not this time, pal," she told her faithful bodyguard. "If I take you along, you'll try to herd the donkeys at the ballgame."

The dog tried to wedge his way in front of her, determined not to be left behind.

"Bruno, lie down," Amanda ordered sternly, using one of the commands she had heard Harjo give the young dog he was training.

Bruno reluctantly dropped down beside the door and stared at her—visually pleaded with her was nearer the mark—with those big, sad, doggie eyes.

"I'll be back. Maybe not in one piece, but I'll return," she promised before she closed the door behind her.

"Lord, what have I gotten myself into?" Amanda asked herself as she drove down the recently graveled road. She barely knew one end of a horse from the other, let alone a donkey! The first and only time she had been on the back of a horse, she had landed on her butt with a grunt and a groan. There was no telling how difficult it would be to keep her seat on a contrary donkey.

But it's for a good cause, Amanda assured herself. Furthermore, the Donkey Basketball game would attracts folks from all over the county. In short, every possible suspect would be in attendance. One careless comment, one carefully phrased question, might give Amanda a lead in this exasperating case—if there actually was a case.

According to Thorn and the medial examiner, there was nothing fishy about Brown's death. Damn it, she could have used some help, but Thorn hadn't been seen or heard from for days. His lack of attention was irritating her, though she had assured herself that Thorn's farming duties had kept him busy. But still . . .

Amanda's thoughts trailed off when she recognized several of the vehicles in the school parking lot. It seemed all the employees from Sam Harjo's road crew had arrived to cheer on their new boss. Ron Newton's old model car with its rusted hood was parked beside Homer and Vinita's battered pick-up. Chuck Gilhaney's rattletrap car was parked beside a flashy black Lincoln that had bumper stickers that read *Vote for Shakelford* plastered all over it. Even the back window of the expensive vehicle boasted a poster with Shakelford's name printed in flourescent lettering.

Shakelford . . . Amanda frowned. She had been so busy gathering facts about the sequence of events leading to Brown's death, and questioning other suspects, that she had almost forgotten about the Republican candidate for District 1. No doubt, Ervin Shakelford would be campaigning to beat the band tonight. Residents from Adios, Vamoose and Pronto would be in attendance.

Amanda eased her gas-guzzler into a parking space

beside Deputy Sykes' squad car. She noticed that the vehicle had been repaired after Benny had wrapped it around a fence post.

She also noticed that Thorn's black 4x4 truck—with its hay fork protruding from the bed—wasn't in the lot. Vamoose's chief of police was either running late or had decided not to come at all.

Slinging her purse strap over her shoulder, Amanda swerved around the side of the brick building to see a semi-truck parked near the side door. The owner of the donkeys was unloading his livestock. The bushy-haired man reminded Amanda of the carnival workers who had milled around the amusement rides during the Vamoose County Fair. His bulging arm muscles were covered by a string of tattoos of various sizes and shapes. "Mother" was printed inside a red heart. The bosomy shape of a woman rippled on the man's left bicep as he popped his whip above the string of donkeys. An *S*-shaped insignia, decorated with green leaves, was tattooed on his right bicep. Amanda didn't speculate about other tattoos on various parts of the man's body. She'd seen enough.

"Okay, y'all, now listen up," the owner said as he tethered the string of donkeys on a nearby supporting pole. "The name's Smythe. John Smythe."

Great, thought Amanda, she was going to have to take instruction from this yahoo who appeared to relish being the center of attention. The way John Smythe held himself, the way he tossed his shaggy head and flexed his muscles, indicated he also enjoyed flaunting his authority.

Amanda frowned pensively. Smythe and Brown obviously shared the same obsession about being in control.

"These here donkeys are my bread and butter, if ya know what I mean," Smythe drawled out. "I expect y'all to treat my animals kindly. There'll be no kickin' or gougin', just because my donkeys don't always go where ya want 'em to go."

Amanda glanced at the string of donkeys. There wasn't a saddle to be seen anywhere. Was she supposed to ride bareback? How could she anchor herself without a pommel and stirrups, when a donkey's back was as flat as a board? There was no center spot to settle into.

"I expect y'all to follow the rules of the game and I'll be the referee," Smythe announced. "Ya gotta be on the donkey to score a basket or pass the ball. If ya fall off or climb down to chase a loose ball, ya gotta keep hold of the reins and take your donkey with ya wherever ya go."

Amanda's hand shot up in the air. "Do we have to dribble the basketball?" She considered it to be a logical question. After all, this was a basketball game.

John Smythe smirked, as if he'd been asked a stupid question. He half turned to locate the idiot who'd asked it. His smirk, Amanda noticed, turned to masculine appraisal, then a rakish smile. It only took a second to realize Smythe did most of his thinking with the gender-specific equipment in his jeans. He was staring at her as if her eyes were on her chest.

"No, ma'am," he purred. "You'll have your work cut out for ya just ridin' from one end of the court to the other and holdin' onto the donkey and a basketball."

He struck a pose that displayed his muscles to their best advantage. Amanda wondered if all that strutting and preening was for her. Must have been. She appeared to be the only woman stupid enough to agree to ride in this dumb game!

"Now, I'll decide who's gonna ride which donkey," he declared as he sized up the riders. He gestured toward Sam Harjo. "You take Sweet Pea since you can handle trouble."

Amanda frowned, wondering how the donkey trainer knew that.

Once Harjo had been issued his mount, Smythe proceeded to dole out donkeys to the cluster of riders who waited on the sidewalk.

"And you, li'l darlin'," Smythe cooed as he handed a set of reins to Amanda, "can ride Buckwheat. He's especially fond of women, just like I am."

Ignoring the suggestive wink Smythe wasted on her, Amanda stared down at the hairy face and dark eyes of the docile creature at the end of the leather reins. Luckily, Buckwheat didn't look like much trouble. The donkey stood with his head drooped in subservient fashion, while the other animals were tugging on their reins and bracing their legs.

This was going to be a snap, Amanda convinced herself. Already, she could envision herself slam-dunking the small-sized basketball while standing on Buckwheat's flat back.

"I need a mount."

Amanda recognized Thorn's voice instantly. She glanced over her shoulder to see Thorn cut an impressive swath through the streetlight that illuminated the side of the school. Without thinking, her gaze darted back to Sam Harjo, who was leaning leisurely against the brick wall, holding the reins to his donkey, his unblinking gaze homing in on Amanda.

"You'll have to take Dumplin'," Smythe said as he thrust the reins at Thorn. "He may be tough to handle, but you look stout enough to do it."

Smythe flashed Amanda one last smile, grabbed a wooden cane that was propped against the wall, then spun on his heels to lead the riders through the side door. "The donkeys have been fitted with rubber horseshoes to help them keep their footing on the gym floor. No need to worry on that count."

As Amanda fell into step in front of Thorn she put aside her concern about making a fool of herself. This might actually be fun. After working herself into exhaustion while calculating tax returns, and beating her head against the wall on this frustrating investigation that was going nowhere fast, she could use entertaining diversion.

" 'How's the stack of tax forms coming along?" Thorn asked from behind her.

"Slowly but surely," Amanda replied. "I only have three left to do—yours, Brown's and Mother's. How are you coming with your farming chores?"

"I finished baling the last hay meadow before the rains," he answered.

Amanda cast Thorn a quick glance as the procession of donkeys and riders paraded to center court to be introduced. Something didn't feel quite right, Amanda mused. Her conversation with Thorn seemed so stilted, so impersonal.

Her attention shifted to Sam Harjo. He was staring directly at her again, same as he had been since Thorn arrived.

"Where's your ring, Hazard?" Thorn asked, his tone noticeably clipped.

"In my purse. Surely you don't expect me to wear it during this ballgame."

"Are you telling me you take it off and on at whim?"

"It's not a slave collar, is it?" Amanda's gaze narrowed on Thorn's disapproving frown. "I don't see you wearing any symbolic indication that we're engaged . . ."

Her voice trailed off when she saw Homer Frizzell sitting on the front row of the bleachers with his platinum-haired wife. Vinita was decked out in a body-hugging knit dress that barely covered her thighs and dipped low at the neck to showcase her bosom. Obviously, Vinita was proud of her nose job and boob job and was anxious to show off assets that had been bought and paid for.

The caked makeup Vinita wore looked fitting for a Broadway stage. Geez, the woman was certainly taking this Donkey Queen contest seriously, wasn't she? Frankly,

Amanda thought Vinita deserved to be crowned Queen of Tacky.

"Hey, how come Vinita isn't riding in the ballgame?" Amanda questioned Velma, who was the manager of Vamoose's Fire Department team.

"You don't have to ride to be in the contest, hon," Velma said as she smacked her chewing gum.

"Now you tell me," Amanda grumbled.

When the announcer called the crowd's attention to the coach of the town team, Amanda watched Ervin Shakelford rise from the bench to wave enthusiastically and smile. The front of his white t-shirt had been stamped with an enlarged color photo of himself. The slogan on the back of his shirt read, *Vote for Shakelford for County Commission District 1.*

Damn, the man was milking this opportunity for all it was worth!

After the members of the teams were introduced, Amanda crammed the protective leather helmet on her head and fastened the chin strap. It was time to play ball.

"Y'all mount your donkeys," John Smythe ordered before he stuffed the whistle in his mouth.

Amanda swung a jeans-clad leg over Buckwheat's back. As if on cue, Buckwheat dropped to his front knees. The crowd roared in laughter when Amanda rolled across the floor and ended in an unladylike sprawl. Climbing onto all fours, she glared accusingly at Buckwheat, who stared at her in his calm, docile manner. Then she glanced back at Smythe, who was grinning around his whistle and studying her butt with attentive interest.

It took Amanda all of one second to realize Smythe had tapped the cane he was carrying on the floor the instant she tried to climb onto the donkey's back. It took her another second to realize Smythe had given her the "trick" donkey.

That ornery cuss, she silently fumed. If she didn't know

better she would swear someone had put Smythe up to
this prank.

The thought prompted Amanda to glance up at Vinita
Frizzell in the front row, grinning so widely that her thick
makeup was about to crack. The rival queen contestant
was enjoying Amanda's humiliation. Why wasn't Amanda
surprised? Velma had indicated that Vinita craved this
absurd title. She had obviously made arrangements to
make Amanda look like an ass in front of everyone.

Amanda's gaze shot back to Smythe in time to intercept
the conspiratory wink he sent toward the front row of
spectators. Amanda wondered how much Vinita had paid
Smythe. Jerks, both of them!

"Hazard, are you okay?" Thorn asked while he sat atop
Dumplin', his long, muscular legs dangling a mere inch
off the floor.

"Just peachy," Amanda muttered. With as much dignity
as the situation allowed, Amanda grabbed the reins, then
dared Smythe to send Buckwheat into another untimely
bow. The tattoo-covered creep had the good sense not to
tap his cane on the floor a second time.

Smythe blew his whistle to begin the game. He tossed
the ball to Amanda, then motioned for her to trot her
donkey toward the north goal. When Smythe tapped his
cane three times, Buckwheat shot forward at blazing speed.

"Whoa!" Amanda yelped as her head snapped backward
and her feet flew up in front of her.

The firefighters charged off in the same direction
Amanda had taken, intent on blocking her shot—provided
she could manage to get one off. As Thorn raced down
the sideline, Amanda cocked her arm and passed him the
ball.

It went sailing over his head and landed in the bleachers.

The crowd guffawed at Amanda's inaccurate pass.

Again, she felt like a damned idiot.

After several laps up and down the floor, donkeys bucking and kicking at irregular intervals, even the best of riders went flying. When Thorn cartwheeled off his donkey, Amanda realized how amusing this crazed entertainment looked to the spectators. Even topnotch athletes looked incompetent while dealing with donkeys.

Scoring a basket was ten times more difficult than expected, Amanda soon found out. Nothing screwed up a shot worse than having the donkey sidestep beneath you while you were in the act of shooting. Her first shot bricked off the backboard and bounced down the court.

At the end of the first quarter of play the score was: firefighters-4, town team-0.

By the second quarter Amanda's backside was bruised from bouncing on the donkey's hard, flat rump. Her arms felt like cooked noodles. She had dismounted and dragged Buckwheat behind her while chasing down loose balls at least a dozen times. Buckwheat never came willingly.

And then her moment of potential glory arrived. Amanda was all alone beneath her team's goal when Sam Harjo intercepted a pass from the firemen. Twisting atop Sweet Pea, Harjo launched the ball the full length of the gym. Amanda let go of the reins to catch the spectacular pass.

Smythe tapped his cane once.

Buckwheat sidestepped.

The ball hit Amanda right between the eyes.

The uproarious crowd rolled in the aisles.

Amanda glared machetes at Smythe.

When the ball bounced off the wall and dribbled across the floor, Amanda vowed to redeem herself. Casting a quick glance at the approaching pack of riders, Amanda hopped off Buckwheat. With the ball tucked under her arm, she bounded onto the donkey. As the riders reached the three-point line and bore down on her, Amanda decided to go for the glory. Dragging her legs beneath her, she stood up on Buckwheat's back to slam-dunk the ball.

The crowd collectively held their breath as Amanda raised the ball over her head. The ball swished through the hoop—touching nothing but net—and the spectators cheered her spectacular success.

"Nice shot, Hazard," Harjo murmured as he rode past her.

Amanda smiled in triumph, until she saw Thorn's squinted gaze bouncing back and forth between her and Harjo. He didn't comment as he reined Dumplin' around to trot toward the opposite end of the court.

Amanda glanced toward the bleachers, noting that Vinita was scowling at Amanda's flashy shot. Homer, however, was still clapping and cheering Amanda on. His upraised arm pumped up and down in an enthusiastic gesture.

"Quit taking bows and get down here, Hazard," Thorn yelled at her. "We're still two points behind."

Amanda swung around and nudged Buckwheat in the ribs. He took off in a bone-jarring trot. Before Amanda reached center court, Thorn had rebounded the firemen's missed shot. Swiveling on the donkey's back, Thorn cocked a brawny arm and heaved the ball through the air.

Determined not to miss the bullet-like pass, Amanda clamped her thighs around Buckwheat and leaned out to snatch the oncoming ball from the air. With seven seconds left before halftime, Amanda tucked the ball under her arm and nudged Buckwheat to lope down court. This was her big chance to tie the score.

"Six seconds left!" the announcer bugled, his excited voice reverberating around the gym. "Can Hazard even the score? Let's hear it for Hazard, ladies and gentleman, boys and girls!"

Amid the cheers of encouragement, Amanda raced toward the goal, her arm lifted into proper shooting position. Nothing fancy this time, she told herself. Time was a factor and she had to do it right the first time. She would bank the shot off the glass at close range and watch the ball plunk through the net the instant before the buzzer sounded.

"Hurry up and shoot!" Harjo yelled from somewhere behind her.

"Go for it, Hazard!" Thorn hollered.

Amanda arched backward when Buckwheat overran the target. The donkey bucked his hind legs as Amanda outstretched herself to take the off-balance shot. The ball ricocheted off the backboard, then bounced from one side of the rim to the other. Amanda felt the donkey skitter out from under her while she kept her gaze focused on the damned ball that was bouncing around as if caught in a pinball machine.

A choked shriek erupted from Amanda's lips when she realized she had lost her ass. She made a pancake landing as the halftime buzzer went off. The ball that had been bouncing around the rim finally plunked through the net.

The crowd cheered, but Amanda was in no condition to celebrate her buzzer-beating shot. She lay there, dazed and disoriented, as the ball dropped through the net and landed on her stomach.

Vaguely, she realized Thorn and Harjo had leaped from their mounts to check on her. When her ears stopped ringing, Amanda realized the crowd had fallen silent.

"Is there a doctor in the house?" the announcer trumpeted.

Amanda's body was still vibrating like a paint shaker as Thorn and Harjo reached out simultaneously. Amanda tried to focus on the hazy images of the two men who towered over her. She saw them stare at each other for a long moment, exchanging glares at two paces.

Although Amanda had been stunned and jarred to the bone, she swore some symbolic moment was passing between the two men. No doubt, it was one of those dumb guy things.

Hell! She could have broken something important and there the two men stood, measuring and studying each other like two medieval knights about to do combat.

"I . . . can't . . . breathe . . . !" Amanda wheezed as she stared at the two fuzzy faces above her. "Do . . . something . . . !"

Ten

Nick glared at the outstretched hand and ruggedly handsome face that was two feet away from his. He saw the care and concern for Hazard in those amber eyes, and he swore under his breath. Hell's bells, things were worse than he thought! Harjo definitely had a thing for Hazard.

When Harjo glanced back at him, Nick sank down on his haunches to lift Hazard's knees. Harjo reluctantly stepped back a pace without touching Hazard. The man had wanted to offer assistance, Nick could tell, but Harjo had remembered his place and backed off.

"Hang tough, Hazard," Nick said as he watched her struggle to draw breath. "I think you just had the wind knocked out of you, but you better stay put until Dr. Simms takes a look at you. If he gives you a clean bill of health, you can get up."

Dr. Simms, in his squeaky Reebok tennis shoes, scurried across the court. Hazard glanced dazedly toward the sound as she snatched in tiny gasps of air.

Sinking down on one knee, the physician smiled compassionately. "Seems like you're always having these little mishaps, young lady." He eased Hazard to her side, his practiced hands skimming up and down her spine. "Now, try to take a deep breath."

Hazard's chest expanded in attempt to breathe, but she sucked air in noticeable hitches.

"Now, move your legs for me," Dr. Simms requested.

Thankfully, all of Hazard's moving parts cooperated.

Dr. Simms positioned one hand behind her purple-tinted head, then slowly eased her into an upright position. "You're going to be fine, but I insist that you let a substitute take your place for the second half."

"Are you volunteering?" Hazard rasped.

"Who me?" Dr. Simms' graying brows jackknifed. "Heavens, no. I'm too old for this stuff. I'm here to have a few laughs and tend injuries."

When Hazard tried to gain her feet, Nick swooped down to scoop her into his powerful arms. The crowd applauded. Nick cut a quick glance at Sam Harjo, who turned away before Nick could interpret his expression. Clearly, Harjo would have liked to have been in Nick's Nikes tonight.

Things were definitely much worse than he thought, Nick concluded as he carried Hazard up the steps to the bleachers. For whatever reason Sam Harjo had been seen in Hazard's company this past week, the man had become emotionally involved.

Damn it to hell. Nick had considered himself on reasonably solid footing when he had competed for Hazard's attention in this county. Most men who had the hots for Hazard not only didn't get to first base, they didn't even have a chance to come to the plate.

Unfortunately, Nick didn't consider Sam Harjo on the extensive list of men to whom Hazard would never give a second glance. The long and short of it was that Sam Harjo—by anyone's standards—was a stud. Hazard would have to be blind in both eyes not to notice.

As Nick perceived the situation, he had a worthy male

rival for Hazard's affection. He didn't know how Hazard felt about Harjo, but it was plain to see that the new commish had taken an interest in Hazard.

Nick set Hazard on the bleachers beside Beverly Hill, then he brushed a light kiss over Hazard's perspiring brow. "By the way, Hazard, nice shot. It was a real Kodak moment. Wish I'd had my camera."

Descending the steps, Nick stared at the brawny figure of the man who had ambled toward the concession stand to buy a cola. Nick almost wished he could convince himself that Dusty Brown's death was more than an untimely accident, because he would have targeted Sam Harjo as the prime suspect.

Is that possessive jealousy or professional judgment speaking, Thorn? he asked himself as he followed in Harjo's wake.

Harjo pivoted, thrusting a paper cup of Coke at Nick. "Here, Thorn, wet your whistle with this before we mount up for the second half."

When Nick stared warily at the drink, Harjo chuckled. "I didn't have time to poison it, if that's what you're thinking."

"Where were you at the time of Brown's death?" Nick blurted out before he realized what he'd said.

Harjo elevated an eyebrow as he stared at Nick over the edge of his own paper cup. "Who's asking? The cop or the fiancé?"

Nick bared his teeth and flung Harjo his most threatening look. "Just answer the damned question."

"I was repairing the fuel line Brown bent out of shape after he tried to leave me stranded on the road in the bulldozer. Then I drove back to the county machinery barn," Harjo replied.

"Who witnessed your departure?"

"Brown."

"Convenient for you that the man who might be able to corroborate your story is dead and buried."

Harjo shrugged a broad shoulder. "I don't need an alibi, because I didn't help Brown into the hereafter."

Nick scoffed sarcastically. "Got any idea how many times I've heard pleas of innocence from guilty criminals?"

Harjo was a hard man to intimidate. Nick had known that since their high school days, when they had participated in sports at rival schools. Nick also knew of Harjo's reputation as foreman of the county road crew. Harjo didn't take crap off anybody and he never backed down. His muscular size and stature were all the reinforcement a man needed.

"Hazard has questioned everyone associated with Brown, with the exception of Shakelford," Harjo commented after he took a sip of his Coke. "She hasn't turned up conclusive proof of foul play. If *she* hasn't, I doubt *you* will. Seems to me that she does your job better than you do."

Nick glared at Harjo. The commissioner glared right back.

"If I discover that you were somehow involved in the incident with Brown, don't doubt for one minute that I won't bust my ass gathering every piece of evidence needed to put you away for life. Defeating Shakelford in the election will be the least of your worries, Harjo."

"Gotta prove it first, Thorn," Harjo challenged before he shouldered his way past Nick to re-enter the gym.

"This is a fine kettle of fish," Nick muttered before he chugged his soft drink.

Determined to prove himself Harjo's worthy competitor, he squared his shoulders and strode off to mount up for the second half of the ballgame.

The instant the game resumed, Amanda found her attention shifting back and forth between Thorn and Harjo. The two men looked as if they were competing against each other, not against the Vamoose Fire Department. The spectacular displays of athletic skill and ability—which had the crowd cheering—had Amanda scowling at the idiotic tendencies of the male gender. Sheesh! she thought with a dismayed shake of her head.

Tiring of the infantile games Thorn and Harjo were playing for her benefit, Amanda focused her concentration on Ervin Shakelford. The Republican candidate was pacing from one end of the bench to the other, showing off his campaign t-shirt to its best advantage. Ervin certainly seemed intent on seizing the moment and winning name recognition.

Twisting in her seat, Amanda scanned the crowd. She blinked in surprise when she noticed Sara Mae and Sonny sitting on the top row, snuggled up like two bugs in a rug, whispering sweet nothings to each other. Amanda pinpointed her attention on Sara Mae's left hand. Sure enough, a shiny gold band encased her ring finger. The couple had obviously eloped.

Some way to spend a honeymoon, Amanda thought. Oh well, this was small-town America and folks in isolated rural locations had their own ideas about what entertainment was. This Donkey Basketball game was the perfect example. Definitely not a night at the opera—not that anyone in the bleachers cared a fig about opera. The countrified members of the crowd were exactly where they wanted to be.

Intent on making the most of the situation, Amanda ignored the pain in her shoulder and marched up the aisle toward the newlyweds. The contented smiles Sara Mae and Sonny were sporting vanished the instant they saw Amanda making a beeline toward them.

Amanda stared pointedly at Sara Mae's left hand. "It appears congratulations are in order," she commented.

"What do you want?" Sonny muttered in question.

"I'm just being neighborly." Amanda tried out an exuberant smile. It didn't fly. Sonny glared at her again.

"No, you aren't," he contradicted. "You still think we conspired to bump off Dusty, don't you?"

"Is that what I think?" Next, Amanda tried out her innocent expression. The newlyweds didn't buy that, either.

"Of course, you do," Sara Mae grumbled.

"You have to admit I have every reason to believe that you had something to do with it," Amanda said. "With Dusty gone, you've got the house where you grew up—"

"How do you know that?" Sara interrupted.

"I asked around. You have the deed to the property that was once in the Harjo family and you have access to the joint accounts that you had been denied."

Sara Mae's eyes popped, but she didn't utter another word. Amanda pressed her advantage.

"Then there's the fact that Dusty's resistance to the divorce proceedings are no long a frustrating obstacle for you. You've got the house, the land, the livestock and Sonny doesn't have to worry about Dusty devising a way to ruin business at the bait shop."

"Now wait just a damned minute, Hazard," Sonny hissed, leaning toward her. "If you don't stop harassing us, I'll—"

"You'll what? Dispose of me the way you did Dusty?" she challenged daringly.

When Sonny tried to bolt to his feet, Sara Mae yanked on his arm, forcing him to sit down. "Don't make a scene, honey," she whispered. "Sam will handle this."

Although Sara Mae had spoken confidentially, Amanda overheard. A cold chill slithered down her spine. No doubt, Sam was in the habit of protecting his younger sister. Warily, Amanda glanced over her sore shoulder to scrutinize Sam Harjo. At the moment, he was leading the pack down the court to score another basket. The crowd applauded enthusiastically.

With all sorts of suspicions clouding her thoughts,

Amanda left the newlyweds on the top bleacher and glanced down at the road crew workers who sat shoulder-to-shoulder in the front row.

Time to double-check the facts, Amanda decided as she made her descent.

Amanda planted herself between Ron Newton and Chuck Gilhaney. Both men scooted sideways to let her squeeze in.

"Sorry about your fall, gorgeous," Ron said as he crammed popcorn into his mouth. "You were looking really great until you fell off your ass."

Ron snickered at his own joke. He laughed alone. Amanda didn't think it was particularly amusing.

"I want to ask you a few more questions about the day Brown died," she insisted.

"Aw, geez," Ron groaned. "Are you gonna ruin a good time with questions? You're spoiling the highlight of my weekend."

"I'm sorry your weekends don't get any better than this," she commiserated.

Ron shot her a puzzled glance. Obviously the man wasn't sharp enough to know he had been insulted. Amanda didn't explain it to him.

"What happened the morning Brown died?" Amanda asked.

Ron slumped in his seat, sighed audibly, then said, "The same thing happened that morning as every other morning. Brown drove up to the machinery barn to bark orders."

"What time?" Amanda drilled him.

"Seven-fifteen. He chewed on my ass for not getting as much done on the bridge as he wanted done before the rains came. Then he gnawed on Chuck for a while. Then he grabbed Homer by the arm and hauled him back to a corner to chew on him for a few minutes."

Now Amanda knew what Brown had for breakfast. He took bites out of his employees to tide him over until lunch.

"Chewing ass was Brown's daily ritual. He wanted the new bridge constructed before everybody found out that it was his pet project. He planned to use the bridge to check on his property and livestock on the other side of Whatsit River so he wouldn't have to take the long way around."

"Long way around?" Amanda repeated curiously.

"The bridge between Vamoose and Pronto is the only passage across the river for 15 miles. Brown wanted the bridge completed before the primary election, just in case Sam decided to use that information to steal Brown's votes.

"Now our ex-commish doesn't have to worry about being re-elected, or checking his cattle south of the river," Ron said. "He's gone for good, and Harjo is saving the county money by serving as commish and road foreman."

"He's collecting two paychecks?"

Ron shook his head. "No, only one. Things are running smoothly now that Harjo is command."

Not for the first time, Amanda's gaze darted to Harjo, then swung to Shakelford, who was waving his arms like a windmill—calling more attention to himself while he pretended to cheer for the town team.

Personally, Amanda didn't think Shakelford gave a rat's ass who won, as long as he was drawing plenty of attention to himself.

"Did Shakelford ever drop by to chitchat after he filed as a candidate for commissioner?" she asked.

"All the time," Chuck Gilhaney spoke up. He pulled a plastic clapper from his shirt pocket, then pointed a stubby finger at it. "Shakelford has been passing out gimmicks like this for weeks."

Chuck shook the hand-shaped clapper several times when Thorn banked a spectacular shot off the glass and drained it through the hoop. Within a few seconds, hundreds of noise-making clappers appeared from pockets and a loud racket filled the gym. Amanda glanced behind her to see the other clappers that had Shakelford's name printed on them.

"Shakelford became a regular at the courthouse and commissioner's barn after Brown started making wise-cracks about him," Chuck continued after he crammed the clapper in his pocket. "Shakelford was purely pissed, let me tell ya. Said Brown was going to pay big time."

Big time? As in winding up dead? Amanda wondered as her gaze zeroed in on the partially-bald head of the man who strutted back and forth on the court below her.

"Was Shakelford at the barn that particular morning?" she asked as she watched one of the fireman tumble off his donkey and skid across the floor.

"Yeah, he was, come to think of it," Ron recalled. "Royally pissed that day, too. Never saw a man's face turn purple before."

Amanda stared pensively at the Republican candidate who had turned his back so the crowd could read the slogan on his shirt—for the forty-eleventh time.

"Brown told Shakelford to stay off the premises, because he was interfering with work," Chuck said as he wadded up his empty popcorn sack and tossed it aside. "Then Brown made one of his rude remarks about Shakelford's wife and daughter."

"What kind of remark?" Amanda wanted to know.

Ron peered questioningly at Chuck. "Should we tell her what he said?"

Chuck shook his wiry red head. "Naw, better not."

"I want to know," Amanda insisted.

"You sure?" Ron asked.

"Positively certain," Amanda affirmed.

Ron leaned close so he wouldn't be overheard. "Brown said he was fucking both women. Said he could understand why Shakelford wanted to run for office—because he wanted to see if he could screw the public better that he could screw his wife."

Amanda battled down a blush. "I'm surprised Shakelford didn't go for Brown's throat, right there and then."

"Oh, he tried, but Homer held him back," Chuck put in.

"That didn't work out so good, because Brown kicked Shakelford in the nuts while Homer was holding him. Shakelford practically crawled on all fours to his car, gasping for breath. Brown just stood there and laughed his head off, then he told all of us to fuel up the machinery and get to work on the bridge."

Amanda frowned. She didn't recall seeing signs of road graders and dumptrucks on that section of the road. "Did you follow his orders?"

"Nope," Chuck said as he peeled the wrapper off his Snickers bar. "That's when Sam came out of his office and told Brown the machinery needed repairs and that he wasn't sending out any graders. Brown got all huffy when Sam disputed his orders. Brown tried to use leverage over Homer, but Sam wouldn't let Brown take Homer to task again."

"That's when Brown insisted Harjo take out the bulldozer or he'd fire the rest of us on the spot," Ron added.

"Could he do that?" Amanda questioned.

"Yep," Chuck replied. "Brown was always pulling that kind of shit on us. Sam was the one Brown really wanted to see quit, but Brown used us to get to Harjo. The jerk had his annoying ways of getting what he wanted."

So Amanda kept hearing.

Scoping out the crowd once again, Amanda noticed Isaac Marcum sitting alone in the third row. While she watched him, she noticed an occasional smile light up his face, making him appear years younger. Her key witness and/or suspect applauded when Harjo launched a shot from the three-point line and the ball swished through the hoop.

Isaac, it seemed, was enjoying himself.

Not, she imagined, as much as he had the day Brown died.

Amanda rose to her feet and inched down the row to the aisle. When she sank down beside Isaac, he grinned slyly at her.

"Still questioning would-be suspects, little lady? Lucky me, I guess it's my turn to get grilled again."

"You could save me a lot of time if you would tell me what happened," Amanda grumbled at him.

"And I keep telling you to let it go."

Amanda stared at Isaac for a long, deliberate moment, then said, "I saw horse tracks, Isaac, and I also saw the horse."

Something akin to anger flashed in Isaac's eyes. For a split second that wild expression rippled across his weathered features. And then it was gone. He was back in control.

"Don't ruin my evening," he scowled, his gaze intent on the game. "First time I've been out in public for a year. No need to remind me why I've been cooped up in the country, and who was responsible for my bitterness and grief." He cast her a fleeting glance. "Go play detective someplace else. I'm not talkin'. I'm never gonna talk. The Viet Cong couldn't make me and neither can you."

Amanda swallowed a frustrated curse as she left Isaac to watch the last minute of the game. She didn't know why it seemed to be a big deal to him. Because of Thorn's and Harjo's antics, the town team was trouncing the firefighters by ten points.

It was almost time for the Donkey King and Queen coronation, Amanda reminded herself. Sure wouldn't want to miss anything as monumentally important as that!

*   *   *

Velma counted the money in Sam Harjo's jar, jotted down the total, then handed the cash to Beverly Hill.

"Like, wow, Aunt Velma, he sure collected a lot of donations, didn't he?"

"Too much," Velma muttered as she bit down on her chewing gum. "Hand me Nicky's jar."

The plastic jar went from one plump hand to another. Licking her thumb, Velma quickly counted the dollar bills, then stacked the change in neat piles of nickels, dimes and quarters.

"Oh, damn!" Velma said, slumping back in the chair in the teacher's lounge. "This is just as I feared."

Bev's eye shadow-caked gaze flew to her aunt. "What's wrong?"

Velma stared somberly at Bev. "Harjo collected more than Thorn did."

Shaking her head in dismay, Bev grabbed the two remaining jars in her pudgy paws. "Here. You count Vinita's and I'll count Amanda's."

With dedicated concentration the beauticians tallied the money.

"One hundred fifty-seven dollars and seventy-five cents," Velma announced. "How much did Amanda get?"

"Two hundred dollars and fifty cents," Bev announced.

Velma's face puckered as she reached into her purse. When Velma laid a twenty-dollar bill on Nick's stack of cash, Bev frowned in disapproval.

"You can't do that. It's against the rules. Like, that'd be cheating, Aunt Velma."

Grumbling, Velma repocketed her money. "You're right." Smack, smack, smack. "But if this fouls up Amanda and Nicky's wedding plans I'll never forgive myself!"

Glumly, Velma plucked up the rhinestone crowns from the cardboard box, then propelled herself toward the door.

"Might as well get this over with," she said as she waddled toward the gym to give the results to the announcer.

While Vinita Frizzell nervously wrung her hands, waiting for Velma and Bev to hand the names of the Donkey King and Queen to the announcer, Amanda surveyed her suspects. She was getting impatient to solve this latest crime in Vamoose. It was, she realized, the worst case ever, because she didn't dislike any of the suspects.

It was the victim she intensely disliked, and she barely knew the man!

Brown had given everyone he knew—personally and professionally—reason to despise him.

Maybe *not* seeing justice served in this case *was* true justice, she caught herself thinking.

Come off it, Hazard, came the stern voice of fair play. *Instinct tells you a crime has been committed. You have to dig until you uncover the truth, whether you liked Brown or not.*

Amanda glanced at the young woman in the slinky black dress who was fidgeting beside her. Vinita was staring anxiously at the announcer. Geez, thought Amanda. Why on earth would anybody work themselves into a lather over this contest?

"And now, ladies and gents," the announcer said for melodramatic effect. "The moment you've all been waiting for. The Donkey Queen is . . . Amanda Hazard!"

Amanda manufactured a smile when she received a round of applause. Vinita's face fell like a rockslide.

"Congratulations," Vinita said through a smile as brittle as eggshells.

"And our reigning Donkey King will be . . ." The folded paper crackled when the announcer held it too close to the microphone.

The crowd waited with bated breath.

Amanda gave the suspects, who were scattered through the audience, one last look.

"The King is Sam Harjo!" the announcer announced.

Murmurs of speculation rolled through the crowd as Harjo ambled toward Velma and Bev to collect the crowns. Amanda darted Thorn a discreet glance. He was staring directly at her with midnight black eyes that bored into her like laser beams.

Talk about your awkward moments, Amanda thought as Harjo approached, sporting a devilish grin.

Amanda suspected that Ervin Shakelford was scowling to himself while he stood beside the pine bench. He would not be pleased that his political opponent was gathering potential votes and name recognition for the upcoming election. Shakelford's campaign strategy for this evening was taking a direct hit. Now, he was nowhere near the limelight—Sam Harjo was.

When Harjo halted in front of her, Amanda took the larger crown from his hand, then reached up on tiptoe to place it on his head at a jaunty angle. "Congrats, Harjo. Chalk one up for public recognition. You didn't have to spend a dime to draw all this attention. Shakelford is over on the bench glaring daggers at you."

The muted whispers of the audience died into silence when Harjo set the sparkling tiara on Amanda's lavender-tinted head. From the corner of her eye, Amanda saw Thorn spin on his heels and exit the gym. Clearly, he had seen and heard enough. He was not being a good sport about the coronation, either.

Amanda refocused her attention on Harjo. His amber-eyed gaze twinkled with mischief as he took a bold step toward her.

The crowd drew an audible breath as the janitor flicked off the overhead lights, dousing the gym in darkness.

Amanda and Harjo were standing at center court, flooded by a bright spotlight. Amanda waited expectantly.

If Harjo planted a juicy kiss, right smack dab on her lips, she wasn't sure how she would react. Yet, kisses seemed to be customary procedure at coronations.

To Amanda's stunned surprise—and the crowd's, obviously—Harjo went down on bended knee, gallantly lifted Amanda's hand, and brushed a feathery kiss across her wrist.

Applause echoed around the gymnasium and cheers rose to the rooftop.

Chalk up another vote of respect for Sam Harjo, she thought as he rose to his feet, then curled her hand around the crook of his elbow. Harjo had effectively assured the crowd of potential voters that he had the kind of class and style that rarely found its way to public office.

Amanda darted another glance at Shakelford as Harjo accompanied her into the foyer. The Republican candidate looked as if he had bitten into something sour. His campaign-slogan t-shirt and clappers had been a waste of money and he knew it.

The only way Shakelford could possibly win the upcoming election was if Sam Harjo ended up in jail.

That, Amanda reminded herself, was still a very distinct possibility.

Nick let loose with several colorful expletives as he stalked from the gym. He thought he could stand there and watch Harjo kiss Hazard's lips off, but at the last second he realized he might be tempted to break one of the laws he was sworn to uphold.

Oh sure, Nick kept reminding himself that he was getting exactly what he deserved—after he had walked out of the relationship with Hazard a few times in the past when he'd been peeved at her—and for good reason!

But damn it! Possessive jealousy was eating at him like battery acid. The green monster he was trying to keep chained was breathing fire and burning a hole in his gut. Nick had decided to leave before he said or did something he would later regret.

"Thorn? Where the heck are you going?" Hazard demanded as she scurried out the door. "You can't leave yet. Billy Jane Baxter and The Horseshoe Band are setting up their equipment to perform at the dance."

"I've got farm work to do," Nick muttered, refusing to glance back to see Hazard's sensuous mouth swollen from Harjo's slobbery kiss.

"At nine-thirty at night? After we've had another round of rain?" she asked skeptically.

"The property I'm planning to work has sandy soil," he explained gruffly. "There shouldn't be a problem." Nick yanked open the door of his truck.

"Thorn? Are you avoiding me?" Amanda wanted to know.

"I'm surprised you've had time to notice."

Fists planted on her hips, she glared at him. "What is that wisecrack supposed to mean?"

"Don't play the dumb blond with me, Hazard," he growled.

Nick saw her spine stiffen and her chin uplift. He knew that he'd hit a sensitive nerve—on purpose, he might add. Good. Now they were even. She was peeved at him and he was pure-dee pissed at her.

"Well fine, Thorn, go crawl on your tractor and ride in circles all night. I'll be here at the gym, subtly questioning the suspects in this case you refuse to recognize—as usual!"

"Suspects my ass!" he shot back, his temper at high tide. "You are enjoying playing the royal couple with Harjo, aren't you? Go ahead and admit it—"

Nick slammed his mouth shut when the door behind Hazard swung open.

"Amanda?" Bev Hill poked her head around the door. "The band is getting tuned up to play the first song. You and Sam are supposed to dance. Like, it's customary, you know.''

When Bev disappeared from view, Nick scooped up the gift he had bought for Hazard a week earlier—and hadn't had the chance to deliver. "Here, your highness, I bought you something.''

Hazard glanced curiously at the gift, then back at him.

Nick thought nothing of spoiling the surprise. "It's a cellular phone. Call me when you want me—if you ever do.''

"Thorn—''

Nick piled into his truck and slammed the door. He could feel the wedding arrangements tumbling down around him like a falling chandelier. Now that Harjo was in the picture, Nick's well-rounded world had become the proverbial eternal triangle.

Scowling, Nick slammed the truck into gear and laid rubber. He drove directly to the convenience store on the outskirts of town. After purchasing a twelve-pack of Budweiser at Toot 'N Tell 'Em, Nick headed for the Allis Chalmers tractor that was fueled and waiting.

He'd have a few beers to take the edge off his frustration while doing his field work. In a couple of hours—if he was lucky—maybe he would get over the fact that Hazard was dancing in Harjo's brawny arms.

Or maybe not!

Eleven

Silently fuming, Amanda stamped back into the gym, adjusting her tiara as she went. Thorn's juvenile attitude toward the Donkey King and Queen coronation was absurd. Besides, she thought self-righteously, Thorn had called off their relationship several times in the past and had flaunted other women to make her jealous. Now, when the boot was on the other foot, he wasn't handling things very well. How mature was that?

Served him right, Amanda mused. Now he knew the angry frustration she had endured during their falling-outs. Let him stew in his own juice and see how he liked it!

"Hazard, everyone is waiting for us to lead off the dance," Harjo said as he fell into step beside her.

Amanda set the gift Thorn had given her aside and smiled brightly. "Lead the way, your majesty."

Billy Jane Baxter, decked out in her gaudy turquoise and silver jewelry, crooned, "There she is, your Donkey Queen, your ideal—yodel-lay-ti-hoo."

Harjo swept Amanda into his arms and waltzed her

across the gym while the spotlight beamed down on them. While the country and western songstress sang, Amanda silently chanted, *Take this, Thorn, you mule-headed bozo. I'm going to enjoy myself tonight. So there! I owe you one—or three.*

"Thorn left in a huff, I noticed," Harjo said as he lifted Amanda off her feet and spun her around in a spectacular twirl.

The crowd applauded Harjo's dance skills. Shakelford, who stood a few feet away, muttered under his breath. Amanda clung to Harjo's broad shoulders until he set her back on her feet.

"Is the engagement still on?" Harjo asked as he leaned close for a brief moment.

Amanda frowned. "I'm not sure."

"In that case, save the last dance for me, Hazard."

When Billy Jane Baxter completed her last nasal yodel, Shakelford strode determinedly toward Amanda, anxious to share her limelight. As other dancers wandered onto the floor to do the two-step, Shakelford led Amanda in jerky motions. The man was not a good dancer, Amanda realized when Ervin trounced on her feet.

"Harjo is really playing this fundraiser to the hilt, isn't he?" Ervin grumbled in her ear.

"It must be standard procedure for political candidates," Amanda countered as she stared pointedly at the color photo stamped on Ervin's shirt. "You haven't fared too badly with your schmoozing tonight. You also received plenty of name recognition while you were marching up and down the sidelines like a human billboard." Then she added subtly, "At least you don't have to contend with Brown's mud-slinging anymore."

Every nerve and muscle in Ervin's bean-pole body went rigid and he missed a beat. The mere mention of Brown's name was enough to provoke intense emotion. While Ervin was off guard, Amanda fired another comment like a scud missile.

"I hear you got into a scuffle with Brown the morning he died."

Ervin jerked upright so quickly that he tramped on Amanda's toes. She grimaced as she watched anger register on Ervin's scarecrow-like features and felt his sweaty palms clamp around hers. Satisfied with the results, Amanda launched another missile at her rattled target.

"After what Brown said about you and your family that morning, I'm sure you would have liked to brain him."

Ervin's slick hand pinched painfully around Amanda's fingers. He bared his recently whitened teeth. "I know what you're thinking, Hazard. When someone around Vamoose ends up dead, you start digging dirt. But you can't pin Brown's death on me."

Oh yeah? Watch me try! "Where did you go after Brown insulted you and punched you in the stomach that morning?"

"Home," he snapped.

"The long way home, following Brown so you could have it out with him in private?" she pressed.

The wide smile Ervin had been flashing all night turned upside down. He gave Amanda a drop-dead look. "Don't mess with me, Hazard. You may be the reigning Donkey Queen of Vamoose, but I've got plenty of connections around here. I will not let you ruin my bid for the commissioner's seat in District 1. I don't want to hear that you're spouting suspicions about my conflicts with Brown. Are we clear on that?"

"Clear as the mud I found Brown in," Amanda replied. "So . . . you do admit there was a conflict between the two of you?"

"I'm not saying one way or the other," Ervin said through his teeth.

"Spoken like a true, fence-riding politician."

"Brown is dead and gone. If you know what's good for you, Hazard, you'll leave it at that."

"Will I?"

"You will."

Wheeling around, Ervin stamped off before Billie Jane could finish her last chorus of yodeling.

Amanda frowned pensively while she stood alone on the dance floor. Her comments had certainly set off a defensive reaction in Shakelford. He hadn't hidden his feelings very well. Hmm, interesting.

"Yo, Hazard, can I have the next dance?"

Amanda pivoted to see Chuck Gilhaney staring expectantly at her. With an agreeable nod, she stepped into his arms.

"Vinita isn't taking her defeat very well," Chuck confided as he kept pace with the fast-tempo country song. "Homer is still in the corner consoling her."

Amanda glanced over Chuck's shoulder to see Vinita blotting her mascara-lined eyes with a tissue. Her husband was patting her arm consolingly. Homer Frizzell, it seemed, was the devoted hubby—unlike her own fiancé, who seemed to prefer spending more time with Allis Chalmers than her!

"Poor guy, he's always having to pamper his temperamental wife," Chuck said before he twirled Amanda in a dizzying circle. Using Amanda's arm like a tow rope, he drew her to him, then spun her away. "Love this western dancing, don't you?"

Amanda's legs wobbled while she tried to recover her sense of balance. "It's swell," she murmured before Chuck sent her into another dizzying whirl. "Do you happen to know if Vinita made contact with that Smythe character who provided the donkeys for tonight's game?"

A wry smile pursed Chuck's lips as he grabbed Amanda to him, then gave her another spin. "How'd you know?"

"Lucky guess. Mr. Tattoo and Vinita exchanged several glances while I was sprawled on the floor. Is Smythe from around here?"

"He has a few acres north of Adios," Chuck reported. "He used to be a rodeo bull rider, but he wasn't good enough to earn a living at it. That's when he decided to get into the donkey business."

Amanda wondered if the tracks she had seen in the mud might have been made by a donkey rather than a horse.

Give it up, Hazard, you're grasping at straws. What possible connection could Brown have with Smythe?

"I'm surprised to see Sara Mae and her new husband here tonight," she said.

Two fuzzy brows arched as Chuck glanced around the gym. "They're here? I hadn't noticed. They tied the knot already? Well, good for them. Sara Mae went through hell this past year because of Brown. I'm glad to hear she's happy."

"I wonder if she arranged that happiness herself," Amanda mused aloud.

Chuck stopped in his tracks, his leathery features frozen in disbelief. "You think Sara Mae and Sonny arranged things?" he croaked. "Geez, you're kidding, right?"

"I believe somebody helped Brown into the Great Beyond," she told him frankly.

Chuck gaped at her, then blessed her with an innocent grin. "Surely you don't think I'm a suspect."

"Brown had more enemies than friends. Can the other workers at the commissioner's barn verify that you worked on machinery the entire morning?"

Chuck skidded to a halt. His good-natured grin disappeared in one second flat. He scowled at her. "Maybe my new boss has the hots for you, but I don't have to bend over backward being nice if I don't want to. You go pointing accusing fingers at me and my buddies and I'll—"

"Club me over the head?" she ventured.

Chuck backed off as if she were a coiled rattlesnake. "Lady, don't get on my bad side," he said before he wheeled around and stalked off.

Amanda's shoulders sagged while she stood at center court—alone again. Never once in her previous unofficial investigations had so many possible suspects been so protective of one another. Usually, suspects pointed her in someone else's direction to take the heat off themselves. But Brown's associates—enemies was nearer the mark—simply clammed up and shoved off.

While Baxter and The Horseshoe Band burst into another fast-tempo country song, Amanda took a load off her feet by parking herself on the front row of the bleachers. She watched the suspects parade past her, doing the Cotton-Eyed Joe.

All except one of the suspects, she noted.

Isaac Marcum limped up the steps to plunk down beside her.

"Still grilling everyone who asks you to dance?" he asked as he stretched out his gimpy leg. "You really eat up this investigation stuff, don'tcha?"

Amanda glared at Isaac's taunting smile. "Why don't you just tell me what happened that morning and put me out of my misery."

"Told ya, little lady, I've got nothing more to say."

"Fine, I'll solve this case by myself. And when I do, you'll be called as a witness—or a suspect—whichever it turns out to be."

"No, I won't," he said confidently. "From what I saw tonight, Thorn isn't likely to believe anything you have to say about this nonexistent case, or any other subject for that matter. Looked mad as hell to me when he left."

Amanda shifted awkwardly on the bleachers.

"I'm right and you know it," Isaac continued. "The minute Harjo got crowned king, Thorn took off. A small setback in wedding plans, I'd say."

Amanda bounded to her feet. She was in no mood to discuss Thorn's noticeable absence or their heated exchange in the parking lot. "Come dance with me, Salty."

"I've got a limp, if you haven't noticed."

She grabbed his hand and hoisted him to his feet. "Then we'll limp together. Besides, it isn't polite to turn down an invitation from the Queen Ass of Vamoose, you know."

Isaac snickered as Amanda led him down the steps. "If you're being nice to me because you think I'll talk, you're wasting your time, queenie."

Amanda had already wasted a considerable amount of time on this perplexing case, so what did she have to lose? There was always a chance that Isaac Marcum might make a slip of the tongue and offer Amanda a much-needed clue.

Unfortunately, Isaac was exceptionally careful about what he said as he sashayed around the dance floor, favoring his stiff leg.

For the next hour, Amanda changed partners after every dance, trying to pick up any tidbit of information she could. Soon, she decided, she was going to have to sit herself down to compile the facts, then rank her suspects in logical order. Those who had the most to gain from Brown's death would head her list. Then she was going to get down to the serious business of pinpointing the culprit and applying enough pressure to make the nut crack . . .

Amanda's determined thoughts were interrupted by the realization that she had to meet her April 15th deadline before she attacked this case. She could dig for clues in what little spare time she had, but she had tax forms to complete. Then she would get to the bottom of this Brown incident—somehow . . .

"Last dance, y'all," Billie Jane called in her twangy voice. "Grab your partners for a slow, romantic western ballad."

"This is our big finale, Hazard," Harjo said from so close behind Amanda that she flinched.

The man had the amazing knack of sneaking up without

a sound—a useful skill if you wanted to launch a surprise attack on your overbearing boss and political opposition.

Amanda found herself drawn close to Harjo's sleek, muscular contours, and felt all the eyes of Vamoose on her. If Harjo was aware that he and Amanda were being closely monitored he didn't let on. He simply glided in perfect rhythm with the music, keeping a close but respectable distance. Yet, there was no ignoring his male presence. Harjo made certain Amanda was aware of him.

Harjo, she decided, knew how to push to the limit without stepping over the borderline of propriety. For that, she admired him, in an exasperated sort of way. If Harjo had bumped off Brown, he had a legion of devoted supporters protecting him. Furthermore, he was pouring on the masculine charm for Amanda's benefit, letting it be known that he had developed an interest in her—whether he actually had one or not. She still didn't quite trust him. The ulterior motive for this budding interest had Amanda questioning Harjo's motives constantly.

And damn Thorn, anyway! If he really cared he would be here. Was he having misgivings about the approaching wedding? Was he bowing out because he had gotten cold feet?

"The dance doesn't have to be over for us," Harjo whispered, staring down at her with his intense gaze. "This could be the beginning of a long, satisfying reign."

Amanda didn't utter one word. She simply stepped away when the refrain of music ended. Fetching her purse, and the gift Thorn had given her, Amanda headed toward the door, then shouldered her way through. Homer Frizzell was a few steps ahead of her, his bulky arm draped over his wife's quaking shoulders. Amanda melted into the shadows so she wouldn't interrupt the touching scene.

"That Hazard woman always gets all the glory," Vinita said between sobs. "I spent two weeks collecting donations for the contest and she wins! I didn't win prom queen, homecoming queen, or rodeo queen while I was in high school. Sara Mae always took those honors, and now it's that Hazard woman! I'm tired of playing second fiddle.''

"You're still *my* queen, honey," Homer cooed as he gave Vinita a comforting squeeze.

It didn't appear to help.

"Queen of the house. Whoop-ti-do," Vinita grumbled. "What kind of title is that? One of these days I'd like to have a real home I can be proud of."

"You will, sugar, I promise."

"Well, at least I got some enjoyment out of the evening," Vinita said. "I got to watch that hot-shot Hazard woman fall off her ass. Smyttie came through for me."

Just as Amanda had suspected. Vinita was a spiteful little thing, wasn't she?

Amanda pulled the rhinestone crown off her head and tucked it under her arm. She didn't think Vinita needed to be reminded of her defeat while she was wallowing in self-pity like a hog in mud.

Slipping quietly toward her truck, Amanda drove away without Vinita noticing her.

Nick chugged another beer as he turned another endless corner on his Allis Chalmers tractor. Riding a tractor was positively the worst place for a man to be when he had trouble on his mind and time on his hands. Blinking groggily, Nick spun the wheel to put the field cultivator he pulled behind him back on track.

"Damn Sam Harjo," he said thickly. "Picked a fine time to turn his attention on Hazard. Hell, after their last slow dance, he'll probably invite himself over to her place . . .''

The picture that popped to mind had Nick scowling and cursing. He crushed the empty beer can and grabbed a full one. His eighth, but who was counting? He hadn't been snockered in ages. Figured he was due, considering the circumstances. His relationship with Hazard was going down the toilet. His sit-back-and-wait strategy was ten kinds of hell.

Dully, Nick fastened his fuzzy gaze on the lights blinking at him in the distance. Probably aliens, the way his luck was running these days. They'd park their flying saucer in this remote field and whisk him away for observation and questioning. Then Harjo would have a clear field of conquest.

The lights approached at blazing speed. To Nick's surprise, the twin headlights halted at his pasture gate. It took his pickled brain a few seconds to realize the shapely feminine figure silhouetted by the lights was Hazard, not an alien.

Nick stamped on the brake, then shifted into neutral. Leaving the tractor idling, he opened the cab door to stare down at Hazard.

"It's nearly midnight and it's sprinkling," she snapped.

Nick leaned negligently against the steering wheel. "Did you drive all the way out here to give me the time and weather report, Hazard? Or are you delivering your John Deere letter in person?" Nick shook his head and sighed. "I mean Dear John letter." He'd obviously been spending too much time on tractors.

Nick saw Hazard jerk herself upright, saw her chin thrust out. "Get your butt down here, Thorn. We have some things to discuss and they won't wait."

That did not sound good, Nick decided as he eased his two left feet onto the platform outside the cab door. This was a Dear John letter delivered in person, he predicted.

This was going to be the big finish. The kaput. The *sayonara*. The toodle-oo. The wedding was about to be called off. Hazard was going to trade the Vamoose chief of police for the new county commissioner.

Nick would take it like a man—with dignity. Then he'd

climb back on his tractor, ride around in circles and drink until he couldn't think . . .

The raindrops had slicked the metal steps of the tractor, causing Nick to lose his balance. His booted feet went flying one way and he went the other. He landed with a thud and a pained grunt on the freshly tilled ground.

"For God's sake, Thorn, you're drunk—and you're a cop!" she muttered as he staggered clumsily to his feet.

"The *cop* in me isn't drunk," he slurred out. "The *man* in me is."

Hazard flung him a withering glance. "I hope you realize you're behaving like an ass!"

"Me?" He snorted as he propped himself against the oversized tractor tire. "I'm not the one who was voted Queen Ass of Vamoose." He squinted toward her jalopy truck. "Did you bring the king with you?"

Hazard backed up two paces when Nick breathed on her. "Good grief, you smell like a brewery."

"Don't change the subject, Hazard. Just give me back my ring and go away. I've got work to do."

Nick wished he could see the expression on her face, but she was standing in the shadows and his vision was seriously impaired.

"This is all your fault, you know." Wheeling around, she stalked back to her truck to dig the ring from her coin purse.

"My fault?" he hooted. "I'm not the one fooling around with Harjo!"

"I am not fooling around!"

"Bullshit!"

Hazard stamped back to him, grabbed his hand, then slapped the engagement ring into his open palm. "If you hadn't insisted on these extravagant wedding arrangements, we could have eloped the minute I finished doing the income tax returns. And by the way, I found some discrepancies in your farming records. You'll have to separate the personal and farm expenses of fuel costs before I complete your 8824 worksheet and Schedule F forms.''

"*My* extravagant wedding arrangements?" Nick smirked sarcastically. "You're the one who wanted all the bells and whistles. And to complicate matters, you've opened another one of your unauthorized investigations. Nothing new about that, I'll admit, but I've told you time and again to keep your nosy snoot out of my professional business as a cop. You're a CPA, not a PI!"

"If you were worth your salt as a cop, and took my suspicions seriously, we could be working this case together!" she fired back at him.

"Right," he ground out. "And Harjo would be my prime suspect. You'd be pleading with me to make sure he turned out to be innocent because you've developed a fond attachment for him, haven't you?"

She turned and stamped off.

"Hazard, come back here. I'm not finished!"

"Oh yes you are," she threw over her shoulder. "You may not know it yet, but you are definitely finished, Thorn!"

Nick let loose with a long string of curses as he watched Hazard throw gravel in her haste to leave. Nick unclenched his fist to see the diamond ring winking in the light from the tractor. He tucked the ring in the pocket of his jeans and pulled himself up the steep steps. This time he kept both hands on the rails for support.

Mom was obviously right, Nick thought as he flounced onto the cushioned seat. Hazard was not the domestic, supportive farm-type wife who would keep the home fires burning. Hell, she'd probably burn down the house when she tried to cook a meal that didn't come with microwave directions!

Better call Mom first thing in the morning and tell her to cancel the trip to the wedding shower, Nick reminded himself as he thrust the tractor into gear. The only shower to be had around Vamoose was the rain that was presently falling on his head!

Grumbling in irritation, Amanda sped down the gravel road that led to her house. She had tracked down Thorn in hopes of having a rational discussion, and wham! He had asked for his ring back. The nerve of him, blaming *her!*

Wasn't that typical of a man, she thought as she surged up the steps to her house. Thorn had wanted a fancy wedding, because this was his first marriage, and she had tried to be accommodating. Now he was accusing her of arranging all the fanfare.

Amanda plugged in the coffee pot, resolving to channel her frustration into a positive direction. She had two more tax returns to compute—Brown's and Mother's. Mother's meticulously organized ledgers would be a snap. Amanda decided to save that one for last.

Brown's income tax ledgers and receipts were another matter entirely. Sara Mae had left a boot box of receipts and loose-leaf notebook papers for Amanda to shuffle through. That would keep her busy for several hours. Certainly she wouldn't have a spare minute to devote to her exasperating confrontation with Thorn.

With Bruno sprawled at her feet, Amanda spread the confused mass of papers on the dining room table. After she had separated the receipts for cattle cubes, hay, and veterinary supplies—piling them in alphabetical order— she sorted out other farming expenses.

A frown knitted her brows as she studied the fuel receipts. Unlike Thorn's long list of fuel expenses for his farm trucks and tractors in his part-time ranch operation, Brown had very few to deduct. The man should have had several hundred gallons of diesel listed in his receipts. And where, Amanda wondered, were the receipts for all those fancy tools displayed in Brown's workshop?

Unless Amanda missed her guess, Brown had fueled up his pick-up—the one issued by the county—and used the vehicle to conduct his farming business. Furthermore, Amanda wouldn't have put it past Brown to drive his hay trucks and tractors by the commissioner's barn to fuel up while no one was around. After all, Brown had a full set of keys to the shop.

Was Harjo also draining the fuel tank for his personal use, same as Brown had?

Ah, the sneaky little perks of public office!

For several minutes, Amanda rifled through the receipts, searching for a partial list of the tools Brown had purchased. She had the unshakable feeling that Brown had ordered the tools through the commissioner's office, then hauled them home. That sounded like something that corrupt jerk would do. He'd obviously used that tactic to cut his fuel costs.

Amanda frowned again. How could Brown swipe the tools from the commissioner's barn without his workers knowing they were missing? The tools would be delivered to the shop, wouldn't they? They wouldn't come directly to him.

Someone had to have known what Brown was doing. That someone had worked closely with Brown and also had access to the commissioner's workshop.

Sam Harjo's name popped instantly to mind. Amanda started to disregard the suspicious thought. Then she remind herself that the foreman—and interim commish— would have that kind of inside knowledge. Was that the information Harjo had planned to use against Brown?

Damn, was Thorn right? Amanda asked herself as she tallied Brown's expenses. Had she reached the point that she was looking for proof that Harjo was *not* involved in Brown's death? Was Harjo such a likable sort that everyone

associated with him wanted to protect him so he wouldn't
be accused of a crime?

Amanda rubbed her stiff shoulders and forced herself
to concentrate on the task at hand. She was down to the
wire on tax deadlines. She had to complete these forms
so Jenny Long could get them typed up and returned to
the clients.

Amanda calculated the totals for Brown's farming
expenses, then sipped more coffee to keep her awake. It
was her civic duty to report her findings to the county
offices, she decided. Brown had cheated the government,
and hard-working taxpayers were footing his bills.

If Harjo had any intention of practicing the same unscrupulous policies, he'd better think again. His attempt to
charm her would not prevent her from seeing that he
followed proper work ethics while he was the District 1
commissioner in Vamoose County.

With practiced ease Amanda tallied Brown's expenses,
but her thoughts kept circling back to the first conversation
she'd had with Sam Harjo. He had claimed that there were
two sides to politics—the one the public saw, and the
ugly side. She wondered if that comment also applied to
politicians. It had, in Brown's case.

Was Harjo implying that he also had two personalities?
The man could be utterly charming, but he was also tough
as nails—or so his employees claimed. Amanda had also
seen Harjo battling Thorn in that ridiculous rivalry at the
Donkey Basketball game. Thorn and Harjo could be down-
right brutal when they thought the situation demanded it.

When Amanda had recorded the figures on Brown's tax
form, she set it aside. And now for Mother and Daddy's
taxes, she thought as she plucked up the file. As expected,
Mother kept perfect records. Since her parents took standard deductions, Amanda breezed through the forms without a hitch.

First thing in the morning, she would drop off the two

forms for her secretary to type up. Then she'd drive out
to Brown's home to take another look around. She had
the intuitive feeling that she had overlooked an important
clue. She would find it or her name wasn't Amanda Hazard.

And if Thorn objected to her unofficial investigation
then that was just too damned bad! When she solved this
case, she was going to rub it in Thorn's face!

Nick stuck his head under the shower, hoping the pulsat-
ing water would clear the cobwebs from his brain. He
needed a clear head since he was in charge of patrolling
Vamoose while Deputy Sykes took the day off.

Damned stupid of you to try to drown your woes in beer, Thorn,
he chastised himself.

Then Hazard had shown up and Nick had taken his
frustration out on her. Male pride demanded that he call
it quits before she could do it . . .

The ring . . .

Had he demanded that she return the ring? Seems like
he remembered saying something like that.

He had, hadn't he!

Geez, Thorn, what the hell were you thinking!

Nick shut off the faucet, dried himself off, then dressed
in his uniform.

What to do. Should he cling to his male pride and end
this relationship with Hazard? Did he want to give Harjo
the chance to move in?

*Hell, Thorn, you're crazy about that woman and you know it.
Even if Hazard isn't the domestic type Mom thinks you need, even
if her craving for investigation drives you nuts, there is still a lot
of good history between you and Hazard. Are you going to blow
the best thing you've had going in years, just because Mom doesn't
approve and Hazard perceives herself as the female version of
Sherlock Holmes?*

Resolved to making amends, Nick grabbed a handful of

crackers to soothe his churning stomach, then headed for the front door. The clatter of machinery and roar of engines drew his suspicious frown. He stepped outside to see Ron Newton behind the wheel of the dumptruck that had unloaded a heaping mound of gravel—right in Nick's driveway.

Squinting in the sunlight, Nick glanced south to see Sam Harjo sitting in the cab of the commissioner's pick-up. Harjo was grinning wickedly.

Nick stared at the impassable mound of gravel, then glared at Harjo's ornery grin. The man was obviously trying to block Nick in his own yard. Well, Nick was not going to lose his temper. He was going to keep his cool.

Digging the keys from his pocket, Nick strode toward the squad car. He revved the engine and surveyed the bar ditch that was standing full of water after the recent rains. As Nick plunged down the steep slope he mashed on the accelerator. Mud and water spurted around him like a geyser.

Teeth gritted, hands clenched on the wheel, Nick cut diagonally up the grassy incline. He smiled in spiteful triumph when flying mud and water showered Harjo's truck. Halting beside the battered truck, Nick rolled down the window to greet Harjo.

"Thanks for the load of gravel, commish. If your boys don't have time to spread it out, I'll use the front-end loader on my tractor to do it.

"And by the way," he added, tossing Harjo a devilish grin. "I plan to do some investigating today. Sure would be a shame if your nose wasn't clean in the Brown case."

Harjo gave Nick a man-to-man look. "Just so you know, Thorn, this thing with Hazard isn't a passing fancy with me. You can investigate all you want in hopes of pinning something on me, but you aren't going to intimidate me into backing off."

Nick bared his teeth. Not to be outdone, Harjo bared his.

For a full minute Nick and Harjo stared each other down, neither man wanting to be the first to look away, the first to leave the scene. It was one of those male macho things again. Nick was prepared to outwait Harjo, even if it took the whole damn day.

Unfortunately, the dispatcher picked an untimely moment to signal Nick.

"Chief, come in."

Muttering, Nick grabbed the mike to the two-way radio. "Thorn, here."

"We've got a stranded motorist three-quarters of a mile south of Vamoose. Hazard's landlady blew a tire and she needs to hitch a ride to Thatcher's Oil and Gas."

"I'll pick up Emma Carter," Harjo quickly volunteered.

The truck sped off before Nick could accept or decline the offer.

"Help is on the way, Janie-Ethel," Nick came back.

Well fine, Nick thought as he followed Harjo's truck down the road. Let the man drum up another vote by doing his good deed for the day. Nick would grab a much-needed cup of coffee at Last Chance Cafe, make his appointed rounds, and ask a few questions about the Brown case.

And Harjo damned well better be squeaky clean, Nick mused. If Brown's death wasn't accidental—as Hazard insisted—Harjo was going to receive the full benefit of Nick's expertise in detective investigation!

Twelve

Amanda dropped off the tax forms to Jenny Long, who was efficiently manning the accounting office on Main Street. She was taking such pride in her work that Amanda complimented her effusively. Jenny beamed and promised to have the returns recorded and copied by closing time.

Before heading out to Brown's house, Amanda wheeled into the parking lot at Last Chance Cafe for a dose of caffeine and a package of Rolaids. Her upsetting encounter with Thorn, and the dozens of cups of her own tar-flavored coffee, had her stomach churning like a vat.

The instant Amanda breezed into the restaurant, Lydia Shakelford glowered at her. Obviously Lydia's father had conveyed last night's conversation. Amanda was receiving the cold shoulder treatment from the young woman who wore campaign pins like a general displaying his stars.

Amanda perched on the stool at the counter and smiled. "Could I have some Rolaids and coffee to go, please?"

"Yeah, whatever."

Lydia didn't pay Amanda the courtesy of glancing in her direction, just swished over to grab a Styrofoam cup and the antacid tablets. Plunking down the cup, Lydia sloshed coffee on the counter, missing Amanda's candy-striped fingernails by millimeters. Amanda caught the Rolaids before they rolled off the counter.

"Seventy-five cents for the coffee and a buck for the tablets," Lydia snapped.

Amanda dug into her purse to retrieve her money.

The bell above the door tinkled when a new customer arrived. The cafe patrons, who had been murmuring in conversation, suddenly fell silent. Amanda swiveled around on her stool to see Thorn, decked out in his police uniform, framed by the sunlight pouring through the glass door. Her heart slammed against her ribs.

"Coffee, please, Lydia," Thorn requested as he approached the counter.

"That'll be fifty cents, chief," Lydia Shakelford said, flashing Thorn a cheery smile.

"Hey, how come I had to pay seventy-five cents for mine?" Amanda wanted to know.

"The extra quarter is for insulting my dad last night," Lydia sniped. "He didn't bump off Brown."

"How do you know? Because *you're* the one who did?" Amanda shot back.

Lydia's flat chest swelled with indignation. "I was on my way to work when Brown had his well-deserved accident."

"Hazard—"

"Prove it," Amanda challenged, ignoring Thorn's attempt to interfere. "And how do you know the time of death? It isn't public knowledge."

"Hazard—"

"I've heard the speculations from customers," Lydia said, tilting her chin to look down her nose at Amanda. "Sometime between eight and nine is the scuttlebutt around town."

"You had plenty of time to club Brown on the head, then report for your shift," Amanda pointed out. "After the tacky remarks Brown made about you and your mother, I suspect you would have liked to retaliate.''

When Lydia's face turned crimson with outrage, Thorn hoisted Amanda off her stool and shoved her outside.

''Damn it, Hazard, why don't you just post an announcement on the bulletin board that says you're searching for suspects,'' Thorn muttered. He opened the door of the squad car, then planted Amanda on the seat. The door shut with a bang.

Amanda sipped her coffee while Thorn detoured to her truck to retrieve Bruno. When the dog was placed in the back seat, Thorn slid beneath the wheel. Damn, she hadn't had time to dump generous helpings of cream and sugar in her coffee before Thorn collared her. The bitter taste of the drink made her lips pucker.

After Thorn cranked the engine, he handed her the file of separated expenses for fuel deductions, as she had requested the previous night.

When Thorn drove away, Amanda frowned. ''Where are we going?''

''For a ride.''

''I plan to snoop around Brown's house this morning while Sara Mae and Sonny are tending to the bait shop.''

''Fine, we'll snoop together.''

Amanda blinked in surprise. ''You're taking my suspicions seriously?''

Thorn stopped at Vamoose's one and only traffic light. ''I'm taking you seriously, Hazard. Always have, always will.''

''Last night you said—''

''Forget last night. My pride was smarting. I tried to soothe it with beer. That didn't work worth a damn.'' He dug into his pocket to retrieve the ring. ''This belongs to you . . . if you still want it.''

Amanda stared at his ruggedly handsome profile as he cruised through town. She was feeling exceptionally sentimental . . . until they passed Thatcher's Oil and Gas. Harjo was leaning against the battered pick-up, staring directly at her. Thorn tossed Harjo a goading grin and flung him a mock salute.

Men, thought Amanda, as Thorn peeled out.

"One question, Thorn."

"Fire away, Hazard."

"Did you, by chance, know that Harjo would be at the service station when you chose this particular route to Brown's house?"

He broke into a devilish grin. "Yep."

Amanda rolled her eyes.

"Harjo got to kiss the queen last night," Thorn continued. "Why shouldn't I have a little revenge?"

"He didn't kiss me, Thorn," Amanda promptly informed him. "Harjo got down on bended knee and kissed my hand."

"Well, shit," Thorn muttered. "That's even worse!"

Amanda did a double-take. "It was respectful and touching."

"Exactly my point. The tough yet tender hunk of a man bowing to his queen. The tactic must have worked. You were impressed by his chivalrous gesture and the crowd undoubtedly considered Harjo worthy of holding public office. Smart move on Harjo's part."

Amanda frowned, contemplating Thorn's comment.

"And you know what, Hazard?" Thorn added as he kept his hands on the wheel and his eyes on the road. "The thing that gets me most is that I actually like that crafty SOB. But if he was involved in Brown's death, I'm going to hang him out to dry."

They rode in silence for several miles. Amanda sipped her coffee and stared pensively at the stripes on the highway.

"Velma called this morning to see if the wedding shower is still on," Amanda said.

Thorn never took his gaze off the road. "What did you tell her?"

"It occurred to me at four-thirty this morning, while I was calculating part of your tax return, that it was Velma who actually told me that you wanted a huge wedding. Did you tell her that?"

"Hell, no. She told me *you* wanted all the pomp and pageantry. I went along with it, because I thought that was what you wanted."

"And I agreed to Velma's plans because I thought *you* wanted to make a big to-do of the wedding arrangements."

"If it had been up to me, we would have flown to Las Vegas the day after your tax deadline. Then we would have scheduled the honeymoon for whenever we could fit it in."

"The whole town expected to be invited, you know," Amanda murmured, glancing at Thorn from over the rim of her Styrofoam cup.

Nick sighed audibly. "I know. Nothing worse than being in the public eye. Everybody anticipated being included in the plans."

"Are you aware that we have been speaking of the wedding plans in the past tense?" Amanda pointed out.

"Are you aware that your engagement ring is still sitting in the palm of your hand?" He glanced at her momentarily, then focused on the upcoming curve as he veered onto the gravel road. "That's what's keeping this conversation in the past tense, Hazard."

Amanda stared at the ring, then at Thorn. "I—"

Her voice dried up when she noticed Vinita Frizzell galloping across the pasture on the same horse Amanda had seen penned up beside Harjo's barn. A missing piece of the puzzle niggled her and her analytical brain shifted gears.

"What's Vinita doing out here?" she asked as Thorn cruised over the hill.

"She lives in a trailer house not far from here," Thorn replied. "Why?"

"The one that sits down the path from Harjo's place?"

Dark eyes drilled accusingly into Amanda. "How do you know where Harjo lives?"

"Because I've been investigating Brown's case and I stopped in to ask Harjo a few questions." Before Thorn got bent out of shape—and he looked as if he were about to—Amanda asked, "Why do you suppose Vinita is riding Harjo's horse?"

"How the hell should I know," Nick grumbled as he blazed over the hill, then veered into Brown's driveway. "Let's don't discuss Harjo, if you don't mind—"

"You are being extremely sensitive about—"

"Drop it, Hazard," Thorn snarled, obviously at the end of his tether. "Now, what goose chase are we on here?"

Amanda ignored his snide tone and stepped from the squad car. "I want to look around the workshop. There are no records of Brown's tool purchases as farming deductions. I have a sneaking suspicion that he was swiping them from the county commissioner's barn and toting them home."

"Breaking and entering is against the law, and I don't have a search warrant," Nick said, grabbing her arm before she whizzed into the workshop.

Amanda shook herself loose. "Fine, you stay out here and keep watch. As for me, I'm doing nothing more than taking inventory of farming property for my client's estate taxes and Schedule F income tax form."

Nick shook his head in dismay. "Hazard, you're bending the law for your own purpose."

"So did Brown, I'm guessing," she said as she strode inside.

Thorn, she noticed, did not cross the threshold, just stuck his head inside to take a look around. The cop in

Thorn wouldn't allow him to stretch the law as far as Amanda was willing to do.

Amanda surveyed the heaping shelves and pegboards where tools hung on hooks. "Yep, I'd say Brown was stealing the county blind. According to my calculations, he was also siphoning gas from the county fuel tanks to power his vehicles.'"

"Well, damn," Thorn muttered. "That means several somebody-elses could have known what was going on."

"Exactly. What those somebody-elses did about it is what we have to find out."

"Somebody like Harjo," Nick murmured.

Amanda glanced sideways to see the spiteful smile spreading across Thorn's full lips. "I thought you didn't want to hear the man's name mentioned again."

Thorn stepped absently into the shop, realized what he'd done, then backed up. "I don't mind hearing it in this context. As foreman of the commissioner's shop, he must have known what was going on."

"He did," Amanda admitted, "but I'm willing to bet some of the workers did, too."

Thorn's thick black brows flattened on his forehead. "Defending him, are we?"

Amanda took one last look around the workshop, then breezed past Thorn. "I'm only pointing out the fact that the road crew could have been aware of Brown's sly dealings and that some of them could have been involved in it."

"But I think I'll start by interrogating Harjo." Thorn smiled wickedly. "I'm looking forward to it, in fact."

Before Amanda piled into the squad car, she scanned the view from Brown's hilltop home. The stretch of road in the valley below could easily be seen.

"Make note of the fact that a stalled truck could have been spotted from up here. And don't forget that Brown showed up at the commissioner's barn at seven-fifteen to spout orders before he swung back by his house at seven-thirty to catch Sara Mae and Sonny trying to haul off more furniture.''

Amanda anticipated Thorn's unspoken question. ''Brown had plenty of time to drive back here, because the county shop isn't far away, and he had asphalt pavement leading to his house, not miles of mud.''

Since Thorn appeared pensive and receptive, Amanda decided to rattle off the facts for his future reference. ''Brown laid Sonny Snittiger low with a punch that morning, then ridiculed the man. Brown stood in the way of Sonny having the woman he's been in love with since he was a freshman in high school.

''Given the conflict between Dusty and Sonny,'' Amanda continued, ''Sonny could have trotted downhill to whack Dusty while he was stuck in the mud, then hiked back up here to drive away, leaving no incriminating tracks.''

''Or Harjo could have jogged over the hill, clobbered Brown, then plowed off on the bulldozer,'' Thorn put in.

''Or,'' Amanda said, refusing to let Thorn dwell on Harjo out of pure male jealousy, ''Isaac Marcum could have seen his chance to have revenge.'' She gestured toward the house perched on the hill to the north. ''As you can plainly see, Salty has a bird's eye view overlooking the valley. I think Salty has a lot of answers, but he won't knuckle under. Believe me, I've tried to twist his arm a dozen different ways, in hopes of getting him to talk.''

Thorn stared in one direction and then the other. ''You think Salty Marcum knows whether this was an accident or a murder?''

Amanda bobbed her head. Layers of hair flapped in the breeze. ''He knows exactly what happened. I'm positive this wasn't a simple accident. If it wasn't, Salty would have said so. He's cantankerous, yet honest enough not to claim Brown died all by himself.''

''Maybe I should interrogate him.''

"You should, Thorn." Amanda seated herself in the car. "Take me back to Last Chance to get my truck. I have a few errands to run before I complete your tax forms."

Thorn slid beneath the wheel and started the car. Taking the new road that led to the highway which passed through Adios, he drove in meditative silence.

Amanda was inordinately pleased to see Thorn contemplating the possibility of foul play. Finally! He'd certainly dragged his feet long enough.

"Hazard, I want you to back off and let me investigate," he insisted.

And then he had to go and say something like that! Amanda fumed. Damn it, she had knocked herself out gathering facts and sniffing for clues. Then this big handsome hunk of a cop stepped in and tried to shrug her aside. When was Thorn going to learn?

"No way, Thorn."

Thorn jerked his head around to pin her with a hard stare. "What is that supposed to mean?"

"What part of *no* don't you understand?" she flung back, angrily crossing her arms over her chest. "*If* we get married, and *if* I investigate future cases, do you plan to brush me aside the way you've doing now, the way you've always done when you finally realize I'm onto something? I initiate the investigation and you step in to take the credit. I hate it when you do that."

Amanda glanced sideways as the patrol car whizzed through the small town of Adios. It hit her just then how the hamlet must have gotten its name. You barely had time to reach the city limits on the south side of town before you whizzed past the north end. There was barely time to say goodbye.

"Hazard . . ."

Amanda was well acquainted with that warning tone in Thorn's voice. She felt the powerful engine of the squad car accelerate to match Thorn's rising temper. Thorn was getting pissed. She could almost see the wisps of smoke rolling from his ears. And on top of his hangover! Yikes, thought Amanda. She should have kept her big mouth shut. She knew her obsessive need to investigate was a sore spot between them.

"Yes, dear?" Amanda smiled sweetly, hoping to dampen his fuse. "What were you going to say?"

It was a waste of a smile, she soon found out.

"Don't try Harjo's buttering-up tactics on me," he muttered. "Just because he's gotten to you doesn't mean—"

"You take that back this very second!" Amanda spouted.

"I'll take it back when I'm convinced there's no hanky-panky going on," he growled, then jerked the wheel when the car veered toward the shoulder of the road.

Amanda was so furious that she was seeing Thorn through a red haze—or maybe it was just the heightened color in his face. She didn't know, didn't care. Thorn was questioning her integrity, her fidelity. He was also trying to brush her off so he could assume command of the case that she had busted her butt to investigate.

"That really tears it, Thorn," Amanda hissed, chin in the air, eyes flashing. "You demanded that I give back your ring, then you wanted me to reclaim it. Then you have the audacity to accuse me of having a lovefest with Harjo!"

"Then why the hell was he seen at your place so early in the morning before he drove you into town?" Thorn asked, and sneered. "Answer that one!"

"Stop the damned car! Right here, right now!" Amanda shouted.

The squad car skidded to a halt. Amanda whipped open the door, only to realize they had reached the city limits of Vamoose. Well, it didn't matter, she told herself. She would walk to town to get her truck. She would not ride in the same vehicle with Thorn while he was behaving like an ass. She had dealt with enough asses the previous night, thank you very much!

The strain between the two of them—one that had been simmering just beneath the surface the past week—was like compressed steam in a pressure cooker. Thorn's comments had blown the lid of Amanda's temper—and vice versa.

Glaring at Thorn, Amanda let Bruno out of the car, then slammed the door. She stalked along the road, watching the patrol car peel out and zoom off.

"Mother should be pleased," Amanda said to herself. Mother had her doubts about Thorn being desirable marriage material. And all this time Amanda had tried to protect Thorn from Mother! Maybe she should have turned them loose on each other and watched the fur fly!

Amanda half turned to stick out her thumb when she heard a vehicle approaching. The rattletrap pick-up, with its rusted tailpipes and chipped paint, squeaked to a stop, rocking up and down on its bad shocks. Amanda smiled when she recognized Bubba and Sis Hix. Bubba Jr. stood between his parents, waving enthusiastically at Amanda. His grimy hands were clenched around a magic marker and a coloring book.

The passenger door creaked open in invitation. The oversized man behind the wheel motioned for her to climb aboard. "Car trouble?" Bubba questioned.

Cop trouble, Amanda silently amended as she gestured for Bruno to hop in the pick-up bed. "My truck is at Last Chance. I need to pick it up."

Sis, who was at least ten months pregnant, scooted awkwardly toward her husband to make room on the seat. When Amanda sat down, Bubba Jr.—dressed in his Atlanta Braves t-shirt, ball cap and training pants—climbed across the back of the seat to park himself in Amanda's lap. He began jabbering in a language only his parents could understand.

"How are things going at Thatcher's Oil and Gas?" Amanda asked Bubba as he shifted into "drive."

"Can't complain. I'm gonna let Sis drop me off at work so she can have the truck this afternoon. She has a doctor's appointment." He smiled like a proud expectant father. "Should be only a few more weeks before our baby girl gets here."

Amanda cast Sis a discreet glance, while B.J. doodled in his coloring book. The poor overweight woman looked as if she should have delivered the baby a week ago.

"Sure will be glad when Sissy arrives," Sis said, patting her ballooned tummy. "I'm tired of waddling around like a duck."

B.J. yammered as he drew squiggles in his book. Amanda smiled affectionately as she glanced down at the greasy two-year-old who had never remained clean for more than a few hours in his entire life. There was no way B.J. could loosen his red magic marker from his fist. There was too much leftover lunch stuck on his fingers. Sis definitely had her hands full with this energetic tike and little Sissy on the way.

Amanda took pity on the expectant mother. After all, Amanda had become B.J.'s honorary aunt a few months back—while Amanda was trying to figure out who left Sheila MacAdo dead in the melon patch.

"How about if I keep Bubba Jr. for you while you're having your prenatal checkup," Amanda offered. "B.J. and I could stop in for some i-c-e c-r-e-a-m," she spelled out to prevent the little tike from bursting into a fit of excitement.

"Oh, no, I couldn't possibly let you do that," Sis replied as she raked her stringy hair from her face. "You've already figured our taxes for free and you paid me to clean your house until I swelled up like a watermelon. I can't impose. You're probably swamped with tax returns, and B.J. might wreak disaster on the papers with his magic marker. He's at the age when he scribbles on everything—Bubba Jr.!"

Sis shrieked. "Keep your doodling on the paper. Do not write on 'Manda's arm!"

Amanda glanced down to see the cherry-red squiggles B.J. had drawn on her forearm. The kid, Lord love him, was smiling proudly as he pointed to the picture he had drawn for Amanda.

"I'm really sorry," Bubba apologized. "My young son loves to draw—on everything."

"No problem," Amanda said, ruffling Bubba Jr.'s mop of matted hair.

"We forgot to congratulate you." Sis smiled as she tried to find a more comfortable position. In her condition, there didn't appear to be one. "We had a grand time watching you win the queen contest and ride in last night's ballgame. Hope you didn't hurt yourself when you fell on the floor. Sure was a great shot though—B.J., stop that!"

Amanda clamped her hand over Bubba Jr.'s fist before he tick-tack-toed her blouse.

The bucket-of-bolts truck ground to a stop in the restaurant parking lot. Amanda noticed that Chuck Gilhaney's clunker and Ron Newton's beat-up pick-up were parked beside her vehicle.

Was it time for a lunch break? Amanda glanced at her watch. It was high noon. It was the perfect opportunity to snoop around the commissioner's barn while no one was around.

When the Hix family drove off, Amanda and Bruno strode to the gas-guzzler. Amanda watched the Hixes pull into the service station so Bubba could return to work. Amanda made note of the fact that Thorn had cornered Harjo at the station before the commissioner could take his lunch break.

Perfect, Amanda thought as she sped down Main Street. She could check the personnel files of the workers in the road crew. She wanted to learn all she could about the men who worked for Dusty Brown and Sam Harjo. The information in the résumés might offer a clue about who had been in cahoots with Brown.

Amanda reached the commissioner's barn, which was located in an unpopulated area between Vamoose and Adios. There was only one pick-up in the driveway. Amanda identified it as Harjo's personal vehicle.

Glancing this way and that, Amanda hurried to the office. The door was locked. She expected that would be the case.

Spinning on her heels, Amanda scurried around the corner to check the office window. It, too, was locked. Amanda pulled her credit card from her purse, then inserted it between the aluminum frames to nudge the latch—a trick she'd picked watching *Magnum P.I.* re-runs.

The thought made her scowl. At the moment, she was none too happy with Tom Selleck's look-alike.

The lock on the left side of the window gave way after Amanda jockeyed the credit card sideways. Smiling triumphantly, she made short shrift of unfastening the lock on the right side of the window. Amanda lifted the window-pane, then flung a leg over the sill. In the blink of an eye she was scrambling through the opening.

Harjo's office was neat and tidy. There were stacks of invoices on his desk—all in alphabetical order.

Ah, a man with a sense of systematic orderliness. Unlike Thorn, who in his whole miserable life never made use of alphabetical filing, or the Dewey decimal system. The big lug!

Hurriedly, Amanda thumbed through the invoices, making certain Harjo's orders for supplies and equipment were on the up-and-up.

Sure enough, they were.

Pivoting, Amanda approached the metal file cabinet. In the first drawer she found a clump of files and correspondence from various supply companies who did business with county road maintenance. The same held true for drawer number two. All the information was filed alphabet-ically, and each file of correspondence was arranged in chronological order.

Squatting down, Amanda rolled open the bottom drawer. Bingo. The personnel files were hers for the snoop-ing. She went immediately to Sam Harjo's file and scanned the information.

Age thirty-five. A college graduate majoring in agricul-tural economics. Previously a nutritional expert for the Ralston Purina corporation. Formerly a rancher who also raised and trained Border Collies. Harjo had been employed by the county for seven years. He had been promoted to foreman after only two years.

The man had a spotless record—until Brown became commissioner, Amanda noticed. Since that time, Harjo's evaluation ratings had plummeted.

Amanda stuffed the file into its proper place, then pulled up Chuck Gilhaney's information. A wary frown knitted her brow when she read the file. Gilhaney had spent time in jail shortly after high school graduation, worked at a fast-food hamburger joint, then applied for a job on the road crew.

Why had Gilhaney been jailed? How long had he served? And for what? Theft?

Unfortunately, the file didn't specify the nature of his crime.

Amanda dug into the drawer to pull out Homer Frizzell's file. ''Well, I'll be darned, another jailbird,'' Amanda mused aloud.

Although Amanda was beginning to see a trend, she lifted Ron Newton's personal file. She wasn't surprised to learn that Newton had spent a spell in jail, in between employment references.

Deciding to be thorough, Amanda thumbed through the files of former employees. And whose name turned up? None other than John Smythe's. Now here was an interesting tidbit of information, thought Amanda. The former rodeo bull rider had also been jailed before applying for a job. Smythe had been employed for six months before he left. To begin training and hauling donkeys, Amanda presumed.

The muffled swish of the office door caused Amanda to spin on her haunches. She glanced up to see Harjo's massive form, spotlighted by afternoon sunlight. His shadow fell across Amanda. She swallowed uneasily.

What was the proper comment to make when you got caught trespassing and rummaging through personnel files? *Oops?*

No, she decided. She needed to come up with something better than that. Unfortunately, she wasn't feeling too creative at the moment.

Thirteen

"Did you enjoy your lunch?" Amanda asked. It was the best she could do on the spur of the moment. She waited, wondering if Harjo was going to blow his stack.

"I didn't get lunch." Calmly as you please, Harjo hung his hat on the hook, then closed the door. "Instead, I was grilled evenly on both sides by the chief of police." Harjo dropped into his chair and propped his booted feet on the edge of his desk. "The Lone Ranger can be a real bad-ass when he feels like it. He was in top form at noon."

Amanda suspected Thorn had taken his irritation for her out on Harjo.

"Thorn was firing leading questions like bullets," Harjo continued. "If you aren't quick-minded, he'll drag you right into a confession, whether you're guilty or not."

Since she had been caught snooping, Amanda didn't try to sneak the file back into the drawer. She simply replaced it swiftly and efficiently. Closing the drawer, she rose to her feet. She waited an uneasy moment, expecting Harjo to use her for a scapegoat after Thorn had fired questions at him. To her surprise, Harjo merely studied her in the light slanting through the window.

"Well? Aren't you going to yell at me?" she prompted, deciding a good chewing was preferable to this uncertain silence.

"No. Did you find what you were looking for, Hazard?"

"Yes. Unfortunately, my findings invite more questions and provide few answers."

"Might as well fire away at me. Thorn certainly did. The only thing your fiancé *didn't* ask was my religious preference. However, he was very intent on knowing my blood type."

"Why?"

"Why what? Why did he want to know my blood type?" Chuckling, Harjo leaned back in his chair. "Just in case he decides to beat the hell out of me—or tries to—I suspect. He must think I'll need a transfusion in the near future."

Amanda eased a hip onto the edge of the desk, noting that Harjo studied every move she made. He was very attentive.

"Who hired the jailbirds to work for the county? You or Brown?" she asked flat-out.

If Harjo was uncomfortable with the question, he didn't show it. He was cool under fire. Rarely did he leave the impression that he had something to hide. "I did."

Amanda found the answer very incriminating, even if Harjo didn't. Although Harjo claimed Brown had offered him a cut in the kickbacks, the statement could have been a misrepresentation of the truth. Who was to say Brown and Harjo hadn't been splitting the kickbacks and perks the past few years?

Amanda made a mental note to check out Harjo's personal workshop to see if he had expensive tools lining the walls. She was beginning to think there was a racket going on here. The *ugly* side of politics—according to Harjo himself.

Harjo and his brother-in-law could have been reaping benefits until they had a falling out. Brown's pending divorce could have been a sore spot between them. After all, Sara Mae was Harjo's younger sister. Being the protective brother, Harjo wouldn't take kindly to Brown's philandering and his nasty comments about his estranged wife.

"Aren't you going to ask why I hired young men who served a little time in the county jail?" he questioned calmly.

"I think I already know."

Her reply put an unexpected expression on his craggy features. Amanda wasn't certain, but she thought Harjo looked a bit disappointed.

Harjo reached over to pick up the phone, then handed her the receiver. "Go ahead and call the big bad-ass cop," he insisted. "Tell him you've got the lead he was trying to wrench from me."

"Funny that you should say *wrench,*" Amanda said, replacing the phone. Marshaling her courage, she stood up to leave. She breathed a sigh of relief when Harjo didn't pounce on her. She half expected him to.

Was the man innocent or guilty as sin? Amanda sincerely wished she could decide which.

"Hazard?"

Amanda halted, her hand wrapped around the door knob. She looked back, wondering if Harjo had lulled her into thinking he wasn't a threat—right up to the moment he launched a surprise attack. She anticipated seeing a pistol aimed at her back.

There wasn't a pistol, only a wry smile aimed in her direction.

"Why don't you come by my place tonight and I'll answer your questions for you—in detail."

Oh sure, she thought. *Nothing like being found alone at*

Harjo's place so soon after she and Thorn had called it quits. The news will be all over town before I return home for the night. Folks will start speculating exactly how long we've been carrying on behind Thorn's back.

Amanda neither accepted nor declined the offer. She exited the office. But to her dismay she noticed two employees lounging outside the shop, smoking an after-lunch cigarette.

Ron Newton and Homer Frizzell took one look at her, glanced toward the office, then grinned at each other.

Amanda tossed them what she hoped was a nonchalant greeting. As she drove away she glanced in the rearview mirror to see Ron and Homer snickering. She'd suspected that would be the case. Her accidental encounter with Harjo was drawing plenty of speculation. Harjo would find that amusing, she predicted. For some reason, the man liked to watch her squirm.

Why? She hadn't figured that out yet.

Although Amanda had planned to complete Thorn's tax returns that afternoon, she decided to put the big lug's 1040 on hold. He was getting his returns on the fifteenth—and not a day earlier.

Heading due south, Amanda took the back roads to Sam Harjo's farm. She was determined to see if Harjo had been stealing tools for his personal use, same as Brown had.

When Amanda turned into the driveway she glanced toward the barn. The blood-red gelding was back in its pen, munching on a block of hay. Apparently Vinita had fed the horse after taking her morning ride.

Amanda frowned, wondering if Vinita, like her hubby and her pal Smythe, had once been in trouble with the law. There was one way to find out—call Thorn and asked him to check.

The thought caused Amanda to scowl. She and Thorn

had heard enough from each other for one day. But, she reminded herself, she couldn't allow personal conflict to interfere in this investigation. She needed facts and MOs. Too bad she hadn't thought to stick the cellular phone in her truck. She could have called Thorn on the spot— *before* she returned his gift to him. Considering the friction between them, she couldn't keep it.

Parking beside the barn so her transportation wouldn't be noticed by passersby, Amanda left Bruno behind. The dog whined when he was forced to remain in the truck. Amanda ignored the canine plea and strode into the barn to have a look-see.

There were several tools lining the walls of the small shop that had been built inside the barn. Amanda checked the brand name to see if Harjo's supplier matched Brown's. It didn't. Harjo's tools looked well used, unlike the brand spanking new ones that hung like trophies on Brown's walls.

That could mean one of two things, Amanda mused. Either Harjo wasn't swiping tools or he sold his share for profits.

Amanda turned to leave . . . and found Vinita Frizzell barricading the exit.

"What are you doing here?" Vinita demanded curtly.

Amanda threw the question back at the silicon blonde. "What are *you* doing here?"

"I live here," Vinita replied icily.

"Oh really?" Amanda glanced around the barn. "Nice living room you have here."

"Real funny, Hazard. You're a laugh a minute. You think you're hot stuff, just because you're the Donkey Queen and you have two men panting after you."

Amanda had no intention of getting into a cat fight with this spiteful female. "Look, Vinita—"

"No, you look," she hissed as she stamped forward. "I

don't want you poking your nose around here. This is private property.''

"If that's so, why are you trotting down from your trailer house to saddle Harjo's horse whenever it meets your whim?"

"Because he said I could do it anytime I please!" she spewed angrily.

When Amanda veered around the human obstacle, Vinita grabbed her by the elbow. "Hey, lighten up, Vinita. You're getting your way. I'm leaving.''

"If I had my way, you'd be—"

Vinita swallowed the remainder of her comment, then glowered. "Don't think I won't tell Sam you were here.''

"I don't think he's going to be the least bit surprised to hear it. After I saw him this afternoon, I think he was expecting it.''

The remark caught Vinita off guard. She was still trying to puzzle out what Amanda meant when the jalopy truck sped off.

Nick plopped down in his living room chair, grabbed the TV remote and channel-surfed. His confrontation with Hazard, and his interview with Harjo, had soured what was left of his rotten mood. Interrogating Isaac Marcum had proved as exasperating as Hazard predicted. The old coot refused to admit he had seen—or heard—anything that fateful day when Brown had been found dead in the mud.

Dealing with the two smart-ass teenagers he'd caught speeding on his way home had topped off a lousy day. By the time Nick turned the police beat over to the part-time sheriff's deputy, who was eager to earn extra cash, Nick was mentally exhausted.

"That's what you get for trying to function with a hangover,'' Nick chastised himself as he landed on the news channel.

When some highhanded journalist began spouting about corruption in police departments, Nick scowled and switched to the weather channel. He could deal with high and low pressure systems—as long as they weren't his.

Lulled by the meteorologist's soothing voice, Nick nodded off. The blaring phone brought him awake with a start.

"Thorn here."

"Nicky, it's Mom. Dad and I are in the city. We decided to spend the night with your brother."

"In the city?" Nick repeated stupidly.

"Well, yes. The wedding shower is at two o'clock tomorrow afternoon."

Aw, damn, Nick muttered to himself. He had forgotten to call Mom early this morning. Considering his falling out with Hazard there couldn't possibly be a wedding shower. Hell, at this point, there might never be a *wedding!*

"Dad and I will be at the farm around noon tomorrow. Rich is coming, too," Mom informed him. "We'll pick up some barbecue and bring it out for lunch."

"Sounds good." Nick decided to let it go at that. He'd break the news about being *dis*engaged over barbecued ribs.

"See you then, Nicky. I can't tell you how anxious I am to meet this Hazard woman."

Nick made a neutral sound, then disconnected. There had been so many distractions lately that he had lost track of the days. He wondered if Hazard was suffering the same mental lapse. Probably not. The woman always seemed to function at peak efficiency. Hazard had undoubtedly remembered to call Velma and cancel the shower, but Nick decided he'd better double-check. Before he could pick up the phone it rang.

"Thorn here."

"It's Hazard," she said in a rush. "I have a request."

What? Drop dead? he thought pessimistically.

"I sneaked into Harjo's office at lunch to rifle through the personnel files—"

"You what?" he howled.

"Can it, Thorn. Just listen for once in your miserable life," Hazard sniped, then plowed ever onward. "You're not going to believe this—"

"Sure I will. I saw you breaking and entering Brown's workshop. Why wouldn't I believe you cased Harjo's office?"

"Look, Thorn, I don't have time for your wisecracks," she went on huffily. "I still have to finish up your 1040 this weekend so Jenny can type them up Monday and get them to you by Tuesday for postmarking on the fifteenth. Unless you want to pay the IRS penalty, you better clam up."

He should never have turned his tax voucher over to Hazard. Wouldn't you know she would hold it over his head.

"Okay, Hazard, what was the big deal at Harjo's office?"

"That's better, Thorn," she said—exactly like a woman who knew she held the upper hand. "Each and every one of the road crew who work for Harjo have done jail time. Even that donkey owner who was in charge of last night's ballgame used to work for the county, and he's seen the inside of a jail, too."

"I'll be damned," Nick murmured.

"I'm sure you will, but in the meantime, I'd like you to use your influence to find out what Smythe, Newton, Frizzell and Gilhaney did to land them in jail. Check on Vinita, too. I'm wondering if there is a theft ring at work in the county commissioner's department. I didn't find any tools in Harjo's personal workshop, but—"

"Lord, Hazard, did you B-and-E his place, too?"

"Didn't have to. The barn door wasn't locked."

"Are there any laws you didn't break today?" he asked sarcastically—he couldn't help himself.

"Yes," she fired back. "I didn't kill you when you left me standing on the side of the road."

"You told me to," he said defensively.

"Since when did you start listening to what I said?"

Nick wasn't going to step on *that* land mine. He had learned better.

"I was mad at you and I didn't know what I was saying," Hazard added.

"I hope you came to your senses and remembered to call Velma and inform her that, since we have become *dis*engaged, tomorrow's wedding shower is inappropriate."

"Shower? Tomorrow? Yikes, I forgot all about it after I found out that the road crew had been in jail!"

Aha, thought Nick. *So the infallible female mind does have a few glitches. That's good to know.*

"Geez, Thorn, what are we going to do? I can't call Velma at this late hour. She and Bev are probably over at the school cafeteria decorating for the shower right now. Velma has invited every woman in town." Hazard groaned into the phone. "And Mother will be there."

"Mom drove all the way up from Texas. She and Dad are already in the city visiting my brother," Nick told her. "So, what are you going to do about it?"

"Me? This wingding wasn't *my* idea, you know."

"Maybe not, but it was your place to cancel it."

The comment was followed by a long moment of silence. Nick suspected Hazard's mind was racing. He could almost hear the gears grinding.

"If it's too late to cancel, without putting the citizens of Vamoose in a tailspin—"

"Not to mention my mom and your mother," Nick put it.

Another long, stilted silence.

"I guess we'll just have to bluff our way through this shower," Hazard said finally.

"Are we going to bluff our way through the wedding, too?" Nick asked. "Just to keep up pretense for the good citizens of Vamoose?"

"Damn it, Thorn. I swear you are enjoying this predicament."

"Where did we go wrong, Hazard?" Nick asked after a moment.

"Somewhere on the road between Adios and Vamoose. The minute you let me out of the squad car, to be exact."

"I'm sorry, Hazard," he murmured.

"So am I, Thorn," she whispered.

If he wasn't mistaken there was a slight hitch in her voice. Maybe all wasn't lost—yet.

"Will you call me back the minute you get the info about the road crew's criminal records?"

"You'll be the first to know."

"Good, because I think I'm finally on the right track. 'Bye, Thorn."

Nick gently replaced the receiver, as if hanging on an extra moment would strengthen the shaky connection between them. He asked himself at what exact point in time things between himself and Hazard had deteriorated. Sure, they'd had their ups and downs, their ins and outs, but that was before—

"Before Harjo," Nick said aloud, then scowled.

Refusing to dwell on his personal problems, Nick kick-started his mind and shifted into police mode. "Okay, Harjo, let's see what kind of undercover racket you've got going in the commissioner's office that might have prompted you to take Brown out."

Nick sat upright in his chair, plucked up the phone and called an old acquaintance at OKCPD. Within a few minutes, faxes were sent to the Vamoose police department. Nick grabbed his keys and headed to town to see what the investigative search had turned up.

* * *

Amanda paced the living room floor, her brain hitting on all eight cylinders. From his customary place beside the door, Bruno watched her circumnavigate the room.

Holy cow, thought Amanda, how could she have forgotten about the wedding shower? This whole marriage thing had snowballed into epic proportions. The recent falling out between herself and Thorn forced them to play along with Velma's shower plans.

Maybe Mother had been right—for once. Maybe Velma did need to get a life, instead of trying to commandeer Amanda's. But the poor, dear beautician had her heart set on giving the grandest shower Vamoose had ever seen. Velma would be crushed if Amanda left a message on the answering machine, declaring the wedding shower had to be called off the night before it was scheduled.

Amanda flung herself around and paced in the opposite direction. Bruno followed her with his eyes. Well, fiddle-dee-dee, there was nothing else to do but follow Scarlett O'Hara's policy of worrying about that tomorrow. Amanda had to process Thorn's tax returns tonight, because she would be otherwise occupied tomorrow afternoon. She was the honorary guest at a shower that might not have the traditional wedding to go with it!

And then there was this exasperating, frustrating case, she reminded herself irritably. As soon as Thorn gathered the needed information, maybe Amanda could get a handle on it. In the meantime, she had to concentrate on calculating Thorn's taxes. She had Schedules A, C, F and SEs to fill out, and Forms 2210, 4562, 4797 and 8824 forms to calculate for Thorn's farming profits and depreciations.

Determined, Amanda plunked down at the dining room table, penciled in the numerical figures, then studied the depreciation tables supplied by the IRS.

Sometime after midnight the phone broke the silence.

Amanda, who was deep in concentration, nearly leaped out of her skin. Heart pounding, she scrambled from her chair to answer the call.

"Hazard's Accounting . . . I mean, hello?"

"It's Thorn."

Amanda forced herself to set aside the emotional turmoil incited by Thorn's husky baritone voice. She was still peeved at him. Their wedding plans were in a holding pattern, and she was beginning to think their relationship would never fly right again.

"Did you have any luck getting info on the road crew?" she asked in an impersonal tone.

"Yes, but I'm not sure I should divulge it to you. After all, you aren't authorized personnel."

"I may not be a cop," she countered, calling on her depleted patience, "but I'm the one who has been gathering information about Brown's associates. Therefore, I can assimilate the facts faster than you can at this point."

"Okay, Hazard, I'll tell you what I found out, because I still . . . like you . . . even though we're . . . you know."

"Yeah, Thorn, I know." Amanda smiled to herself. The sexy country cop was trying to call a truce. Her irritation with him dropped a few degrees. "So . . . what's the scoop on the road crew?"

"Ron Newton served time in the county jail for possession of marijuana," Thorn reported. "Frizzell landed in the slammer for drunk and reckless driving. Gilhaney was arrested for speeding and driving without a license, turning off lights to avoid identification and resisting arrest. In all cases, no one could go the bail so the boys spent time in the county jail."

"What about John Smythe and Vinita Frizzell?"

Thorn chuckled. "Now here's an odd one. The brother and sister rodeo team—"

Brother and sister? Amanda blinked, startled. Then she reminded herself that in small-town American you couldn't swing a dead cat without hitting somebody's relative. Kissing cousins, shirttail cousins, aunts and uncles were as thick as swarms of mosquitoes.

"John and Vinita were arrested for horse theft after they participated in a rodeo at Pronto."

Amanda recalled that Vinita claimed she hadn't been selected as rodeo queen. That also explained why Vinita took Harjo's horse out for an occasional spin. Amanda also remembered hearing that John Smythe had been a bull rider.

"So the story goes," Thorn continued. "John claimed he won the horse in an all-night poker game. When the drunken card player sobered up, he filed charges for horse theft."

"Who wound up with the horse?" Amanda quizzed.

It was a long moment before Thorn responded. "Harjo did."

Damn, the man's name kept cropping up with amazing regularity. "The horse didn't happen to be a blood-red gelding with a palomino mane and tail, did it?"

"Hold on a sec. Let me check."

Amanda tapped her foot impatiently while Thorn scanned the faxes.

"Yep. Your description matches. John and Vinita were released from jail after the *misunderstanding* was settled. A man named Clarence Reams was paid—in cash."

"When did the incident take place?"

"Almost two years ago."

"Thanks for the info," Amanda murmured, immersed in thought.

"Well? Do you see any connection?"

"At the moment, no, but it'll come to me eventually," Amanda replied.

"I expect to be the first to know when it does," Thorn demanded. "Don't go off half-cocked, the way you usually do, when you think you're ready to wrap up a case. If it's

Harjo you need to go after, I intend to be the one who arrests him."

"Sure, Thorn, whatever you say."

"Don't patronize me," he growled at her. "I want your word on it."

"What word?" she muttered when he got pushy.

"You know what I mean. I expect you to call. That's why I bought you that damned mobile phone!"

The line went dead. Amanda hung up, then returned to the tax forms that were scattered across the table. According to Thorn, the road crew's conflicts with the law were low-risk crimes that required minimal support and control needs after release. Not particularly noteworthy, Amanda noted. No one on payroll was drawing unnecessary suspicion.

Interesting.

So what was Harjo's angle? she wondered.

Amanda was still asking herself that question when she fell asleep at the table, her head resting on tax vouchers. She awoke sometime later. Trudging off to bed, Amanda reminded herself that it would take time to solve the case. Once all the bits and pieces of information gelled in her mind, she could formulate her theory on who, how and why.

Collecting facts and gathering clues in investigation was like making wine, Amanda thought as she collapsed on her bed. She simply had to wait for all the ingredients to ferment in the vat of her mind.

On that optimistic thought, Amanda fell into an exhausted sleep. She had met the tax deadline, finishing Thorn's 1040 just under the wire . . .

Nick left the faxes on the seat of his truck and strode toward the school cafeteria. The place had been locked up tight. With flashlight in hand, Nick stared through the

glass doors. He wanted to take a gander at the decorations
Bev and Velma had spent the evening thumb-tacking into
place.

As the beam of light swept across the cinder block walls,
Nick groaned aloud. Velma had somehow managed to get
her hands on photos of Nick and Hazard. Preschool and
adolescent snapshots had been enlarged into posters.

God, Nick's reputation as an efficient chief of police
would be ruined forever! There was a poster of him in
diapers—his thumb stuck in his mouth!

Nick snickered as the beam of light tipped upward, illu-
minating the photo of a young girl who had her share of
baby fat. Hazard's hair fanned out in all directions—kind
of like a disturbed porcupine prepared to fling quills.

It seemed that bad hair hairdos had been in Hazard's
destiny.

Focusing the flashlight on the head table that sat against
the north wall, Nick appraised the napkins, plastic dishes
and centerpiece. With a disbelieving shake of his head, he
asked himself where Velma and her niece had come up
with their weird ideas for the shower. When Hazard's
sophisticated-minded mother saw the decor, she would be
howling in astonishment.

The centerpiece was not made of the customary flowers,
it was constructed from supplies found in the beauty shop.
Hair rollers of various sizes and shapes had been glued
together to form flower petals. Bobby pins and plastic hair
clips served as artificial leaves. Hair nets, sprayed stiff with
lacquer, had been substituted for baby's breath greenery.
The entire conglomeration had been spray-painted in passion pink and Prussian purple to match the satin bows and
balloons which were taped to the walls and ceiling.

Good Lord, Nick thought, as he surveyed the miniature
arrangements that had been placed on each table. The
shower decorations were too ridiculous for words!

Flicking off the flashlight, Nick returned to his truck.

He could imagine Mom's reaction to the decorations. Mom had already made it known that she frowned on this "mixed" marriage. Big city girls and down-home farm boys had no business getting hitched.

The shower was going to be a disaster, Nick predicted as he drove home. As for the wedding, he wasn't certain there would be one. Nick had the unshakable feeling that his prospective wedding hinged on Sam Harjo's guilt or innocence in the Brown case.

"Helluva development," Nick muttered to himself. He needed to devote his time to opening an official investigation, but his parents and his brother would arrive at noon tomorrow. When was he supposed to squeeze in time to determine if someone actually had hammered Brown on the head and left him dead in the mud?

Fourteen

Amanda crawled from bed and staggered toward the bathroom. She was not looking forward to today's activities. She hoped a refreshing, eye-opening shower would enable her to face the hectic encounters awaiting her.

Squeaky clean, Amanda stepped from the shower, feeling like a new woman. She returned to her bedroom, hoping she had scrubbed enough shampoo into her hair to remove the tint and glitter. One look in the mirror told her she hadn't. Her hair still had purple highlights.

"The things I let Velma do to my hair in my quest for truth and justice," Amanda muttered as she combed out the tangles.

With blow dryer in hand, Amanda made an effort to style the latest cosmetic calamity. Tufts of hair, embedded with glitter, stuck out in every direction, making the shingled hairdo even more pronounced.

No matter what method Amanda tried, she couldn't tame down the thick mass of uneven hair.

"Face it, Hazard, you're going to look like a French poodle . . ."

Her voice evaporated when she noticed that soap and water hadn't erased the magic-marker squiggles Bubba Jr. had drawn on her arm the previous afternoon. The little tike had given her a tattoo that refused to be washed away.

A fragment of memory tumbled into place in Amanda's mind. Her magic-marker tattoo reminded her of the one she had seen on two occasions.

"Holy cow!" Amanda crowed when another scrap of half-forgotten memory hit her between the eyes.

Heart pounding, Amanda wheeled around to grab her clothes. She glanced at her watch as she jerked on her jeans. She had enough time to drive out to confront her suspect with her knowledge, then hightail it back home to dress for the wedding shower.

Worming into a t-shirt on her way down the hall, Amanda snatched up her purse, keys and the cellular phone. Bruno met her at the front door.

"Come on, pal, we have a case to crack."

Bruno didn't bother with his customary good-morning growl as he trotted past the three-legged dog that was sprawled on the porch. The Border Collie hopped into the truck the instant Amanda opened the door.

Amanda put the pedal to the metal, slinging new gravel as she sped away.

Taking the highway that circled toward Adios, Amanda veered past Brown's home, then caromed toward Sam Harjo's farm. She noticed Sam's personal transportation parked in the driveway as she whizzed past. She also noticed the horse was not in its pen. Good. She preferred to deal with Homer Frizzell—alone.

Amanda followed the narrow dirt path to the trailer house. She glanced down at the cellular phone that was sitting beside her. She had better call Thorn—as he'd demanded.

Amanda opened the black leather case and punched in

the number. Nothing. Not a dial tone, not even a beep or squall.

"Worthless piece of electronic junk," Amanda grumbled as she climbed from the truck. She would simply have to call Thorn later. It was *his* fault that stupid phone didn't work.

Shoulders squared, feet braced, Amanda rapped on the door. Homer Frizzell answered after the second knock, then blinked in surprise.

"What the heck are you doing here?"

Amanda stared at Homer's bare chest, then focused absolute attention on the bulging bicep of his left arm. She gestured her candy-striped finger toward the red squiggles on her own arm.

"Notice the resemblance?" she asked.

Homer frowned warily. "What are you up to, Hazard?"

"It's not what *I'm* up to," she contended. "It's what *you* have been up to, which is no good—"

Amanda yelped when Homer's hand snaked out to clamp around her forearm. Before she could react, he hauled her inside and locked the door.

It was then that Amanda sincerely wished she had called Thorn before leaving home. She could have used a backup. Now, Homer had her in a bear hug—his brawny arm hooked around her neck, restricting her air supply.

"You just couldn't leave it alone, could you?" he growled in her ear.

Amanda couldn't reply. The pressure being exerted on her throat caused her vocal apparatus to shut down.

"Now you've screwed up everything."

Homer stuffed Amanda into the chair by the table. Before she could bolt and run, he snatched up the tablecloth and tied her to the chair.

"Homer, don't make things worse than they are," Amanda wheezed, straining against the makeshift rope.

"Hell, they're as bad as they can get, thanks to you!" Homer yelled at her. "You've ruined my life!"

"You didn't do much for Brown's life, now did you?" she pointed out.

Big mistake, she realized too late. Homer let loose with a string of four-letter words that would have had Salty Marcum blushing.

"The world is better off without Brown in it," Homer snapped. "Too bad you couldn't have kept your nose out of it. Now you leave me with no choice."

The comment did not sound encouraging. Homer was getting desperate. Amanda could see his eyes darting around the compact trailer, the beads of sweat popping out on his forehead.

Homer began pacing back and forth, mentally plotting his next move. Amanda decided she had better distract him before he devised a plan to dispose of her.

"I realized that what I thought was an *S* drawn in the mud was actually a snake that resembled your tattoo. Brown was trying to identify his killer," she blurted out while Homer paced the floorboards.

He stopped short, then rounded on her. "That's how you figured this out?"

Amanda nodded. "I also know that you took off after Brown left the commissioner's barn that morning. Vinita had a hair appointment, but since she doesn't drive, you had to pick her up. You tracked Brown down while Vinita was getting a bleach job. Of course, it didn't take you long to locate Brown because you knew exactly where he would be, didn't you?"

"Yeah, I knew," Homer muttered. "The son-of-a-bitch was out there giving Harjo hell. I'd had all of Brown and his dirty dealings that I could stomach and I wanted to tell him so."

Amanda nodded in understanding. "You were the one who swiped the tools from the shipments that arrived at the commissioner's barn. Then you handed them over to Brown.''

Homer blinked in surprise. "How'd you come up with that?"

"Simple. You're the head mechanic at the shop. It's only natural that you would be the one to inventory the tools and equipment that arrived.''

"Damn it," Homer grumbled. "We're both going to wish you weren't so smart before long.''

"What happened, Homer?'' Amanda pressed, refusing to give him time to plan his means of escape. "What did Brown do that made you so desperate to shut him up? Was he going to blame your thefts on Harjo? Did Brown want his political opponent to take the rap? Did Brown need you to corroborate his story?''

Homer's frizzy head bobbed up and down. "That's exactly what Brown had in mind. He was going to try to talk Harjo into taking a few kickbacks, but I knew Harjo wouldn't do it. He's too honest, too decent, too damned good-hearted.

"I couldn't let Brown take Harjo down," Homer went on, his words pouring out in a rush. "If it wasn't for Harjo, none of us would have jobs on the road crew. Harjo hired young men who had gotten off to a rocky start. He supervised us, instructed us, laid down rules and saw to it that we toed the line until we got our acts together.''

"And when Harjo decrees that you can have only one beer after a hard day's work, you observe his policy,'' Amanda added thoughtfully.

Homer nodded again. "We do what Harjo says because we know he has our best interests at heart. He's turned misbehaving boys into men. He's gotten all of us out of scrapes at one time or another, but we don't hold a grudge when he comes down hard on us, because he's made the effort to save our asses when nobody else—our own families included—ever bothered.''

Amanda frowned pensively. "So why did you betray him by joining forces with Brown?"

"Betray him?" Homer howled. "I would never, *ever* betray Harjo. Hell, he lets me park my trailer here for nothing. He gives Vinita a lift when I'm tied up. He lets her ride the horse whenever she pleases. Harjo is like a big brother! When Brown hounded me into swiping the tools and hauling them out of the shop, I thought I was doing Harjo a favor."

Amanda blinked, bemused. "A favor?"

Homer nodded his bushy head. "Brown assured me that he and Harjo had ordered the tools and shop supplies through the companies the county dealt with because they could get them at wholesale cost. Brown said the goods would be paid for separately. I was supposed to load the stuff in Brown's truck so he could drop it off to Harjo on his way home. At the time, I had my trailer house parked at Pronto, not up here," he explained.

"I didn't realize I'd been suckered into Brown's extortion scheme until the invoices began to arrive. I kept my mouth shut because I'd already made the delivery, and I was too embarrassed to tell Harjo that I was stupid enough to fall for Brown's sneaky trick."

"But Brown wouldn't let you off the hook after he had lured you in," Amanda continued for him. "He used your devotion to Harjo to his advantage, didn't he? Let me guess, Brown swore he would make you look the culprit if you breathed a word about it to Harjo."

Homer nodded bleakly. 'The son-of-a-bitch held it over my head every time he decided to add a new line of tools and supplies to his personal workshop. Brown threatened to fire me if I didn't continue to cooperate with his embezzling scheme. He even forced me to accept a few kickback checks, cash them, and turn the money over to him."

Amanda groaned inwardly. Homer had fallen into Brown's trap and the snare had closed around his throat.

But obviously Harjo had gotten suspicious when he checked the invoices. Amanda had been in Harjo's office. She knew he thoroughly examined correspondence and invoices, because she had seen them on his desk, and stored neatly in the file cabinet.

"So you're the reason Harjo was reluctant to use the information against Brown during the election campaign," she assumed. "Harjo didn't want you implicated, did he?"

Again Homer bobbed his fuzzy head, while continuing his nervous pacing. "I knew I had to stop Brown before he twisted the facts and accused Harjo of embezzling. The bastard ordered me to haul the tools from his workshop and plant them in Harjo's barn so he could make public accusations about misuse of funds."

"That's why Brown towed you into the corner for a private conversation that morning," Amanda guessed. "He let everyone think he was chewing on you, just as he had chewed on them."

"Yeah, he was a cunning bastard," Homer replied. "I knew he was going to offer Harjo a cut of the kickbacks and profits, then set him up for the fall. I knew Brown would take me down, too. I had to stop him. For Harjo's sake, I *had* to!"

Amanda winced when Homer's voice elevated ten decibels. She appraised her apprehensive captor, watching dribbles of perspiration stream down his face. He swiped at the sweat that burned his eyes.

Yes, Homer was definitely getting overanxious. He wasn't sure what to do next. Amanda vowed to keep him talking, hoping she could worm loose and save herself before Homer's desperation took him over the edge.

"So you decided to dispose of Brown while he was stuck in the mud," she said before Homer could turn his thoughts to his escape plan.

"Hell no!" he snapped at her.

"No?" Amanda repeated, confused. "But I thought—"

"When Harjo drove off to the commissioner's barn on the bulldozer, I climbed on the horse and trotted through the ravine," Homer interrupted. "Brown was jacking up his flat tire when I arrived. He told me to change the tire, then round up the cattle that had broken through the fence. I told Brown he could fix his own tire and chase his cattle, because I was through taking orders from him. He got mad and kicked the horse, causing it to slam into the side of the truck. The jack slipped in the mud, knocking Brown off balance. When he got mud all over himself he started yelling his head off, blaming *me* for it."

Geez, Amanda thought, Brown should have written a book entitled, *One Thousand and One Ways To Be A Jerk*.

"I told Brown, right there and then, that I'd take the blame for embezzlement, but no way was I naming Harjo as an accomplice. I intended to name *Brown*. Even if I went to jail because of it, I wasn't going to let Harjo take any heat."

"And Brown lost his temper—for the umpteenth time that day," Amanda put in.

"He blew his top all right. He grabbed the jack handle and took a swing at me while I was still on horseback." Homer presented his back, gesturing to the elongated purple bruise that stretched from his shoulder to his spine.

"You came off the horse to get even," she presumed.

"Damned right I did—or at least I tried to," Homer gritted out. "I'd had a belly full of Brown. But the SOB hit me on the leg before I could get my hands on him. My leg buckled under when I leaped from the horse. Brown raised the jack handle to hit me and—"

Homer slammed his mouth shut like a crocodile, then paced some more. "None of that matters now. I've got to think, got to plan."

That was the very last thing Amanda wanted Homer to do! Desperate men concocted desperate schemes. She preferred to escape from this mess alive.

"And then what happened?" Amanda demanded to know.

Homer stopped short, lurched around, then glowered at her. "Oh no you don't, Hazard. That's all you're going to hear from me."

The fact that Homer refused to finish the story caused warning bells to clang in Amanda's mind. She had the unmistakable feeling that Homer hadn't gotten out of the scrape by himself. If Brown held the jack handle and was prepared to make another strike, someone must have come to Homer's rescue.

Hmm . . . interesting. So who had arrived on the scene to save Homer from getting his head bashed in? She ruled out Harjo, because he had driven off in the bulldozer. That left Sonny Snittiger and Salty Marcum.

Amanda made an educated guess and plowed ahead, watching carefully for Homer's initial reaction. "So Salty Marcum sneaked up behind Brown, grabbed the jack handle and clubbed Brown before he could clobber you again."

Sure enough, Homer's initial reaction gave him away. She was right on target.

"Salty pounded Brown before he knew what hit him," Amanda hurried on before Homer could deny Salty's part in the incident. "Suppressed anger and revenge packed a mighty wallop, I suspect. Brown didn't know who had hit him, did he?"

Homer's head dropped to his bulky chest. His hands knotted into fists. "I lunged at Brown while his arm was raised to strike. Everything happened so fast that Brown probably didn't know exactly what had happened."

"So Salty shooed you on your way before either of you were spotted," Amanda guessed. "He knew Sonny and Sara Mae were up at Brown's house and that they had a bird's eye view of that stretch of road."

Homer nodded, still flexing and contracting his fists in

a nervous gesture. "Salty helped me climb back on the horse so we could round up the stray cattle. Bruno bounded from the back of the truck to help."

Homer, Amanda imagined, knew which commands to give Bruno. He had probably watched Harjo train his dogs a hundred times.

"Once we had the fence patched up, we went back to see if Brown had roused. We didn't realize he was facedown in a tire rut that stood full of water until it was too late. Hell, we didn't know he'd drowned!"

"Salty sent you off to pick up Vinita from the beauty shop," Amanda ventured. "That's why the two of you made a pact to keep silent, only you got nervous when I brought Salty home with me. You were the one who was sneaking around my hen house."

"Yeah, I was afraid Salty was going to blab since he had wished Brown dead for so long. I swear that crazy old man would have taken the rap himself if I hadn't talked him out of it. He saved my life and I couldn't let him take the blame . . ."

When Homer's voice trailed off, Amanda inwardly flinched. She could see a sense of resolve flooding over Homer. The man had arrived at some distorted sense of resolution.

That was not good!

"I won't let Salty take the blame," he said firmly. "I'm not going to let Harjo get tangled up in this mess, either. There's only one thing left for me to do."

Uh-oh, Amanda thought when Homer stared grimly at her.

"Harjo always said that a man wasn't a man if he didn't accept his responsibilities. I guess this is what he meant."

Double uh-oh, thought Amanda. Homer saw himself as some self-sacrificing crusader. She was in mega-trouble!

A firm rap rattled the door hinges. Homer spun around,

presenting Amanda with an unhindered view of the nasty bruise on his back.

"Homer, is this Hazard's truck out here? What's going on?"

"Shit!" Homer hissed, glancing wildly around.

Amanda gulped hard. The very last man Homer Frizzell needed to encounter right now was Sam Harjo, his mentor, his idol, his guardian angel. Homer was too ashamed to admit that he had botched up badly.

"Homer, open up," Harjo demanded.

The command sent Homer into a distressed frenzy. He raced down the hall, returning a few seconds later with a double-barrel shotgun.

Amanda hit the panic button. "Take it easy, Homer. We can work this out. You've got to keep your head." *Or I'll get mine blown clean off!* "I'm sure that after I explain the entire situation to Thorn—"

"Thorn! That's it!" Homer burst out in sudden inspiration.

The speaking end of the weapon stared Amanda in the face. "What's it?" Cross-eyed, she gaped at the death-maker, too rattled to think straight.

Homer ignored her question and stared at the locked door. "Go call Thorn," he hollered at Harjo. "I'm holding Hazard hostage. I want safe passage out of the country or I'll burn down this trailer and blow Hazard to bits."

There was an uneasy pause. Homer flicked off the safety lock and fiddled with the trigger of the shotgun.

"Damn it, Homer, don't do anything crazy," Harjo called back.

"Get Thorn on the phone," Homer blared. "Tell him I want a chopper out here and an airline ticket PDQ or Hazard will be history."

"Homer—"

"Call Thorn now or Hazard's dead meat!"

The clatter on the wooden steps indicated Harjo had raced home to make the phone call.

Nick breathed a sigh of relief when Mom drove off to the shower. Since the moment Mom arrived, she had been doing her damnedest to persuade Nick to cancel the wedding plans.

"All I can say is that Hazard better make a good impression on her mother-in-law-to-be this afternoon," Dad commented, shaking his dark head. "Your mom hasn't taken the news of your engagement to a big city girl well, not well at all."

Nick flashed his brother a quick glance. Rich was sprawled on the sofa, channel-surfing, grinning in devilish delight. As Nick recalled, Rich had faced the same objections before his own short-lived marriage. Since the divorce, Mom reminded Rich—repeatedly—that she had told him the marriage would be a mistake.

The jingling phone jostled Nick from his musings. Reflexively, he strode off to take the call.

"Thorn here."

"Thorn, we've got a problem."

Nick scowled when he recognized Harjo's voice. *"You* are the problem. Why don't you butt out!"

"Hazard is being held hostage at Homer Frizzell's trailer house," Harjo hurried on.

"Yeah, right. What are you trying to pull now?" Nick smirked in question. He glanced down at his wristwatch. "Hazard is at the wedding shower."

"No, she isn't. Her truck is in Frizzell's driveway. Unless you want to attend Hazard's funeral, you better haul ass. I don't know what the hell's going on, but Frizzell is having a panic attack. He wants a helicopter to take him to Will Rogers Airport so he can fly out of the country. By the time I jog to the trailer, it's going to dawn on him that he'll need cash, too."

"What the hell—?" Nick swallowed air. He had the uneasy feeling he knew what had set Frizzell off. It must have something to do with the Brown case. Hazard must have reached her conclusions, then gone off half-cocked—just as Nick had expressly told her *not* to do! Damnation!

"I'm on my way, Harjo. Get your butt back over there and try to talk sense into Frizzell. Tell him that he'll only make matters worse with this stunt. I'll take care of the arrangements and I'll be there as soon as I can."

When Nick lurched around, Rich was already on his feet, staring expectantly at him. Rich had plenty of experience with the OSBI. He recognized the sound of trouble the instant he heard it.

"Hazard is in danger again," Rich said. It wasn't a question, only a grim statement of fact. "Worse than last time?"

"Her chances of survival are never good," Nick muttered sourly. "That woman is never going to learn to keep her nose out of places it doesn't belong." Nick snatched up his police-issued pistol, a rifle and his keys. "I need a chopper at the Harjo place—three miles east of Adios. Then call the airport and have a commuter plane fueled and waiting. If I can't defuse this situation, Hazard may be taking an unplanned vacation."

All business, Rich rushed toward the phone. "I'll be there to back you up as soon as I make the calls. Dad can stay here and relay calls over the CB radio if anything new develops."

Nick was out the door before Rich made contact with the OSBI. With sirens screaming, he raced toward the highway.

Was he ever going to get used to Hazard putting her life in jeopardy in order to solve a case? he asked himself. Damn it, he'd even bought that daredevil female a mobile phone so she could contact him. Did she use it? Hell no.

Hazard simply piled into her jalopy truck and roared off. She sent Nick into cardiac arrest every damned time she pulled one of these harebrained stunts!

Fuming, Nick blazed toward the Harjo farm.

"Harjo? What's going on here?" Vinita Frizzell questioned as she ambled back to the trailer house. "What's that woman doing here with my husband? Isn't it enough that she won the donkey crown? Is she trying to add my husband to her list of broken hearts?"

"Homer!" Sam called out. "Vinita's back from her horseback ride. You better come out here before she gets the wrong impression."

"Vinita, honey?" Homer bellowed. "Get out of here— now. Have Harjo take you to town. I don't want you around when the shit hits the fan!"

"What are you talking about?" Vinita demanded anxiously.

"Homer, listen to me," Sam implored. "We can work this out. Haven't I always taken care of you and the other men? Now won't be any different."

"It's different because I screwed up—big time. I gotta do this, boss," Homer insisted. "If I don't take all the heat, it'll mess up your chances of winning the election."

"Damn it, man, this is the wrong time to turn martyr. You're going at this backwards!"

"Take the heat for what?" Vinita asked. "What's Homer talking about?"

The screaming siren broke the strained silence. Harjo glanced back to see Thorn—armed to the teeth—bound from the squad car.

Nick swore under his breath as he stalked forward. Vinita had commenced crying when she spotted the rifle and pistol Nick was toting. As for Harjo, he was striding toward the front steps, without waiting for back-up.

Great, just what Nick needed. A hysterical woman screaming to her husband to watch out for the heavily-armed cop and a prospective boyfriend hell-bent on saving Hazard's neck.

"Back off, Harjo," Nick rapped out. "This is my turf."

"Yeah well, that's my employee in there. I carry more clout with Frizzell than you do."

Sam halted at the top of the steps and stared at the locked door. "Homer, I'm coming inside to talk this out."

"No!" Homer roared in objection. "Stay back or I'll set this place on fire. Vinita is tired of living in this crummy tin can anyhow. I'll buy her a real house ... I'll need money, too. I forgot to have you tell Thorn that. Better add cash to my list of demands."

Nick wedged his way up beside Harjo. "Homer, it's Thorn. We've already seen to traveling money. Better come on out. The 'coptor will be here shortly."

"I don't hear the whirlybird yet. I'm not coming out 'til I do."

Nick could tell Frizzell was getting nervous. The man's voice was shaking noticeably. Frightened captors were the worst kind, Nick reminded himself. When they panicked, only God knew what would happen next.

"Hazard? Are you okay?" Nick called out.

"I—" Her voice became an instant mumble. Nick assumed Frizzell had fitted his hostage with a gag.

"She's got nothing to say," Homer yelled. "She already messed up everything and forced me into this."

"Calm down, Homer," Harjo insisted. "You've already got Vinita in tears. She doesn't understand what's going on and she's worried about you."

"It'll be okay, sugar," Homer tried to console his wife. "This is just something a man has to do to make things right, no matter what the personal sacrifice."

Vinita bawled her head off. Mascara ran like black rain down her puffy cheeks.

Nick glanced over his shoulder to see his 4x4 truck careening around the curve. Rich leaped out, his pistol in hand. The whack-thump of helicopter blades echoed overhead.

"Your ride is here, Frizzell," Nick informed him. "We'll back off so you can come out the front door."

Furniture clattered. Hazard's muted yelp resounded inside the house.

"Don't hurt her!" Harjo bellowed. "Damn it, Homer, behave yourself!"

Nick yanked Harjo back, forcing him down the steps and out of the way. The door creaked open. Hazard— with a pillowcase tied around her mouth and a tablecloth wrapped around her torso like a straightjacket—was escorted onto the wooden deck. Her eyes were rounded and her hair stuck out in all directions. Nick doubted fear was entirely responsible for her wild 'do. Bad hairdos had become the rule, not the exception with Hazard.

Homer kept his arms pinched tightly around Hazard's neck. The shotgun was pressed to her head. Homer was using Hazard as his shield of defense.

Things did not look good, in Nick's opinion. One fumbling step and Homer could trip and fall. His quaking hand was wrapped around the shotgun, and the man was sweating profusely. That usually proved to be the case with amateur criminals. Homer was as scared as a cornered cat and he'd gotten in over his head. Homer believed Hazard was all that stood between him and disaster. He wasn't about to turn her loose until he deplaned in a foreign country.

Nick felt Harjo tense beside him. Damn it, this was no time for the hulk of man to attempt daring heroics. Harjo was going to try something stupid, Nick could feel it in his bones.

The instant Homer Frizzell started down the steps, Nick saw Harjo coiling to pounce. There wasn't time for a scathing lecture on letting cops do what they were trained to do. Besides, Harjo wasn't a stand-aside kind of guy. He had no intention of letting Frizzell and Hazard reach the chopper which had touched down in the pasture near the trailer house.

The instant Bruno realized Hazard needed his protection, he leaped out the open window of the truck. Snarling in protest, the dog bounded toward the steps.

Then everything happened at once . . .

Fifteen

Nick tossed aside his weapons and sprang forward at the exact moment Harjo pounced. The dual action caught Homer unaware. Harjo had Frizzell in an instant headlock, levering the shotgun upward. The weapon discharged a split-second after Nick clamped his arms around Hazard's waist and used his forward momentum to break the hold Frizzell had on her. Nick and Hazard hit the ground, and Nick rolled over, protecting her with his body. What he received for his efforts was a vicious snarl from Bruno.

Using wrestling holds learned in high school, Harjo put Frizzell in a double chicken wing and pinned him to the grass. Vinita was screeching at the top of her lungs, begging for Harjo to show mercy.

Hazard lay unmoving beneath Nick's sprawled form. Nick was hesitant to look down, for fear her head had been forcefully removed from her shoulders by the shotgun blast. He didn't smell the coppery scent of blood, but then he wasn't sure he trusted his clogged senses at the moment.

Reluctantly, Nick did glance down. The matted, Prussian

purple-tinted hair—glittering with silver—was intact. Undeservedly, Hazard had escaped unscathed.

Nick bounded to his feet when he heard his brother racing forward to take command of the field. Rich had his pistol stuffed up Homer's nostrils in nothing flat.

"Okay, Harjo, you can let him go. I've got the bastard covered," Rich growled.

Harjo disentangled his arms from Homer's neck, then rose to his feet. Vinita dropped to her knees to bleed black-mascara-colored tears on Homer's heaving chest.

"OSBI. You're under arrest," Rich barked. "You have the right to remain—"

Hazard sent up a muffled protest. Harjo hurried over to unfasten her gag. Nick frowned, noting how quickly Harjo had come to Hazard's assistance. The man really had it bad, Nick decided. He ought to lock Harjo in the slammer for obstruction of justice—or some other technicality—to ensure the man kept his distance from Hazard.

"Frizzell is not under arrest because I'm not filing charges," Hazard stunned everyone by saying. "This has been a giant mistake, hasn't it, Homer?"

Frizzell—still at gunpoint—blinked in confusion.

Hazard stared into the distance, but damned if Nick knew what she was looking at. There seemed to be a lot going on around here that he didn't understand.

"Rich, get that gun out of Homer's face," Hazard demanded as Harjo assisted her to her feet so he could untie the confining tablecloth.

Rich glanced at Nick for instruction. Nick shrugged, then motioned for his brother to back off.

"What the hell is going on, Hazard?" Nick asked, trying desperately to control his irritation—and failing miserably.

"Homer just got overly excited, is all," she said with a dismissive flick of her wrist. "Things started happening before he had time to think them through. Isn't that right, Homer?"

Homer blinked. "Yeah, I guess they did."

"Homer thought he was protecting Sam Harjo. Homer held himself personally responsible for the trouble Brown caused around the commissioner's shop, even if the problems weren't Homer's fault. Isn't that so, Homer?"

"Um . . . well . . . I . . ."

Hazard cut Homer off when he hemmed and hawed. "That's what happened," she declared. "No harm done."

"No harm done?" Nick erupted. "You could have been incinerated in that trailer, or you could have had your damned head blown off when Harjo attempted his stupid heroics. And damn it, this would not have happened if you had used the mobile phone to contact me as you were told to do!"

Hazard's chin went airborne. "It's your fault I had an inoperable phone. I tried to call but the stupid thing didn't work."

Nick wheeled around and stalked to the truck. With leather pouch in hand, he stamped toward her. "The *stupid thing* won't work unless you plug the adapter into the cigarette lighter or charge the battery."

"You didn't mention that," Hazard huffed in self-defense.

"You could have read the instructions," he snapped back.

Rich stepped forward, placing himself between Nick and Hazard. "Before the two of you get into a shouting match, let's break it up, shall we? If charges aren't being filed, we can all go home. Nick, you can follow up on this incident later. I suspect Mom will be back from the shower soon."

"The shower!" Hazard hooted. "With all the excitement, I forgot. What time is it?"

Nick glanced at his watch. From the corner of his eye he saw Harjo's lips twitching in devilish amusement. That rascal was enjoying the fact that this fiasco had caused Hazard to miss her wedding shower.

"It's three-thirty," Nick muttered. "You're not only late, Hazard, you didn't show up at all. And if—"

Rich grabbed Nick by the arm and towed him toward the squad car. "Come on, little brother. You better cool off before you say something you can't take back."

Nick figured Rich was right. He allowed Rich to stuff him behind the steering wheel.

Rich glanced speculatively toward Harjo. "Looks like trouble to me, little brother. I guess you're getting paid back for the turmoil you put Hazard through while we were trying to figure out why Will Bloom ended up dead in the dirt."

"Go soak your head in kerosene, Rich," Nick said, and scowled.

"Hey, don't take your frustration out on me. I'm just giving you my assessment of the situation. Any idiot can see you've got competition for Hazard's affection."

"Thanks for reminding me," Nick grumbled sarcastically. "Like I don't know that. You always did know how to cheer me up."

Rich leaned down to confront Nick eye-to-eye. "While we were working the last case, you told me Hazard had become cynical and mistrusting of men after her first marriage. I can relate to that, believe me, bro. Now that you've restored Hazard's faith in men, this was bound to happen. Hell, the woman is a knockout. Surely you didn't expect other guys to back off just because you put an engagement ring on her finger. If you get all huffy every time some guy shows an interest, you're going to screw this wedding thing all to hell."

"It's already screwed," Nick mumbled. "She's not wearing my ring, because I asked her to give it back."

Rich stared at him as if he had lost his mind. Then he threw back his head and burst out laughing.

Nick didn't think it was a damned bit funny.

"Nicky boy, you are really asking for trouble. You just

declared open season on one well-stacked female. Good luck trying to keep ahead of the pack. Hell, I might even give you a run for your money. Dumb move, bro, really dumb!''

Rich was still sniggering as he sauntered off to speak with the chopper pilot. Nick drove away, cursing the disaster his life had become. When he wasn't swearing, he asked himself why Hazard had let Homer Frizzell off the hook. By damn, he was going to get to the bottom of this case—just as soon as he dealt with Mom.

"That should be fun," Nick grunted as he drove home to face Mom's rapid-fire questions.

Chaos whirled around Amanda. Vinita was wailing and blubbering all over Homer. The helicopter took to the air, creating a blast of wind that set Amanda's purple-tinted hair on end, disrupting her attempt to gather her thoughts. Harjo was raking Homer over the coals for his misguided sense of loyalty.

Rich Thorn called out a farewell to Amanda as he jogged toward the four-wheel-drive pick-up. Amanda had no idea why Rich was grinning and winking at her. She strode toward her clunker truck. Bruno came to heel, refusing to be left behind.

"Hazard! Hold up a minute," Harjo called out. "I want to talk to you."

Amanda spun around to survey the handsome commissioner who ambled toward her. Then her gaze strayed to the squad car that was making tracks.

"Hazard," Harjo said, halting directly in front of her, "I—"

"I've got a favor to ask, Harjo."

"Name it."

"I'd like your crew to clear out the blind intersection south of Salty Marcum's home, ASAP."

"Done. I'd like to see you, under entirely different circumstances," he said without pausing for breath. "In case you haven't noticed, I—"

"There's something I have to do and it has to be done now," she interrupted. "We'll talk later, Harjo."

Amanda piled into her truck and drove off. She wasn't sure she was ready to deal with Harjo. She needed a little time to think the matter through. The first thing she needed to do was bring this case to a satisfactory closure.

She also needed some time off, she decided as she pointed the pick-up due west. Between the hellish demands of income tax season, and the on-again, off-again wedding arrangements, Amanda felt as if her emotions were whirling like the spin cycle in a washing a machine.

What she needed was to hibernate for a couple of days— maybe three. Then she would deal with the soap opera her personal life had become.

Amanda applied the brake, waiting for the camouflaged figure tucked in the tree-choked ravine to step into view. The truck idled for five minutes before Salty Marcum reluctantly moved toward her.

"Just can't get rid of you, can I, little lady?" he muttered as he climbed through the strands of barb wire fence.

"Nope." Amanda motioned him to the truck. "Get in. I have a bone to pick with you.'"

Salty slid onto the seat, forcing Bruno to scoot over. The dog growled. Salty ignored him. "You broke Homer down, I see. Thought you would, if you ever figured it all out." A faint smile pursed his lips. "You're damned good, little lady. Even while you pestered the hell out of me, I must admit that I enjoyed watching you do your thing. Too bad you aren't working for army intelligence forces. They could use you."

Salty settled himself more comfortably on the seat. "So . . . are you hauling me over to Thorn's place?"

"Nope." Amanda veered north, heading directly for Salty's house on the hill.

The crusty old vet blinked in surprise. "Why the hell not?"

The jalopy truck ground to a halt in Salty's driveway. Amanda twisted to confront Salty face-to-face. "I won't have to deliver you to Thorn's doorstep, because you're going to go see him on your own."

"Oh yeah? Says who?"

"Says me," Amanda replied firmly. "You saved Homer's life that day on the road. If not for you, Brown would have ruined a few more lives, and reputations."

Salty snorted. "Don't make me out to be some kind of hero."

"But I think you were a hero in 'Nam, and I think you're one now," she contended.

"Never expected a woman like you to wrap fancy trimming around the truth," he growled at her. "I didn't clobber Brown just for Homer's sake. I did it for my little girl and you damned well know it. My only regret is that the SOB didn't know I did it. Wouldn't you know that stupid bastard would cause trouble, even when he died. And hell, who would've thought the asshole would drown in six inches of water."

Amanda watched turbulent emotions flash in Salty's eyes. The poor tormented man didn't realize—would not admit—that he was a hero in every sense of the word. Bitterness would continue to poison Salty until he let go of his troubled past and found something to live *for*. Amanda intended to badger Salty until he let go, then she was going to devise a way to give his life new purpose.

"Now you listen to me, you old goat," she said, wagging her finger in his face. "You are going to Thorn's house and tell him exactly what happened that morning on the road. Then you're—"

"The hell I am!" Salty erupted, glaring at her.

"You *are* going to see Thorn—now," she insisted. "If you don't, I'll nag you until you do. You think I was a pest while I was digging for information about this case? You ain't seen nothing yet, pal."

"That figures," he grunted, giving her the evil eye.

Amanda was pretty sure that Salty's rough, tough facade was mostly bluff. The old coot was softening up toward her, but he didn't want her to think he was a pushover.

"I am relatively certain Thorn will drop this case, given the circumstances," Amanda told him.

"Thorn would never have given it a thought, if not for you," he didn't fail to point out.

"True, but my inquiring mind had to know what really happened—and why. As it turned out, there *was* more to the incident than met the eye."

Amanda paused momentarily, then decided to hit the old rascal where he lived, giving him the nudge that would push him over the edge. "Your daughter would have expected her beloved father to clear up this matter, wouldn't she? Molly would have wanted you to get the truth out in the open. After all, you're the one who taught her to be honest and responsible."

"Damn you, Hazard, you really know which buttons to push to get your way, don't you?" A mist of tears glazed his eyes. He stared out the window for a long moment, then nodded his gray head. "Okay, little lady, I'll go see Thorn—but only because of Molly."

Amanda leaned over to press a kiss to Salty's cheek. "After you talk to Thorn, I'd like for you to come by my house. I'll fix supper."

"What? More shit on a shingle?" Salty smirked. "You may be hell on wheels when it comes to investigation, but you don't cook worth a damn. I'll do the cooking or I won't come."

"Deal."

Amanda offered her hand. Salty's callused fingers closed around hers in an affectionate squeeze.

"Know something?" he murmured.

"What, Salty?"

He stared her squarely in the eye and said, "I wish Molly could've grown up. I would've wanted her to turn out just like you."

On that parting remark, Salty climbed from the truck and limped away. Amanda blinked back the tears as she drove home.

"You must be tired, Hazard," she diagnosed. Either that or Salty's quiet compliment had hit *her* right where she lived.

Bone-weary, Amanda trudged through her front door. Her jaw dropped to her chest when she spied the opened gifts that had been stacked in the corner of the living room. Kitchen appliances, pots and pans, bowls and platters—to name only a few of the items—had been delivered from the wedding shower.

Who had picked the lock on her door to haul in this stuff? she wondered.

"Hi, Half Pint. 'Bout time you showed up."

Amanda gaped at her paternal grandfather who hobbled around the corner of the kitchen. Pops—as she affectionately called him—ambulated toward her with the aid of his aluminum walker. His bald head and wire-rimmed glasses reflected the light streaming through the window.

Now Amanda knew who had unlocked her door. She had given Pops his own key when he lived with her a few months earlier. Obviously, Mother had decided to get Pops out of her hair, and out of her house, for another extended vacation.

"I heard you missed a whiz-bang wedding shower," Pops

said as he hobbled across the room. "Your mother and Thorn's mom—whoa!"

Amanda dashed forward when Bruno took it upon himself to protect her from the intruder. Pops teetered precariously. Amanda latched onto his arm before he hit the wall and collapsed on the floor.

"Bruno, back off," Amanda ordered as she propped Pops upright.

Pops flashed his gritted false teeth at the dog. Bruno growled in counterthreat.

"This is my new bodyguard," Amanda introduced.

"No kidding." Pops clamped both hands on his walker, then inched toward the recliner. "For a minute there, I thought that dad-blamed mutt was going for my throat."

Pops maneuvered backward, then plunked into the chair. "You keep that mutt in the house with you?"

Amanda nodded her lavender-tinted head.

A wide grin spread across Pops' wrinkled features. "A house cat and a house dog? Your mother is really gonna have a fit about that."

Pops looked as if the prospect delighted him. Ah, but he did love to give Mother hell every change he got.

"Since you didn't show up for your own shower, you're mother decided to punish you by pawning me off on you," Pops informed her.

Amanda tossed her purse and keys on the coffee table and shrugged casually. "You know you're welcome to come whenever you like."

"Well, don't let your mother know that. It would spoil all my fun of razzing her about it." He propped up his feet and grabbed the remote. "So . . . how come you missed the shower? Were you cracking another of those cases your mother has no idea you're investigating?"

Amanda frowned pensively. "Yes, but I think it would have been better if I had left this one alone. Mostly, I just stirred up trouble and caused some ill feelings. This turned out to be a complicated case of self-defense—or something to that effect."

"It's always better to have the truth out in the open. Then folks don't have their consciences nagging them to death for no reason," Pops said philosophically, then grinned. "Except in your mother's case. I never tell her a damned thing if I don't have to. It drives her crazier than she already is."

"Did Mother mention meeting Thorn's mom?" Amanda asked tentatively.

Pops bobbed his shiny head. "Yep, she sure did. Those two women put their heads together and decided you and Thorn were definitely not right for each other. That's about the only thing they did agree on, except that the shower decorations were atrocious."

Amanda inwardly cringed. She could almost hear Mother howling about Velma's decor.

"I better start supper. I invited a friend over," Amanda said.

"Not Thorn?" Pops studied her through narrowed eyes. "What's going on, Half Pint? Are you and the country cop having problems again?"

"He asked for his ring back before the shower, and it was too late to cancel," she confided.

"What the hell's a-matter with that boy?" Pops demanded indignantly.

"It's a long, involved story."

"I've got time to listen. If your mother has her way I'll be here at least a month."

Amanda glanced away before Pops pinned her with a probing stare. "I'd rather not discuss it now. It's been a long, exhausting two weeks."

Pops, God bless him, didn't pry. "Why don't you go take a nice, relaxing shower. I'll fix supper for this . . . er . . . new friend of yours."

"It's not what you think, Pops." *At least not with this*

particular friend, she silently stipulated. "Salty Marcum is a reclusive war vet who walks with a limp and carries a chip on his shoulder."

"And you plan to sand it off," Pops presumed.

"He needs a friend."

"Then we should get along just fine," Pops said, with great assurance. "I could use one myself. The ones my age keep dropping off."

A spurt of sentimentality gushed through Amanda's veins. Impulsively, she leaned over to hug the stuffing out of her grandfather.

"You're choking me," Pops teased playfully. "Go shower. I'll put supper on the stove. I haven't had a chance to cook since the last time I was here. Your mother—the fussy broad—won't let me near her kitchen."

Smiling gratefully, Amanda left Pops and Bruno to become acquainted. She doubted it would take long. After Pops tossed the dog a few nibbles of supper, Bruno would be Pop's friend for life.

While Salty and Pops swapped war stories over baked beans, fried potatoes and ham steak, Amanda sat in silence. She was glad the two men had hit it off so well. Now Salty would have an excuse to re-enter society. He and Pops could tool around town while Amanda was running her accounting business.

Amanda was also relieved to hear Thorn had decided not to press charges in the Brown case. As it had turned out, it *had* been an ironic twist of fate that caused Brown's demise, and Thorn had let it go at that.

Ironic, wasn't it, that this was the first time Amanda actually appreciated the fact that Thorn had not begun an aggressive investigation. Who would have thought it?

"How about a friendly game of dominoes?" Pops suggested while Amanda cleared the table. "Do you play, Salty?"

"Doesn't everybody?"

The lighthearted tone of Salty's voice, and his relaxed smile, was a sight for Amanda's sore eyes. Salty, she concluded, was getting back on the right track after months of seclusion.

"Want to join us, Half Pint?" Pops invited.

"No thanks, I'm going out for a little while," she said, on the spur of the moment. This looked to be the perfect opportunity to let Salty and Pops become better acquainted.

"You sure?" Salty questioned, studying her intently. "Everything okay with you, little lady? You look mighty tired to me."

"I'm fine," she assured him. "I won't be gone long."

By the time Amanda grabbed her keys, the two men were deeply engrossed in their game of dominoes. With Bruno at her heels, Amanda ambled outside. The Oklahoma moon beamed down like a spotlight and a galaxy of stars winked from above. Ah, there was no place like the wide-open country to make you appreciate the peacefulness of the night, she thought to herself.

Amanda piled into the gas-guzzling truck, then headed west. She was in a tired, indecisive mood, she realized a half mile later. She wasn't sure where she wanted to go. One minute she felt the impulsive urge to drive out to Harjo's home so she could thank him for helping to save her neck. She also needed to apologize for thinking the worst about him during her investigation. She had been impressed to learn that Harjo had taken it upon himself to guide and direct young men who obviously hadn't had many breaks in life. Amanda admired that.

Harjo was going to make a conscientious, efficient commish, she predicted.

Personally, she didn't think Shakelford had a prayer in

the upcoming election, no matter how many campaign clappers and promotional gifts he distributed throughout the county.

And then there was Thorn. She wanted to drive to his farm and express her gratitude. Not for the first time, he had risked his own life to remove her from harm's way. She also wanted to thank him for going easy on Salty.

No doubt about it, Thorn was one helluva cop.

Amanda stopped at the country intersection and shifted into neutral. She frowned pensively, trying to make up her mind which direction to take. If she turned left, she would reach Thorn's farm . . .

What to do? Amanda asked herself as she stared south, then north.

Nick picked up the phone and dialed from memory. While the phone rang on the other end of the line, he glanced down the hallway. His family had gathered around the TV to watch the evening news. It was the only time Nick had had to himself since he returned from Frizzell's house. Then he had found Salty Marcum on the doorstep, requesting a private conversation. Once Nick had the Brown case squared away, he'd had to listen to Mom list all the reasons why a big city girl like Hazard could not possibly fit into his countrified life.

"Answer the damned phone, Hazard," Nick grumbled impatiently.

"Hazard's residence!"

Nick frowned at the booming voice that greeted him. "Pops, is that you?"

"You'll have to speak up!" Pops yelled. "My hearing aids keep going on the blink! I'm gonna have to buy some of those Energizer bunny batteries real soon!"

"Pops, is Hazard there?" Nick shouted.

"No, she drove off a few minutes ago. Didn't say where

she was going. I've got to hang up now. Salty and I are playing dominoes and it's my turn!''

Nick scowled when the line went dead. He had a pretty good idea where Hazard had gone—to Harjo's house.

Damn it, Rich was right, thought Nick. Asking for the engagement ring back was the stupidest thing he'd ever done. Hell, he had practically handed Hazard over to Harjo on a silver platter—or at the very least, put her on the menu!

Glumly, Nick rejoined his family. He was going to have to play his cards right if he was going to win Hazard back. No more flashes of temper, he promised himself, no more skepticism about her suspicions. The next time Hazard cried foul play, Nick was going to pay close attention. She'd love that.

He would begin his campaign of reconciliation tomorrow, he decided. He wasn't going to lose Hazard to a handsome, competent county commissioner like Sam Harjo. Nick wanted Hazard to be happy, but not *that* kind of happy!

Sam Harjo plucked up the phone and punched in the number. Three rings later a man answered.

"Hazard's residence!"

Sam held the receiver away before the loud voice blasted his eardrum. "May I speak to Hazard, please?" he said politely.

"What? Speak up! I can barely hear you!" Pops blared.

"Can you put Amanda on the phone?" Sam hollered back.

"She's not here. She left awhile ago. Don't know where she went or when she'll be back!"

Grumbling to himself, Sam disconnected. He didn't have to be clairvoyant to know where Hazard had gone—to Thorn's farm. Maybe Sam had stepped out of line when he tried to make his interest known, but damn it, a woman like Hazard didn't come along very often in life—if at all.

Since Hazard had not been wearing her engagement ring recently, Sam knew this was his big chance to get to know her better. Sam had nothing personal against Thorn. Hell, he admired and respected that cop. But Sam wasn't going to bow out gracefully. He'd be an absolute fool not to give a relationship with Hazard his best shot.

Fifteen minutes later, Amanda was still sitting in her idling truck, stroking Bruno's head, trying to decide which way to go. Should she turn right to visit the hunk of a county commissioner who was a younger version of Clint Eastwood? Or should she turn left to resolve her problems with that stud of a country cop who reminded her of Tom Selleck?

Amanda supposed there were a few women out there who would have begged to trade places with her, because they didn't think she had anything to complain about. What could be more flattering than having two gorgeous hunks tugging on your emotions?

Okay, Hazard, quit stalling. What's it going to be? Eastwood or Selleck? Break new ground or rebuild a broken bridge . . . ?

Amanda was jostled from her indecisive thoughts when the old truck gurgled, sputtered and sucked air. She glanced down at the fuel gauge.

Well damn, she had been driving around all week and she hadn't taken time to stop by Thatcher's Oil and Gas to fill up.

Glancing heavenward, Amanda smiled tiredly. "Are you trying to tell me something, Big Guy?"

Climbing from her stranded truck, Amanda turned on her boot heels and hiked home—where she probably should have stayed in the first place. Truth was, she was dead on her feet and her brain was no longer operating at full tilt. Instead of trying to decide whether to turn left or right, she should have taken her own good advice and hibernated until her exhaustion wore off. Maybe then she could think straight.

"Come along, Bruno," she called to her devoted body-guard. "There are times when the best companion a woman can possibly have is a dog. The only thing the men in this world are good at is complicating a woman's life."

Ambling down the recently graveled road, with Bruno trotting beside her, Amanda left her decision—and her jalopy truck—to be dealt with on another day. *Definitely* not tonight . . .

Dear Readers,

I hope you enjoyed accompanying me through my investigation of *Dead in the Mud*. The next book in the Amanda Hazard series, *Dead in the Chevy,* will be released in April 1998. Please join me in my continuing quest for truth and justice in small-town America. Hopefully, by then, I will have resolved my dilemma. Thank you, dear readers, for your indulgence.

Yours truly,
Amanda Hazard, CPA

AMANDA HAZARD MYSTERIES
BY CONNIE FEDDERSEN

DEAD IN THE CELLAR   (0-8217-5245-6, $4.99)

DEAD IN THE DIRT   (1-57566-046-6, $4.99)

DEAD IN THE MELON PATCH   (0-8217-4872-6, $4.99)

DEAD IN THE WATER   (0-8217-5244-8, $4.99)